THE
WILD SIDE

Books by Fern Michaels

On the Line
Fear Thy Neighbor
No Way Out
Fearless
Deep Harbor
Fate & Fortune
Sweet Vengeance
Fancy Dancer
No Safe Secret
About Face
Perfect Match
A Family Affair
Forget Me Not
The Blossom Sisters
Balancing Act
Tuesday's Child
Betrayal
Southern Comfort
To Taste the Wine
Sins of the Flesh
Sins of Omission
Return to Sender
Mr. and Miss Anonymous
Up Close and Personal
Fool Me Once
Picture Perfect
The Future Scrolls
Kentucky Sunrise
Kentucky Heat
Kentucky Rich
Plain Jane
Charming Lily
What You Wish For
The Guest List
Listen to Your Heart

Celebration
Yesterday
Finders Keepers
Annie's Rainbow
Sara's Song
Vegas Sunrise
Vegas Heat
Vegas Rich
Whitefire
Wish List
Dear Emily

The Lost and Found Novels:
Secrets
Hidden
Liar!

Holiday Novels:
The Brightest Star
Spirit of the Season
Holly and Ivy
Wishes for Christmas
Christmas at Timberwoods
Santa Cruise
Falling Stars

The Godmothers Series:
Far and Away
Classified
Breaking News
Deadline
Late Edition
Exclusive
The Scoop

Books by Fern Michaels (cont.)

E-Book Exclusives:
Desperate Measures
Seasons of Her Life
To Have and To Hold
Serendipity
Captive Innocence
Captive Embraces
Captive Passions
Captive Secrets
Captive Splendors
Cinders to Satin
For All Their Lives
Texas Heat
Texas Rich
Texas Fury
Texas Sunrise

Anthologies:
In Bloom
Home Sweet Home
A Snowy Little Christmas

Coming Home for Christmas
A Season to Celebrate
Mistletoe Magic
Winter Wishes
The Most Wonderful Time
When the Snow Falls
Secret Santa
A Winter Wonderland
I'll Be Home for Christmas
Making Spirits Bright
Holiday Magic
Snow Angels
Silver Bells
Comfort and Joy
Sugar and Spice
Let it Snow
A Gift of Joy
Five Golden Rings
Deck the Halls
Jingle All the Way

Published by Kensington Publishing Corp.

THE
WILD SIDE

FERN MICHAELS

KENSINGTON
PUBLISHING CORP.

Prologue

Present Day

Melanie Drake was absentmindedly tapping the pen she was holding on top of the yellow pad that sat beside her daily planner. Not quite forty and living in the midst of technology, she was still hooked on pen, pencil, and paper. She was convinced the act of writing something down made a stronger connection to one's memory. It was also a popular means of communication among criminals. No electronic footprint. But more on that later.

Yes, she had a cellphone. Yes, she kept things in her phone calendar, but for Melanie that was backup. As soon as she returned to her office, she would jot down whatever new appointment had been made. Then she would scribble it on the wall calendar that was hanging in her linen closet. If it was in front of her face, there was an excellent chance she would remember.

She glanced at her schedule for the day: routine grammar school guidance counselor agenda. She checked the clock above her door. The yelling, shrieking, laughing voices were about to descend on Jesse Moorer Elementary. Her first task of the day was to maintain order in the hallway.

Miss Drake stood outside her office door and greeted the children as they attempted to stampede their way to their classrooms. "Good morning, everyone. Slow down, please. Mind your manners. Be polite." She must have repeated those words at least a dozen times before the early morning bell rang. Every. Single. Day. And always with a genuine smile on her face.

After years of investigating criminals who clearly didn't follow the rules, she believed bad behavior should be nipped in the bud, meaning at a very young age. She loved being on hand to help shape a new generation of respect and integrity. If she could save one child from a life of felonious activity, then she'd done something good for the world. And that was why Melanie "MelDrake" Drake ultimately became a guidance counselor.

This was the first year of Melanie's second career. Admittedly, it was a bit unusual for someone to start working in the educational system just as they were about to turn forty. Normally it went the other way around. Teachers and counselors entered the field right after college and graduate work; and after twenty years, they retired or entered a different field or started a small cottage business. But Melanie's prior career had taken its toll on her: physically, emotionally, romantically, and spiritually. Yep. It damaged pretty much everything, but it was a means to an end. Luckily it didn't end *her*.

PART ONE

The Rules

Chapter One

The Summer of Change

It was 1992 when Melanie became a stickler for rules. She was between second and third grade and spending most of the summer in traction with a broken leg, broken arm, and healing from stitches that ran from her right eyebrow to her earlobe. Someone had run a red light and T-boned the family car. She was in the right rear passenger seat and got the brunt of the collision. It took many conversations with her parents to convince her she was lucky. "It could have been worse." Of course, an eight-year-old who was stuck in bed while her friends were outside playing couldn't imagine anything worse.

Melanie was also very bright. One day she asked her father, "Why did this happen?"

He contemplated the answer. Instead of getting into a philosophical discussion with his eight-year-old, he decided to keep it simple: "Because someone wasn't following the rules." She thought about what he'd said as she furrowed her brow. Those words would be forever etched into her consciousness.

That particular summer, the internet was in its infancy. For the general public, it required a dedicated dial-up phone line. It also required a personal computer, something that was lacking in many households at that time, leaving Melanie with meager choices of activities that could be pursued from her stationary position.

Yes, Melanie's options were limited. Visitors would come, but it was summer. No one wanted to be stuck inside on a sunny day. When friends came over, they would play board games until they literally became bored. When she didn't have kids her age around, she worked on puzzles or reading. She had a boom box, but the selection of music on the radio was all over the place. It ranged from hip-hop to ballads and everything in between. The DJ's favorite seemed to be that "Achy Breaky Heart." It was a catchy tune. It didn't hurt that Billy Ray Cyrus was cute, either. But how many times could you listen to it? Besides, it made her want to get up and dance, which was out of the question. Back to the books.

Because she was sequestered in her bedroom, her parents decided to put a small TV in her room. Depending on who was babysitting, TV programs ranged from *Perry Mason* to *Dukes of Hazzard*. Oddly enough, Melanie preferred *Perry Mason*. She was transfixed, scrutinizing the characters, following every twist of the plot. Her ability to spot the criminal was uncanny. Her parents were concerned the content of the show was a bit sinister for an eight-year-old, but her aunt Lucy insisted it sharpened her grand-niece's mind.

Then *Columbo* went into syndication, and they added another show to their roster, laughing at the disheveled detective, knowing his cunning would solve the crime. Even though the audience knew who the perpetrator was at the beginning, it fascinated Melanie to see how *Columbo* figured it out. So Melanie and her aunt made a pact. They wouldn't tell her parents what they watched when they were together. They claimed they were watching game shows. Melanie knew she was fibbing, but she wasn't breaking any rules. At least not obvious ones. Her parents never prohibited her from doing anything. They were confident their clever daughter had the sense to understand what was good and bad, even at her young age.

When Aunt Lucy wasn't around and Melanie was stuck with the ditsy babysitter, Melanie opted for seclusion with her stack of books. She devoured the Nancy Drew series and then entered the world of *Harriet The Spy*. Her penchant for solving mysteries led to solving puzzles. She could whiz through at least one puzzle book a day. By September, she had far outpaced her classmates' reading skills, giving her an edge over her fellow students. But Melanie didn't brag about it. She liked the idea of having a special skill she could call upon to wow the teacher and stun the classroom. A talent in the making: gathering information.

One afternoon that summer, her uncle Leo visited and brought several decks of playing cards. She pouted at first. She was sick of Go Fish and Crazy Eights. But when he made several cards from an Uno deck disappear, she was enthralled. She wriggled in the only possible way she could with one arm flailing and her good leg lightly bouncing on the bed. He was delighted his niece was interested in his much-loved hobby and promised to teach her a new trick every week. By the time her cast came off, she had mastered a good number of magic tricks. Sleight of hand was one of her favorites. One of her discoveries was how to write secret messages in lemon juice. But she needed an adult to iron the paper to be able to read what she wrote. She would keep that particular talent in her personal mental vault. She also appreciated the unspoken rule about never divulging the secrets of the tricks.

The casts came off in mid-August, allowing Melanie time to regain her strength before school started. She knew she wouldn't be able to play most games, so she memorized the rules of soccer, softball, and hockey, another bit of knowledge she could put in her repository of talent and information.

She scrutinized her appearance with a handheld mirror and stared at the zipper-like scar that ran along the side of her face. Her father told her it was a "badge of honor," although she couldn't figure out what the "honor" part of it meant. To her, it was an ugly red mark about which she was sure to be teased. She believed if she had a limp *and* a scar, it would certainly arouse mockery, and she tried valiantly to mitigate the potential for ridicule. She let her short black hair grow past her collarbone and practiced tilting her head to cover the scar. She realized she couldn't walk around with her head cocked to one side, though. Her mother found a scar-treatment serum she applied several times a day. But it was obvious to her that the scar wasn't going anywhere. Therefore, she was diligent about her physical therapy, and by the time school started, she walked with a normal gait.

Chapter Two

Back to School

Secretly Melanie dreaded the first day of school. Her anxiety about the reception she would get was growing with every step down the sidewalk. But friends she hadn't seen were happy to greet her, and much to her surprise, her classmates seemed intrigued by her accident and scar. Some of them even thought it was "cool."

Melanie thought otherwise. She was waiting for the moment when someone called her Frankenstein. But it never came. Maybe it was pity. Kids were weird. It was hard to say what would cause them to make someone the brunt of a cruel joke. At least she didn't limp. *A limp and a scar*. Both would have been too much to bear. She'd started the school day full of anxiety, but by noon, Melanie was feeling normal. Maybe kids weren't as cruel as she imagined. When she showed some of her tricks during lunch, they were in awe and begged to learn how she did them. She stared her audience down with a deadpan expression. "I cannot tell you. Do not ask me again." Her response earned different reactions. The girls giggled, and the boys began to call her "MelDrake the Magician." Part of that nickname would stay with her for years to come.

While Melanie insisted on following rules, she was not a tattletale. No. Rather than be branded a snitch, she took matters into her own hands.

One morning, right after the Pledge of Allegiance, just as the class was sitting down, she noticed Richie Burke pull something from his sleeve. It was a plastic straw. She tilted her head to catch a glimpse of what he might be up to. He was in the last seat in the row next to the windows. Melanie was in the adjacent row, and one seat up. They were seated catty-corner to each other.

Richie had the reputation of being a troublemaker, so she didn't want to stare at him and risk invoking his nastier side. Instead she glanced at the window and watched his reflection. She could see him making spitballs and then lining them up on the edge of his desk, close to the student in front of him, blocking his handiwork from the teacher's view. When their teacher, Miss Bender, began writing math problems on the blackboard, Richie popped a spitball into the end of his straw, aimed, and fired at the back of Jenny Lennon's head. Richie watched as Jenny reached around to feel her hair, but the spitball bounced to the floor. Richie's face was turning red as he valiantly tried to stifle a laugh. Instead he snorted, causing everyone's head to turn in his direction. He feigned a cough. A few shrugs, and it was all eyes back on the blackboard.

Miss Bender asked if he was okay. He nodded with his fist against his mouth, trying desperately not to let snot shoot out of his nose. As the class settled down, Miss Bender reviewed the basic math problems. "Any questions?" If someone did voice a question, everyone else in the class would moan, so there weren't any most of the time.

Once again, the teacher pivoted toward the blackboard.

Once again, Richie aimed and fired. And once again, Jenny scratched the back of her head. Richie was about to explode with his own amusement. He waited until the next opportunity and blasted another spitball, this time hard enough that Jenny whimpered. With that, Melanie got up from her seat, leaned toward Richie, and yanked the straw out of his hand. Then she brushed the two remaining balls onto his lap with her sleeve, marched to the front of the classroom, tied the straw into a knot, and dropped it in the wastebasket. As the little drama unfolded, Miss Bender watched with her mouth agape.

"What's this all about?" she queried.

"Pardon, Miss Bender." She pointed to the artillery in the trash bin. "I found it on the floor and didn't want anyone to trip over it." *Trip over a straw?* It was the best she could come up with. She brushed her hands together as if she was sweeping off some dust. As Melanie returned to her seat, her eyes burned a hole in Richie's face. Even though he towered above her by several inches and outweighed her by fifty pounds, Richie Burke was convinced never to cross Melanie Drake. Ever.

As time went on, Melanie got the reputation of having the ability to chew a person up with just one look, but for some odd reason, most people responded by asking if she wanted dessert. It was part of her charm, although *charming* didn't necessarily describe her as a kid. It was something she nurtured and developed and used when necessary.

Due to her accident, her sports activities were limited that school year, so she spent most of the time carefully watching her schoolmates play softball and soccer. Having the rules etched in her memory, she was fascinated to see how often someone would try to cheat. Even just a little. She would wait until she could catch the transgressor's eye and then give them one of her stare-downs. She was intrigued to discover she could stop someone from cheating with just one look.

Over time, that particular skill would become one of her best personal weapons.

The rest of the fall season was chock-full of eye-popping news. Bill Clinton beat George H.W. Bush in the presidential election, and Sinéad O'Connor ripped up a photo of Pope John Paul II on live television. The world seemed to be growing less predictable. But on a brighter note for Melanie and her friends, the Cartoon Network was launched, so she was able to watch *Looney Tunes* more often. Melanie wasn't known for telling jokes or funny stories, but something goofy could make her laugh out loud. She couldn't decide which rivals were her favorite: Wile E. Coyote vs. Road Runner, or Daffy vs. Bugs. She appreciated Bugs's attitude. No one was going to best him. She liked that about him and the twisted way he got his justice. She would put that in her mental tool kit.

Young Melanie was intrigued by the notion of opposing forces, and 1993 brought more of them to the forefront. It seemed as if the world was listing. Out of balance. Bombings were occurring right here in the United States. Six people were killed and over a thousand injured at the World Trade Center. Then there was the horrific siege at Waco, Texas. When three eight-year-olds were murdered in West Memphis, Melanie thought her childhood was over at the ripe age of nine. Times were changing more quickly than ever, thanks to technology. Over ten million mobile phones were sold internationally. Things were beginning to move fast and not necessarily in the right direction.

Chapter Three

Mr. Leonard

The summer between third and fourth grade was less dramatic than the school year and surely much better than the summer before. Melanie was able to spend time outside and took on swimming as her summer sport, along with reading more complicated novels. Her voracious appetite for books brought her reading to a sixth-grade level.

By the fifth grade, Melanie was reading at a seventh-grade level. She had already ripped through the pages of all the books required by her English teacher that year. There wasn't a question he could ask that she didn't know the answer to, but she refrained from monopolizing the class. Just as she wasn't a tattletale, she also wasn't a show-off, but she was bored. During a reading lesson, she tried to stifle her yawning, and at one point, she caught herself nodding off. Her teacher, Mr. Leonard, was not known for being particularly kind. He always seemed to be mad about something. He approached Melanie's desk and slammed a yardstick down so hard, it broke into pieces. Melanie jumped from her seat as the rest of the class gasped.

"Am I keeping you awake, Miss Drake?" he snarled.

Melanie sat up tall, blinked, and answered. "No sir."

"Then would you like to tell the class about *Treasure Island*?"

Melanie stood up and began, "*Treasure Island* was written by Robert Louis Stevenson in 1881. Some of his other books include *A Child's Garden of Verses*, and the creepy *Dr. Jekyll and Mr. Hyde*." She paused and scanned her audience. She wasn't aware that "reading the room" was a thing. For her, it was intuitive. Her classmates were wide-eyed and at the edge of their seats. None of them wanted a yardstick smashed in front of them.

Melanie shared the synopsis of the book, outlining the story of a young boy named Jim Hawkins whose family owned an inn. An old sea captain, named Billy Bones, was one of the residents, but he died, leaving behind a mysterious chest. Melanie's description of the plot was animated as she proceeded to describe the treasure map, the pirates, the mutiny, and the rescue. When Melanie thought she'd given Mr. Leonard enough to thwart his attempt at embarrassing her, she took a slight bow and sat back in her seat. The class was mesmerized and clapped with enthusiasm. Mr. Leonard was red-faced. "You have your mother call me," he demanded.

"Okey dokey," she replied calmly.

"What did you say?" he roared. She swore she saw steam coming out of his ears.

"Yes, sir," she corrected herself. When he turned around, she gave her fellow classmates one of her classic eye rolls. Kids were biting their lips trying not to laugh. No one wanted to send Mr. Leonard on another bashing spree. Melanie craned her neck to see if there were any more yardsticks. Nope. Just a pointer. One more weapon left. She wondered if the janitor noticed all the missing rulers. She recalled at least five other occasions when Mr. Leonard had destroyed school property. *Why didn't anyone say anything?* She thought about the conversation she was going to have with her mother.

Perhaps that would put an end to his tyrannical behavior. Either that, or she would be grounded. She knew she would have to choose her words carefully and not sound like a whiny schoolkid.

That evening during dinner, everyone had their turn discussing the events of the day. Her parents owned a real estate agency in Harrison, just an hour southwest of Washington DC. With the influx of politicians and lobbyists, her parents were a very busy couple. Her mother discussed showing one of the McMansions, and her father bemoaned his paperwork. Melanie waited for her brother Justin to boast about his basketball scores before she dropped the Mr. Leonard bomb on her mother.

"Mel? And how was your day?" her father asked with his fork in midair.

She took a big breath. "Well . . . you remember I told you that Mr. Leonard has a bad temper?"

Both parents nodded. They knew kids had active imaginations, although Melanie wasn't prone to exaggerating. "Today he was talking about *Treasure Island.*"

"You read that last summer," her mother said with confidence and a smile.

"Yes, so I was bored." Melanie made a grimace. "I guess my eyes were closed, and Mr. Leonard broke a yardstick over my desk." She was very matter-of-fact.

Her father plunked his fork on his plate. "He did what? A yardstick?"

Melanie frowned and nodded. "Yep. I mean, yes."

"Oh my goodness! What happened? Did anyone get hurt?" The smile left her mother's face instantaneously, and she placed her hand on Melanie's arm.

"No, there were just a bunch of splinters all over the place. I don't think they hit anyone," Melanie said thoughtfully.

More questions came at rapid fire.

"Why would he do such a thing?"

"Has he done this before?"

Then finally, "Are you okay?"

"Like I said, my eyes were closed. I guess he thought I wasn't paying attention."

Justin snickered. "You probably weren't." Justin knew his sister was a model student. He simply liked to tease her.

"No need for that, son," his father responded with a frown.

Melanie attempted to kick him under the table, but she couldn't reach without disengaging herself from her mother's death grip. Instead she gave him one of her death-ray looks.

Her father spoke again. This time, he was calm. "What happened after he broke the ruler?"

"He made me get up and tell the class the story," Melanie answered with confidence.

Justin snickered. "Bet you got him good on that one!"

"Yes, but now he wants Mom to call him tomorrow."

"Call him? Were you misbehaving?" Mrs. Drake asked with surprise.

"No!" she said defiantly. "I did exactly what he asked me to do." She tightened her lips.

"So why on earth does he want me to call him?"

Melanie shrugged and asked a rhetorical question: "Because he's mean?"

"You can tell Mr. Leonard if he has anything he wants to discuss with me, he can call our number. How dare he!" Mrs. Drake was exasperated.

"Do you want me to handle this?" Mr. Drake interjected.

"No. I want Melanie to tell that brute to pick up the phone himself."

"We don't want Melanie to suffer any further repercussions," he said evenly.

"Repercussions, my hiney! The man is a brute, picking on children."

Melanie furrowed her brow and looked up at the ceiling.

Children. She never considered herself a child. A kid, yes. A child, no. In her mind, the word *children* meant immature. Well, if it worked in her favor, her mother could call her anything she wanted, and Melanie had no problem delivering her mother's message.

The next morning, as the kids were scrambling to their seats, Mr. Leonard pulled Melanie aside. "Did you tell your mother to call me?"

"Yes, sir, I did."

"And?"

Melanie looked him straight in the eye and quoted her mother verbatim. "She said, 'If he has anything he wants to discuss with me, he can call our number.'" Melanie quickly glanced at the blackboard. Only that one pointer remained. Would he use it? She held her breath. She knew no matter what transpired next, her parents were on her side.

Mr. Leonard's face reddened for the second time in less than twenty-four hours, and she thought his head might explode. He snarled, "Fine. I will do that. Now go to your seat." He flung the lesson plan book toward his desk, but it missed and went careening over the side and into the wastebasket. The class erupted in howls and giggles, which made things worse. "Shut up! All of you! Tonight you are going to write, 'I must behave' one hundred times." There was silence. Melanie thought her classmates would be angry with her, but they knew Mr. Leonard enjoyed doling out punishment, even when it wasn't warranted.

That evening at dinner her mother, asked how it had gone with Mr. Leonard. "Okay, I guess."

"What do you mean, 'you guess'?"

"Well, he wasn't very happy with my answer, so he threw his lesson plan, and it ended up in the garbage."

Justin's soda came spewing out his mouth, her father tried to stifle a laugh, and her mother looked on with horror.

"That man has a terrible temper!" she exclaimed.

Melanie refrained from an "I told you so," but she went on to mention their punishment assignment because the class laughed at the lesson plan disaster. Her mother was on the verge of throwing her own temper tantrum. "That's enough bullying as far as I'm concerned. Peter, you and I are going to have a meeting with the principal. Someone who is easily unhinged should not be teaching children."

Children. That word again, but if it got rid of Mr. Leonard, she didn't mind what she was called.

"You're right, Dorothy. I'll call Mr. Rigley in the morning." He huffed. "There's already enough violence in the world. We don't need it in the classroom." Mr. Drake couldn't possibly know the kind of devastating events that lay ahead.

"Maybe you'll get him fired," Justin wisecracked.

Melanie wondered if that would make her a hero to her classmates. Not that she needed the adoration, but it would be kinda cool.

The next morning, rather than wasting a phone call, the Drakes decided to go straight to the principal's office. They waited a reasonable amount of time for the man to get settled into his routine before they pitched a fit. In a courteous but firm manner, of course.

They arrived wearing business attire. "Good morning, Mrs. Chesterfield. May we have a few moments with Mr. Rigley?"

Mrs. Chesterfield had been the school secretary since Dorothy (Gleason) Drake went to Hamilton Elementary School. It was over twenty-five years ago, and Mrs. Chesterfield was ancient back then! Funny how one's perception of "older people" changes as you become one of them. Dorothy Drake wondered if the pink glasses and pink pearl eyeglass holder were the same ones the secretary had sported years ago. She still had the pink hair, too. Mrs. Chesterfield hadn't changed a bit.

"May I ask what this is about?" The secretary peered over

her spectacles. She had a cherub's face. It was a wonder she'd survived all these years dealing with the kids. And their parents.

"It's somewhat of a private matter, Mrs. Chesterfield." Mr. Drake glanced over at the two students sitting in the waiting area.

She got the message. It wasn't a matter for eavesdropping kids. She picked up the phone and buzzed her boss's office. "Mr. Rigley, Mr. and Mrs. Drake are here to see you." She paused and looked up as if she had to count. "Yes, both of them." She nodded. "I will. Thank you." She hung up and told the Drakes to take a seat. Mr. Rigley would be out shortly. "He has a matter he needs to attend to." She tilted her pen in the direction of the two youths, who were slouched in their seats.

Mr. Drake indicated he understood and shuttled his wife to the two chairs opposite the teens, whose expressions showed signs of indifference.

Several minutes later, Mr. Rigley came out. "Ross? Henry? In my office." He turned to the Drakes. "I'll just be a minute." He followed the boys and then closed the door behind him.

Mrs. Chesterfield leaned in and whispered loudly enough for them to hear. "Those two are a bucket of trouble. They're in here at least once a week."

Dorothy didn't want to ask why, and she didn't have to. Mrs. Chesterfield relished the opportunity to gossip. She also believed that if she was speaking the truth, then it wasn't really gossip.

"They keep getting caught smoking marijuana. Imagine that? Eleven and twelve years old! They don't realize they stink of it when they come back from their hidey-hole." She shook her head. "I overheard some kids talking in the hallway, saying they are selling it to other students, but nobody's been able to prove it. One has to wonder where their parents are and how they're getting their hands on the stuff." She clicked her tongue.

Dorothy squeezed her husband's hand. She knew Melanie would never touch marijuana, but Justin might. He was in junior high school, at a very impressionable age, and a much bigger risk-taker than his sister. At least for now.

As if he knew what was on his wife's mind, Peter said, "Justin is a smart kid." He paused. "Besides, if he was smoking weed, we would smell it on his clothes, his hair, and his breath. I have to agree with you, Mrs. Chesterfield. One has to wonder. Unless they change their clothes before they get home and do their own laundry, that smell stays with you."

Mrs. Chesterfield laughed out loud. "That'll be the day when either of those two see the inside of a washing machine. They probably slip a few dollars to the maid. They both have them, ya know. Full time. Plus they have nannies or some kind of sitter. Parents are political big shots and are never around. I was dead serious when I said, 'one has to wonder.' Spoiled rotten, I say." She grunted. "Times have surely changed since you went to school here, Mrs. Drake. Funny, calling you Mrs. Drake now."

"Dorothy is fine. Really." She smiled at the spry senior.

Their conversation came to an end when the principal's office door opened. The two boys shuffled out. No smiles on anyone's faces. "Mrs. Chesterfield, please notify their parents and have whoever is supposed to be in charge of them pick them up. They're suspended for two weeks. I just hope it won't be treated as a vacation." He was careful with his words. They lived in an upper-middle-class community, and the parents had delusions of entitlement. Mr. Rigley stared the two boys down. He was well aware these two youths were unsupervised a good portion of the time. With the exception of the live-in housekeepers, no one was keeping an eye on them.

Ross had a cocky grin on his face. He knew Mr. Rigley couldn't bring in the police without proof, so they were suspended for unruly behavior. *Big deal.*

Ross began to sulk.

"Here is what's going to happen. You go home and think about where you could end up if you don't follow the rules. We'll give you the paperwork to bring home to your parents. They will have to monitor your homework and keep a log."

Both boys groaned; then Ross chimed in with sarcasm. "My parents are invisible."

Rigley knew that was the crux of the problem. No parental guidance or supervision. Who would teach these boys morality? Integrity? Honesty? He thought about the 1978 documentary, *Scared Straight.* Delinquents spent three hours in prison with hardened criminals. He imagined the uproar if someone suggested it now.

"They're going to be so pissed," Henry whined. He could not picture his mother sitting down to supervise homework. It would interfere with her evening racquetball lessons. At least that's what she told his father she was doing at the club.

"Or do you prefer that I go to their place of work and tell them in person?" Rigley was bluffing, doing his best to shake some sense into the teens. "Better to give them the news in the comfort of their own home, don't you agree?" Mr. Rigley asked calmly. "You wouldn't want them to be humiliated, would you?"

Henry knew his father was going to hit the roof. If he heard about the suspension in his office, he would go ballistic. *There goes my allowance.* "No." He gave Rigley a sour look, while Mrs. Chesterfield phoned the boy's custodians.

Rigley turned toward the Drakes. He'd never had an issue with Justin while he was at Hamilton, and Melanie was a straight-A student. He wondered at the reason for this unexpected visit. "Please come in." He gestured toward his office.

Once again, he closed his door. "Have a seat." The Drakes sat in the two chairs facing Mr. Rigley's desk. "What brings you here today?"

Dorothy and Peter looked at each other. Dorothy spoke first. "Melanie came home with a very disturbing story last night."

Peter spoke next. "Mr. Leonard slammed a yardstick over Melanie's desk, and it broke into several pieces."

Mr. Rigley looked alarmed. Peter continued. "From what I understand, it wasn't the first time."

Mr. Rigley let out a big sigh. "Do you know what brought on Mr. Leonard's behavior?"

"According to Melanie, Mr. Leonard was discussing *Treasure Island* and Melanie closed her eyes for a minute. After the drama, he demanded she stand up and tell the class what the book was about," Peter said.

"Melanie read the book over the summer and had no trouble reciting the story. When she was finished, Mr. Leonard ordered her to have us call him," Dorothy explained. "But we told her to let him know if he had an issue, he should call *us*."

Peter continued. "The next morning, she approached Mr. Leonard and conveyed our sentiments about the phone call. Apparently, he got angry and flung the lesson plan across the desk, and it landed in the trash can. The students thought it was funny and laughed."

Dorothy picked the tale up from there. "That infuriated Mr. Leonard further, and he gave the class a punishment assignment. They were to write *I must behave* one hundred times. We told her not to do it. And this is why we are here."

"This type of hostile behavior by an adult, a teacher no less, has no place in school," Peter added.

Mr. Rigley took a few more notes. "Students often exaggerate, especially if they don't like the amount of homework they're given."

"With all due respect, Mr. Rigley, our daughter Melanie

does not exaggerate, nor does she shirk any of her assignments," Dorothy observed.

"Point well taken," Mr. Rigley said thoughtfully. "What I would like to suggest is that I interview some of her classmates privately and ask them what they've experienced in Mr. Leonard's class."

"That's a very good suggestion. How long do you think this process will take? We do not want our daughter being exposed to more severe conduct." Peter Drake was firm.

"I'll handle it right away," Mr. Rigley promised. "Today."

Dorothy let out a sigh of relief. "Thank you, Mr. Rigley. You know we are not nagging, helicopter parents."

Peter added, "Melanie is bright and astute. She didn't come running to us with this issue. We simply asked how her day went, and then she told us what transpired."

"I completely understand." Mr. Rigley stood behind his desk. "I'll get to the bottom of this before lunch," he reassured them.

With that cue, the Drakes stood, shook hands, and conveyed their appreciation. They bid adieu to Mrs. Chesterfield, wished her a good day, and left the building. Dorothy locked arms with Peter. "I'm glad we did this in person."

"So am I," Peter replied. "I wonder what will happen to the explosive fifth-grade teacher."

"I don't really care, darling, so long as he leaves Melanie alone." She pecked her husband on the cheek as he opened the passenger door for her.

Mr. Rigley walked to Mr. Leonard's class carrying a clipboard. "Sorry to interrupt." He glanced at his notes. "May I have a word with Mark Tucker, Maggie Sullivan, Keith Parent, and Yolanda Fleming?" Mr. Rigley chose four different students to give him a mix of points of view. Granted, they were ten and eleven years old, but they were still their own people with their own opinions.

"What's this about?" Mr. Leonard asked suspiciously.

Mr. Rigley motioned for the students to accompany him. "This won't take long," he replied, purposely ignoring the question.

Once they were out of earshot of the classroom, Mr. Rigley let the students know they were not in trouble. He just wanted to ask them a few questions.

The four kids sat in the same four chairs in the vestibule previously occupied by Ross, Henry, and the Drakes. One at a time, they were called into Mr. Rigley's office. Each one was warned not to discuss the matter with anyone, and then he proceeded to ask questions about Mr. Leonard's vitriolic behavior. Initially, all of them were intimidated and concerned about the consequences of being a tattletale, but they knew it was important to tell the truth. Within forty-five minutes, Mr. Rigley had gleaned enough information to know he needed to explore Mr. Leonard's behavior further. But not at the expense of the children.

The next morning, a nicely dressed middle-aged woman greeted the class. "Good morning, everyone. I'm Mrs. Hawthorne. I will be taking Mr. Leonard's place for the time being."

Eyes darted around the room from Melanie to Yolanda, to Maggie, Mark, and Keith. Whispering and giggling followed. Melanie shrugged and wished she could clap her hands instead. She knew her parents must have made a good case in order for Mr. Rigley to question her classmates. She was convinced Mr. Leonard would somehow be punished for not following the rules. She wasn't sure what rule he had disobeyed, but there had to be one about breaking things on students' desks and being a jerk.

Chapter Four

Mr. Flynn

After the Mr. Leonard incident and her presentation on *Treasure Island*, Melanie began to have a reputation for being cool, calm, and collected. Granted, some of the kids were wary of her. She seemed to have an edge on them, more of a "big picture" approach, but others found her company appealing, perhaps because Melanie's take on things was slightly more mature than that of her peers.

With Mrs. Hawthorne at the front of the class, the rest of the school year passed without incident, and they were promoted to the sixth grade.

Melanie wanted to have a summer job, but at eleven, there weren't many options. Instead she fashioned one of her grandmother's shawls into a cape with the words "MelDrake the Magician" written in hot-pink glitter. Every morning, on her way to work, Dorothy would drop Melanie off at one of the community's nursing homes or the local hospital, where she would perform card tricks for the patients.

As the new school year approached, she went through her closet with her mother. Melanie had grown two inches since the prior year. She was about to turn twelve and was five feet, four inches tall with long legs. She tried not to feel like a freak, since most of her friends were hovering around five-feet-two. But sixth grade proved she was not the only one going through growing pains. Many of the boys began to show signs of acne, and girls were experimenting with their hair.

By the time she entered junior high, she was increasingly aware of the biological changes she and her female classmates were going through. Everyone around her was in some phase of a hot mess.

The phys ed teacher had her hands full with all the hormonal fluctuations. For the first time, everyone had to change into a gym suit, and the girl's locker room became a gawking place where a variety of breast expansions and boxes of feminine products were visible. It was time for the teacher to educate the class about menstruation and what it meant. Some of the girls were looking forward to this big change, because they believed it would make them more mature. Little did they know it was just the beginning of an often-bumpy ride on the road of womanhood.

By high school, cliques, mean girls, spoiled girls, nerds, geeks, and jocks were among the many new things to navigate, including the notion of being "popular." For the girls, stereotypical blondes and cheerleaders were at the top of the pyramid. Melanie did not meet either criterion. For one thing, she wasn't blond. For another, she didn't have boobs. Her mother promised she would "develop," but Melanie was skeptical. She would have to depend on her keen sense of observation and her smarts.

One afternoon a few boys made a snide remark about her friend Audrey's "knockers." *Better to be known for your brains than your boobs,* she encouraged herself. Of course, that would ultimately depend on who was in charge, and who was following the rules of proper behavior. That theory was tested in 1998 during the Clinton and Monica Lewinsky scandal, and we know how that turned out.

Melanie wasn't a loner by any means, but her priorities were a little different from those of her friends. She studied, volunteered, and pleased audiences with her magic tricks during the school talent shows. If she got invited to a party, she went. If not, she didn't give it much thought. She wanted to be considered one of the brightest students, and that ambition propelled her forward.

As the idea of college loomed in the distance, she appreciated her parents' view of education. It was important and available; and if you were a good student, it was free or almost free. With that in mind, Melanie was determined to continue her run of getting straight As. Biology was a problem for her, though. She did not want to cut up dead worms or frogs. Even the smell of formaldehyde made her nauseous. She knew it would take some extra credit work to circumvent the dissecting part of the curriculum and decided it was necessary to discuss her situation with her teacher, who had already become impatient with her "queasy dramatics."

Right after the class was dismissed, she approached her teacher. "Mr. Flynn, may I speak to you for a moment?" Melanie was now a mature fifteen-year-old. "I need some advice."

The cranky, bald man with the beady eyes looked at her suspiciously. He was flabbergasted. "Advice?" No one ever asked for his advice. "Yes. I have a few minutes." He really had lots of minutes, hours even, but no one needed to know that. He gestured toward the desk in the first row. Melanie chose to stand.

"Mr. Flynn, I do not want you to think I don't respect the requirements of sophomore biology, but is there some way I can do something besides cutting up invertebrates?"

Mr. Flynn blinked in surprise. She had been paying attention. At least once. "I'll have to speak with the principal. Deviating from the curriculum is highly frowned upon."

"I understand. But it's not as if I want to shirk my studies. With your experience, I am certain you could find something comparable to the knowledge I would garner from the dissections."

Flynn blinked rapidly. Yes. Yes, he was experienced, even if the rest of the faculty thought he was a dullard. He stood and started to pace slowly, resting his chin between his thumb and forefinger.

Melanie recalled a cartoon. She couldn't remember the character, but it depicted the inside of a man's head with wheels turning as the nuts and bolts flew off and spilled out of his ears. She bit her upper lip, repressing the urge to laugh out loud. She quickly regrouped and put a pleasant smile on her face, hoping to encourage a favorable answer.

He turned on his heel. "I think you may be onto something, Miss Drake. There are many other aspects of biology that can be substituted. I will have to get permission, but in the meantime, we will call it an 'experiment in education'."

"Thank you, sir." Melanie smiled again. "I appreciate your interest in the fundamentals of education and how they apply to real life." Melanie had an impeccable grasp of the English language. If you didn't know she was fifteen, you would think you were having a conversation with someone older. More educated. More mature. And she was. Both those things. Having been a voracious reader since grammar school, Melanie had a far larger vocabulary than her fellow students. Probably a good many adults, as well.

Flynn nodded as she exited the room and decided he *was* quite brilliant.

The following week, during the regular lab period, Mr. Flynn called Melanie up to the front of the class. "Ms. Drake will be cataloging your results, so be sure your writing is clear."

He handed her a clipboard and waved her off.

And that's how it's done, she thought to herself. Asking advice is one of the biggest compliments you can give to another person. Insert a dash of puffery, without sounding smarmy, and you have an excellent chance of achieving your goal. More info for the vault, she noted.

Melanie's personal life could be considered boring to those who simply wanted to have a good time. Not that she was averse to fun; she was simply able to compartmentalize her life and maintained a healthy balance. She had little interest in dating boys. That could wait. Besides, they were immature. She was easily bored with their conversation. She did, however, have a study buddy. It was her fifth-grade friend, Mark Tucker. Mark had been impressed with Melanie's presentation of *Treasure Island*, and from that point up until the time they finished high school, the two bonded over their shared love of books.

Chapter Five

The Tipping Point

It was the fall of 2001 when Melanie began her senior year of high school. Her economics teacher insisted they read *The Washington Post* every day, and when he was met with whining, he reminded his students, "A year from now, you will no longer be in a microcosm where there are countless opportunities for information, guidance, and freedom. Yes, freedom." He paused to let the word sink in. "I know what you're thinking. *Freedom?*" Mr. Cosgrove went around to the front of his desk, leaned against it, and folded his arms. "I am sure most of you would argue that you have curfews, and homework, and chores. But you also have a lot of free time to hang out with friends, go to sporting events, parties, watch TV, listen to music, play video games. You have time to do those things now, but once you graduate, there are going to be expectations beyond turning in a homework assignment or going to practice. You will be expected to hold a job, go to college, or vocational school. That, my friends, will be your routine. The road to responsibility." Another pause. Students started to slouch in their seats. "You're probably thinking, 'What does that have to do with a newspaper?'

Why am I telling you all this? Because I want you to be aware." He moved to the blackboard and wrote the words BE AWARE and underlined them three times for emphasis. "Be aware of what is happening around you, in your community, your country, and the world. If you are aware, then you will be better prepared." He stood silently for another moment. Then he snickered and grinned. "Meanwhile, enjoy yourself, but try to be aware. Look around you. Look ahead. You don't want that light at the end of the tunnel to be an oncoming train."

There were a few uncomfortable guffaws, but the mood of the classroom became slightly more contemplative.

Melanie soaked up those words like a sponge. *Be aware.* It occurred to her that if she put them together, the result came dangerously close to the word BEWARE. *More info for the vault.*

As the first two weeks passed, she was grateful for the requirement. Not that the news was good, but each day she became better informed. She read about the expanding energy crisis, and the formation of a national energy policy. She was aware of the words *climate change* before they became part of the everyday lexicon. She was also aware of the need to develop nuclear safety measures, here and abroad. If she hadn't been forced to get her fingers covered in ink, she might not have been as aware of the world outside the innocent hamlet of Harrison, Virginia. Because of her heightened state of awareness, Melanie knew it was important to pursue a career that could make a difference. She just wasn't sure what that career should be.

Then it happened. The devastating day when our country was attacked by terrorists. We were a stunned nation, and the horror continued to unfold over the coming weeks. Months. *What is happening to us? Where do we go from here? Is there a place to go? Will we recover?* People were terrified as they faced the unknown.

That life-changing event gave Melanie clarity. A lot of people were making up new rules, and they weren't good. There were also secret organizations that had no rules at all. Rules were meant for commoners. Something had to happen to get the planet back on course. Humans had to change their behavior. But how?

She remembered her conversation with Mr. Flynn and how she'd negotiated an arrangement that suited both of them. Melanie wrote up the students' notes; therefore, he didn't have to. In exchange, she did not have to face a preserved frog. *Diplomacy. Negotiation.*

Melanie believed when there was conflict, one should confer. Consult. Be reasonable. Melanie knew she couldn't change the world by herself, but she believed in the butterfly effect—a small change or variance in one state could create a large change in a later state. She was not going to be a victim. She was going to be a butterfly. It was better and cheaper than going to war. But, in time, Melanie would learn that some people are unreasonable, implacable, bull-headed, stubborn, and just plain evil.

She was on a mission. She applied to the few colleges that offered the curriculum she wanted. There was no doubt she would be accepted to all of them. While the Drakes enjoyed many nice things, they weren't rich, and college was expensive. Add in housing, books, food, and transportation, you're looking at a big chunk of change. A scholarship, at least a partial one, was very possible. She hoped the school that offered it wouldn't be too far from home, but she made finances the determining factor. By January, she had been accepted at Yale, Georgetown, Stanford, and the University of Virginia College of Arts & Sciences. She and her family were elated when Virginia came through with all of her requirements.

The last few months of her senior year moved at a quick

pace. She was moving away from home. There would be new people. New places. Big places. She was ready.

Along with graduation came the senior prom. Melanie wanted to go to mark the transition, but she surely didn't want to go alone. Mark! They could go together. She knew she could convince him, and they would make it fun. Mark wore a red tuxedo jacket with black pants and a black bow tie. He finished off his look with a black bowler hat. He looked kind of cute, actually. Melanie was dressed in a blue and white beaded kaftan, with a matching scarf tied around her head, the knot below her ear. She stared in the mirror. She knew she had to put something on her face. The cover stick she occasionally used wouldn't cut it. The occasion required a little more effort. This would probably be the last time she would see most of these people. Ross and Henry had been out of the picture once they got to junior high. Ross ended up in a juvenile facility, and Henry was sent away to military school. No one ever discovered what happened to Mr. Leonard. Rumor had it he was in a straitjacket in an asylum. At least that's what everyone wished.

She peered at her scar, which had morphed from looking like a zipper to more like one of those creepy worms from biology. She decided to adorn it instead of hiding it. She pulled the magic kit from the closet. Inside was a collection of metallic face-paint tubes including turquoise, silver, and purple. Perfect! She began to make fine twinkle-looking strokes along the scar and finished it off with a butterfly at her temple. *Yes, perfect!* Her father was right. It was a badge of honor. Had it not been for the accident, she might never have become such an avid reader. Her life could have taken an entirely different course.

As promised, she and Mark had a ball making fun of the way some of the guys danced. "Don't athletes require some kind of coordination?" he asked sardonically.

"It appears their talents have been left out on the field," Melanie replied with a similar tone.

The summer flew by, as Melanie juggled working as a receptionist at her parents' office and getting ready for the big move. She was confident, but also nervous. It was going to be a very big change. She was accustomed to studying, but this next level would be entirely different. Her career path would depend on the outcome.

PART TWO

The Job

Chapter Six

As soon as she was able, she declared to major in politics and foreign affairs, with the goal of being accepted into the Distinguished Majors Program. Her thesis was on the subject of *The Politics of Religion and The Religion of Politics*, and how the lines are constantly blurred. College was grueling and competitive, but Melanie had a steel will and let nothing distract her from her studies. Not even boys. She decided to increase the age when the male gender had a clue about life and the real world. Maybe they would catch up to her around age thirty.

After graduating from college, she discovered most companies, including the government, required a master's degree of job candidates. For the first time since the third grade, Melanie was deflated. Getting a master's degree would cost money, and she wasn't about to dig herself into a hole of debt that would amount to a lifetime of financial liability.

One evening, she was uncharacteristically bemoaning her situation to her brother. He had an easy answer for her problem. "Apply for a job at OSI. They have programs for continuing education." Justin was referring to the Office of Special Investigations for the U.S. Air Force. He was a decorated pilot and was more than willing to write a glowing recommendation. Though she protested against such nepotism, he did it anyway. But her record spoke volumes.

Melanie graduated from University of Virginia with a 4.0 grade point average; she was a member of the International Relations Club, and occasionally, the Women's Soccer Club.

She researched the job postings and put an application in for an entry-level position. Over a month had gone by and she was getting discouraged when she received a registered letter with information regarding an initial screening with Human Resources. The packet contained reams of paperwork asking for school records, medical records, permission to do a background check, and, should she be considered, her agreement to undergo a mental capacity test. *Whoa.* The instructions were to fill out all the forms and bring them with her to the initial screening. She would also have to bring a photo ID. If that process went favorably, then her application would be evaluated, scored, and ranked by a review board of OSI special agents.

The following week, she was in front of the security gate at Quantico, Virginia. For the first time, she had the jitters. She wasn't sure if it was because she was going on a job interview, or because she was in this hub where some of the world's most important decisions were made. She took a deep breath. Probably a bit of both. It was intimidating.

The Marine guard checked his list of expected visitors and phoned the OSI human resources office. He gave her a pass and instructions as to which door she should enter. From there, she went through very tight security. She could not take any personal items with her except for the paperwork and was given a large orange tag in exchange for her purse, coat, and phone. She was escorted to an office, where a person in his mid-fifties sat behind a desk. He oozed authority.

He was polite and very much down to business. He said nothing as he perused her paperwork. Her hands were beginning to sweat. It was impossible to tell what the man was thinking. He finally looked up. "You seem to check off all the boxes." A smile. Finally.

"So tell me, why do you want to be in service to the OSI?"

Melanie was fully prepared for that question. "I realize this will sound cliché, but I want to make a difference. The world seems out of balance. We need people who are willing to work to regain that balance."

He smiled again. "I am sure whatever your endeavors, you will make a difference. You have an impressive dossier."

"Thank you." Melanie gave him one of her softer stares. "Sir? What do you think?"

He folded his hands over the paper file that sat on his desk. "Your application will be evaluated, scored, and ranked by a review board of OSI special agents."

"I understand. But if you don't mind my asking, what do *you* think?" She knew she was treading a fine line.

"I think you would make an excellent candidate, but you are overqualified for the posting you applied for."

"Thank you. I think. But please understand, my goal is to gain an entry-level position at PAQ." She was referring to Palace Acquire Program, a counterintelligence agency branch of Special Investigations.

"That is rather ambitious, but I have seen people with less savvy and intelligence succeed." He paused, causing a lump to form in Melanie's throat.

Lump gone. "Thank you, sir."

"It will take several weeks. It's the government, you know. That will be something you'll have to get used to." He chuckled. "Hurry up and wait."

Melanie finally let out the breath she had been holding for what felt like an hour. "Every bureaucracy operates that way."

"I think you'll do just fine." He guffawed. "Sit tight, and you'll be hearing from HR soon." He didn't want to overstep and tell her she was perfect for an entry-level job, just in case one of his superiors didn't think she would pass muster. He stood and shook her hand. "Pleasure to meet you." She fixed her eyes on the officer. "I am willing to start wherever I am needed."

He watched as she exited his office. She was poised and exuded professionalism. He hoped the higher-ups didn't blow it. OSI needed people like Melanie Drake.

Almost a month later, she was informed she had ranked high enough for another interview. This time it would be in front of a panel of OSI special agents and would include a psychological assessment. If she got past this round, her application would go to the Executive Director for validation. At that point, they would tentatively match her with a position location based on her request and the needs of the agency. She thought if she indicated she was flexible, it would increase her chances of getting a job. Again, weeks went by before she heard anything. At the moment, they were in need of a communications administrator. Translated: clerical assistant. It wasn't exactly what she had in mind, but what she had in mind would come with more experience. For now it was a foot in the door. No, it was two feet in the door. Next up was a medical exam. She hoped her scars wouldn't hint at any disability that could disqualify her. She was handed a piece of paper with a very rudimentary outline of the human body and instructed to mark the areas where her bones had broken. The facial scar spoke for itself. The exam took two hours, and she still wouldn't know if she had a job or not. They thanked her for coming in, made her sign more documents, and sent her on her way. "Someone will be in touch with you regarding the rest of your application."

She thanked them in return and wondered how much longer this was going to take. According to her calculations, she'd begun this process almost three months before. *Bureaucracy. Rules.*

Ten days later, she received a phone call informing her that her application was in the suitability part of the process, which would take another forty-five to sixty days. She was getting twitchy. She had arranged to stay with her parents during her job hunt, not realizing it would take months. They agreed she could work in their office until she was gainfully employed. She was on the verge of embarrassment. After all the work she'd put into her studies, how had she ended up living with her parents? She kept telling herself it was temporary, but six months isn't temporary. Not as far as she was concerned.

Hurry up and wait. He wasn't kidding. She made an appointment with a placement agency. She had to get some kind of job. Anything. The morning she was supposed to meet with the headhunter, she got the call. Melanie was accepted into the Palace Acquire Program, where she would be on a three-year training and career development track. She would have a mentor and opportunities to receive additional training. She was given a date to report to HR to receive her instructions.

When she arrived, she went through the metal detector checkpoint. All people entering the building were required to secure their personal possessions, including cellphones, in a high-security area. She was then directed to the HR area, where she was issued two khaki shirts, two pairs of black trousers, and a handbook. There was a small locker room where she changed with two other women with identically unfashionable wear. She was told in advance sneakers were unacceptable, not that she would have worn them.

She was given a key for the locker for her clothes, and then directed to a small area where she had her photo taken, laminated, and strung on a lanyard. From there, she went to a classroom. She was the only one there.

After a few minutes, Major Polly Beale entered. Melanie didn't know if she should stand and salute. Definitely stand. The woman in her late forties introduced herself. "Major Polly Beale, Director of Cyber Activity and Practices. We keep an eye on the movement and flow of information through hundreds of servers."

Melanie nodded her head. Beale continued. "I am going to be evaluating your skill at spotting an anomaly. Depending on how well you do, you will be assigned to a system and be responsible for monitoring said system."

Melanie thought it was a tremendous amount of responsibility for an entry-level job. Beale sensed Melanie's doubt. "You will be supervised by one of the more experienced personnel, but I am confident you will be able to handle the work."

"Thank you, Major," Melanie replied.

"Call me 'Boss'." Polly smiled. "Shall we get started?"

Beale powered up a computer with simulated scenarios of what Melanie would be staring at all day. Melanie's computer mirrored what the major was viewing. "I want you to study the flow of traffic." She was speaking about internet traffic. "Watch the screen for a few minutes and click when you notice any changes coming from any direction."

Melanie stared at the monitor. It reminded her of a computer game. Even though this was a simulation, eventually she would be playing for keeps. She followed the dozens of bright green bars connecting from one access point to another. She clicked on anything that deviated. The test lasted for thirty minutes, and she had no idea how well she was doing, or not. At the end of the exam, a buzzer went off, causing her to flinch. She hoped that wasn't a nonstarter. Major Beale took a few minutes to evaluate Melanie's score. She smiled. "Good work." Melanie didn't ask the major to elaborate. Curiosity was killing her, but she didn't ask. She was surrounded by top-secret information. They only told you what you needed to know. If Major Beale thought it was appropriate, she would share whatever she thought was useful, or necessary.

Beale escorted Melanie down a hallway lined with doors that read RESTRICTED or AUTHORIZED PERSONNEL ONLY, plus a multitude of cameras facing in every direction. They came upon an open area of cubicles, where a dozen others sat with headsets and monitors. "Welcome to cybersecurity." She nodded toward an empty booth. "That's where you'll be working." She snapped her fingers to get everyone's attention. "Folks, meet Melanie Drake. She will be working with us starting today. Be nice." People smiled, nodded, and a few waved. Beale powered up Melanie's computer and handed her a headset. "And there you go. Not very exciting, but seriously important. I'll be in my office if you need anything." She gestured to the glass-enclosed space a few feet away.

"Thank you." Melanie donned her electronic device, took a seat, and began to study the large screen in front of her. This was not what she'd imagined. Now she had to figure out how to move from staring at computer screens all day to getting her master's degree in foreign diplomatic work. She realized she'd let the cost of continuing education narrow her focus. Well, here she was, and for however long it took, she was going to make the best of it.

After a few days, Melanie got the hang of completing her work without becoming bleary-eyed. She noticed a rhythm and a pattern. Slight deviations were easy for her to spot, and she reported them immediately. Melanie was able to maneuver end-of-day shift reports as deftly as her card tricks. Major Beale was immediately impressed by her efficiency and how quickly she caught on. Melanie thought it was simply a matter of time before she would catapult herself into a more challenging position. Maybe not catapult. Getting noticed by the senior members of the team was important, but her interaction with them was limited, as was most of the building. She had little access to anything except the floor where her cubicle was located, the small breakroom, and the bathroom. Most people brought their lunch and spent the half hour they were allowed to eat in the sterile breakroom, exchanging a little chatter but nothing significant. Mostly sports.

Major Beale would make her rounds, ensuring some face time with her crew. She knew it could be unnerving to her subordinates, but if they couldn't take the pressure of tossing a salad or chomping on a sandwich with their boss hanging around, then they weren't cut out for such sensitive work. Beale also made it a point to sit with Melanie. The young woman was smart, poised, and efficient. Having navigated her way through a primarily male-dominated organization, Polly Beale felt a kinship with the new hire. True, there were other women in the department and in the building, but most of them had achieved their goals, and Beale knew how difficult it was to be starting out.

Polly Beale had entered OSI through the Air Force. She had almost twenty years under her wings and was now a major in the cybersecurity division. Beale's area of expertise was digital forensics: the fingerprints of technology. Polly was all about intrigue and finding the truth. She was married to a fellow officer, also a major. They were career military personnel. They had no children. It was a matter of circumstances. As they were coming up the ranks, they never spent enough time in one place to raise a child properly.

Polly was direct without being blunt. That was something she and Melanie had in common. Their mutual love of books was another, and Melanie was pleased she and her supervisor had something in common besides their determination to stop cybercrime.

After about four weeks on the job, some of her colleagues invited Melanie out for drinks. This was something new for her. She was sociable, but not necessarily a social person. Still, she was pleased to have the opportunity to mingle with seasoned agents. Pick their brains.

Cordial but guarded, Melanie Drake wanted to get to know people before they knew her. She had a knack for ferreting information without revealing too much of herself. But when someone was finally allowed into the land of Mel-Drake, there was one thing she made abundantly clear: Follow the rules, especially hers. Don't lie. Don't cheat. Don't hurt other people or animals, or risk being banished from MelDrake. Off the Christmas card list. She acknowledged some rules made no sense but, for the most part, they were not unreasonable.

Melanie wasn't the only one who wanted to get to know the people around her. They surely wanted to know more about this newbie who seemed to have caught the attention of their superior. *Who was Melanie Drake? What was she up to? Was she a mole?* Collectively they decided to furnish her with a few cocktails, hoping to get to the bottom of the Melanie Drake mystique.

When not in her work clothes, Melanie sported attire that was classic and worn well on her five-foot, seven-inch frame. Simple, but always with one accent piece such as a brooch, statement necklace, or the saddle shoes she wore with her double-breasted pantsuit. But unless she brought a change of clothes, she looked like everyone else. No one was allowed to bring anything that was not OSI-issued past the heavily locked and coded security door, which meant she would have to change in her car. Not happening.

The group was gathering in one of the local bars that was between Melanie's apartment and work. She'd run home and change into something less official, while some of the others pulled sweaters over their regulation shirts in the parking lot. There was a locker room available, but it was a long walk from their security entrance, so most came to work in their required attire of black trousers, khaki shirt, and black boots.

With the exception of the line running from her eyebrow to her earlobe, Melanie had a pretty face and a lovely smile, enhanced by a wry sense of humor. When asked, she could converse on a variety of subjects, from the latest scientific news to Pantone's "color of the year," and debate who had the best Super Bowl halftime performance. Melanie could hold her own regardless of whose company she was in. Instead of giving her colleagues a better idea of who she was, she danced around their questions, her sophistication and knowledge making her even more of an enigma.

After the second month, her coworkers realized she wasn't a mole. At least not for their superiors. If she had been, a few of them would have been dismissed by now for implying certain people were sleeping with people they weren't supposed to be sleeping with.

She resisted making judgments, but she didn't approve. *Rules.* One of the commanding officers was breaking at least two of them. She was married, and her playmate was her subordinate. Melanie couldn't ignore the truth of the matter. Betrayal. It simply wasn't right. Careers ruined. Families broken. *And that's why there are rules.* She kept her conversations banal and never gossiped. Better to hear what was going on than become the subject of scandal.

By the third month, Melanie had no feedback as to what was next on her career path. She was hesitant to say too much regarding her goals, but she knew, at some point, she would ask Polly for career advice. She hoped the opportunity would present itself sooner rather than later. But in her position, you didn't ask questions unless it was regarding the work you were doing at the moment. You spoke when you were spoken to.

Since the day she'd submitted her initial application, her experience with OSI had been confounding. She was anxious to know what opportunities lay ahead. It had taken her long enough to get to this point, wherever it was. Where was she going? She knew there was no turning back, but dang, she wished she had a clue.

By the fourth month, she could no longer stand the ambiguity and asked if she could have a private meeting with her boss. She felt as if she were groping in the dark. Or was that part of the program? An observation period, perhaps? *Interesting.* When she entered the major's office, it appeared her boss knew what was on Melanie's mind. She smiled and gestured to the chair across from her wooden desk. "I am sure you have been wondering when you would get your next assignment?"

Melanie didn't want to appear too forward, as if she assumed she was in line for a promotion. "To be honest, yes. I had a lot of ideas before and during college."

Major Beale relaxed into her chair. "Tell me."

"After 9/11 I wanted to get involved. Help people to talk to each other instead of blowing each other up."

Beale knew Melanie had been only seventeen when the attack happened. She was at an impressionable age. She was idealistic. Bright. But reality could be extremely ugly. Beale believed evil existed. Not in the Biblical sense of a demon with horns and a pitchfork. People were the demons. The question still remained, *why?*

Beale focused her attention on Melanie. "And you think by sitting down and having a conversation with someone, you can keep them from killing innocent people?" Beale leaned forward.

"It's my hope." Melanie smirked, realizing how fanciful and naïve she must sound. Academia could do that to the brightest person. "It would appear that getting people to sit down together is often the big issue."

Beale tilted her head and snorted. "You got it. Unfortunately, those types of people do not want to sit down and have a cup of tea. They are hardwired to go in the direction of destruction. For now, we can only do our best to thwart their efforts. Should they succeed, it's up to us to investigate and bring our enemies to justice. Avoiding disasters is key. Until bad people are willing to stop being bad, we have to remain vigilant." She sat forward, realizing she was pontificating. "And that's the way it is," she concluded, quoting the most revered newscaster in the history of TV, Walter Cronkite. "Now that you know about the reality of the situation, what do you want to do about it?"

Melanie continued. "I wanted to work in international affairs and foreign relations. My brother recommended I start here."

Major Beale sat back and smiled. "He should be proud. You've been doing great work. Among other things, you were able to identify unusually heightened activity coming from West Africa."

Melanie smiled. "Trying to do the best job I can."

"On another occasion, you identified an additional anomaly that turned out to be a scheme targeted at people with diabetes."

Melanie gave her a quizzical look. She was only aware of the geographical locations, not the identity of the originator. Everything was numbers. IP addresses. Lots and lots of numbers. Coordinates. Numbers and more numbers and locations escalating through the dark web.

Beale continued. "I know scammers do not seem to be a threat to national security, but in many ways they are. The scammers procure contact information, reaching out to unsuspecting people. In this case, they notify diabetes patients that they have a newer, cheaper prescription approved by the government. Unfortunately, too many people fall for it. Their personal data gets breached, bank accounts, mortgages. It's a total disruption. And disruption is a form of sabotage."

Melanie listened intently, but her mind kept wondering when Beale would get to the subject of Melanie's career?

"Unfortunately, such scam emails go out by the tens of thousands every single day." She grimaced. "It keeps us on our toes." Major Beale explained that by ferreting out phone scammers, her department was able to uncover information buried in the dark web. "You never know where it will lead." Beale paused. "I am not at liberty to discuss any breaches, but I can assure you, you've been doing a fine job."

It was time. Melanie was getting ants in her pants. "Speaking of where it will lead. Can you give me an idea of the advancement process in the department?"

"Right. That's why we're here. Correct?"

Melanie nodded.

"It depends on how quickly you learn the systems and what you excel at. Based on what I've seen, you'll probably be moving on to Bolling by the end of the year for further training. The military is in the process of combining efforts. The goal is to have a joint base by 2010. If things go according to plan, you'll be part of the transition team. By that time, we'll know your strengths and weaknesses."

Weaknesses. Not normally in her vocabulary. And training? *Training for what?* This mystery career path was exasperating. Melanie was accustomed to knowing what the project was, completing it, and moving on to the next one. But here, everything was top secret, including her future. Melanie quickly discovered it was never up to the employee or recruit to decide their future. In order to get the maximum results, people were placed according to how well they fit in, and where their talents could be used best.

Beale's mind drifted. Melanie seemed keen on understanding why people didn't want to make nice. Perhaps she should explore the area of counterintelligence and psychological profiling. Beale jotted down a note, but didn't mention it to Melanie. She wanted to be sure there was an opportunity there before she approached Melanie on the subject. "We'll have further discussions."

Melanie knew it was her cue to scoot. "Understood. Thank you, Boss." She felt a sense of relief. At least she would be moving in *some* direction.

Mixing with her coworkers became a monthly thing. The group ranged from five to seven people, depending on who was available. Melanie looked forward to winding down with her colleagues. She decided being sociable wasn't such a bad thing, until Wayne Howell asked her to go out with him. It threw her for a loop. *What was the protocol for that?* She didn't dare ask him. *Maybe talk to Polly?* She stalled him by mentioning other plans and asking for a "rain check." She had to admit, she enjoyed his company. Another unusual circumstance for Ms. Drake: she'd found a guy who wasn't boring. He was smart and charming. And kind of cute. This was a new frontier for Melanie: dating. She had little experience. And sex? She had *no* experience. Just one round of heavy petting that scared the whoopie out of her. She didn't want to be prim, but her body was feeling strange twinges that she couldn't seem to control. Enough of that. She would deal with it later.

Now it was "later" and time she found a BFF she could talk to about such matters. She was about to turn twenty-three, and she knew jack about the opposite sex, with the exception of growing up with a brother and a loving father. They did not count.

Melanie's challenge was how to approach the subject with Polly. Was it a big no-no, asking your superior for personal advice? It occurred to her to approach it as a hypothetical question. She practiced silently: *Major Beale, Boss, I have a hypothetical question. What if one member of the crew asked another member to dinner?* Melanie knew Beale would answer the question with a question: *Who asked you out?*

When she arrived at the office the next day, she pulled her boss over and whispered, "Can we meet in five minutes?"

Polly loved intrigue, and it was obvious from Melanie's tone she wanted to discuss something other than computer monitors.

Beale looked at Melanie. "Ladies' room or my office?"

"Ladies."

Melanie looked around the cubicles. No one was getting up from their seat. She hurried to the restroom and peeked under the stalls. Empty. Her hands were beginning to sweat. Maybe this wasn't such a good idea, but before she could change her mind, Major Beale came through the door.

Beale knew it had to be personal. The ladies' room is always personal. She leaned her back against the door so no one could enter unexpectedly. She folded her arms. "What's up?"

"Off the record?" Melanie asked.

"We are not having this conversation."

Melanie thought her boss meant Beale wouldn't speak to her. "I'm sorry to have bothered you."

"I meant we are not having this conversation because when we are done, the conversation never happened. *Capisce?*" Beale was grinning.

Melanie let out a huge sigh of relief. "Thank you, ma'am."

"Don't call me 'ma'am.' It's 'Boss,' but right now I think you need a friend. Am I right?"

Another big gust of air left Melanie's lungs; then she jumped into it. "Wayne Howell asked me to dinner." There it was. Out in the open.

"Are you asking me if you should go? Or are you asking my permission?"

"Both." Melanie was beginning to blush. "I'm not a seasoned dater. I've always been buried in schoolwork."

Beale pursed her lips. "This is what I suggest. Go out on a date, but DO. NOT. SLEEP. WITH. HIM." She was adamant.

"Oh, I wouldn't!" Melanie gasped, although she knew if the date went well and there were others, it would be expected at some point.

"Good. But here's the deal. The military has strict rules about personnel of different levels fraternizing with each other, as well as a slew of other regulations. Thankfully, my husband and I entered at the same time and moved up the ranks together. But neither of you are military, so those rules don't apply to you. Technically. If you're asking, 'Is it a good idea?' My answer would be no. It doesn't matter where you work. Civilian, military, or otherwise. There is a reason for the expression *don't do it where you eat.*" Of course, Beale had cleaned up the phrase, but Melanie knew what she was referring to.

Beale softened. "I know it's hard to meet people, especially working here. You're locked up all day, and after work, your brain is fried and you just want to go home, take a shower, and shove something in your mouth. So if you keep it platonic, fine. It's nice to have a companion."

Melanie thought there was going to be a *but*, but there wasn't. She got the message, loud and clear. "Thank you."

It would be nice to have someone to do stuff with. Take advantage of the many places to explore. She wasn't interested in anything serious, was she? There was a loud knock on the door. The conversation that never happened was now over. Beale was the first to leave the ladies' room. Melanie moved toward the sink, washed her hands, and counted to ten before she made her exit. She didn't want anyone to see them leave the room together. Beale watched Melanie walk past her office without looking in her direction and go straight to her station. *Good strategic move.*

Beale phoned the director at Bolling and inquired if there were any entry-level positions open in Criminal Investigation Training, specifically psychological profiling. The answer was yes, in just a few weeks. The timing was ideal. Melanie would finish this phase of her preparation and then move on to technical training in Glynco, Georgia. That part of the program was twelve weeks, and she would learn all aspects of law enforcement. In two years, Melanie should be well ensconced as a federal agent.

At the end of the day, Wayne stopped by Melanie's workstation. "How about getting together next week?"

She looked up from her blue-ray glasses. "What did you have in mind?"

"How about the National Arboretum?" he suggested.

It had been years since Melanie had been to that enchanting place filled with gardens of all kinds from all over the world. Wayne had just scored a few points in Melanie's mind. That was it! A point system. It was the only way she could handle dating. There had to be a method to the madness. If not, she would devise one. She wondered at what point Wayne should get the privilege of sex? That was a question she couldn't ask Major Beale. *Let's not get ahead of ourselves, girl.* Perhaps a sliding scale would work. Perhaps dividing up his characteristics in sections with a running cumulative score could work. Yes, he would be graded on his generosity, integrity, responsibility, loyalty, and kindness.

Melanie's thoughts had drifted a bit too long.

"Mel? Drake?" He gave her a curious look.

"Oh, sorry. Yes, wonderful idea! I was reading about the reopening of some of the gardens. The Bonsai Museum and the National Herb Garden are close to the National Capitol Columns. Would be a nice walk." Melanie was referring to the twenty-two Corinthian columns that had once graced the original East Portico of the Capitol Building. They were removed in 1828 and now stand on the twenty acres of the Ellipse Meadow.

Wayne was grinning. Score!

"I'll pick you up around ten." Wayne was still grinning.

Melanie wrote down the address of the apartment she was renting. "I'm looking forward to it." Then she felt it. A tingle. A hint of goosebumps? She chalked it up to having something to look forward to. *It isn't an attraction*, she told herself. *No. No, it isn't.* Maybe if she said it enough times, the feeling would go away. Giddy. *Not good. But yes, good. Why hadn't her parents encouraged her to date more when she was in high school?* As with any of the other challenges she faced, she would be methodical and open-minded. Just like most things, dating was a process.

Saturday morning arrived, and she was on her third outfit. She couldn't decide what to wear. It was early spring. Slacks or black jeans? Blazer, poncho, or denim jacket? She thought about it. They would be in a car for over an hour and then outside for a couple of hours, and walking would be involved. Black denim jeans, cream-colored long-sleeve turtleneck, short black denim vest. Ankle booties and a pair of gloves. Hair? What should she do about her hair? Ponytail? It was just long enough to be in a short ponytail. She pulled it back. Nah. Headband? She groped through her box of hair ties and found a cream-colored band. Excellent choice. It would be a nice contrast to her black hair, and it matched her sweater. She stood in front of the mirror and stared. "Time to conjure up that spunky, confident kid, Melanie Drake. It's not an interview." She stopped abruptly. "What if it is?" She was arguing with herself out loud. She burst out laughing.

"Get a grip!" She gave herself the thumbs-up and met Wayne at her front door.

The ride to DC took longer than expected. Traffic was particularly horrendous as they approached the infamous Beltway.

Wayne kept his patience, even though other drivers were blowing their horns. He leaned his head against the headrest. "Why are people such idiots?"

"Interesting question. Would you care to hear my theory, or my opinion?"

"That, too, is an interesting question. Let's have both."

"People who shouldn't have children, do. What I mean by that is, there are people who should not have custody of any other human being."

Wayne did a double take. "You're going to have to go deeper."

"You have to take a test to carry the mail. However, you do not have to take a test to carry a baby." Melanie gave him one of her sideways glances. "Correct me if I'm wrong."

"Good point. Continue."

"We need parents to teach generosity, integrity, responsibility, loyalty, and kindness." She instantly realized she was espousing the same principles she was going to use to grade Wayne.

"I totally agree," he replied, as he edged his way toward an exit ramp. "I'm taking the back roads."

Good. He agreed. More points.

They had no trouble finding things to talk about on the ride to the Arboretum. Melanie was pleasantly relaxed. She silently reminded herself she was looking for companionship, not romance.

Wayne pulled into the New York Avenue entrance and parked the car near the visitor center. From there, they strolled to the National Bonsai and Penjing Museum, which featured the legendary miniature Chinese and Japanese trees.

Melanie began to recite what she remembered about the trees. "The art of Bonsai originated over 1,000 years ago. Legend has it that an emperor from the Han Dynasty had a miniature replica made of his domain so he could look at it every day."

"You are a walking encyclopedia." Wayne grinned.

Except when it comes to the letter M and men, Melanie thought to herself. *So this is what I missed in high school.* "I am also a magician." Melanie thought it would be fun to drop her hobby into the conversation. Take him off guard.

"Are you going to make me disappear?" Wayne assumed she was joking.

"No. Not yet." She raised her eyebrows. In hindsight, she wished she had.

After the Bonsai Museum, they walked down the beautifully landscaped path that led to the twenty-two National Capitol Columns. The massive pillars loomed ahead in a meadow atop a hill. A large rectangular reflecting pool lay at the bottom of the steps that led up to the columns. The image in the water looked surreal. On the other side was a meadow of lavender, creating a purple haze over the scenery. And it was quiet. A peaceful place for contemplation.

The rest of the afternoon was easy. A few casual shoulder bumps between them, but no hand holding. Simply two friends enjoying an afternoon at the National Arboretum. It was around four o'clock when Wayne suggested they grab a bite and start their journey home. If traffic cooperated, the drive back to Dale City, where Melanie lived, would take around ninety minutes.

They stopped at a pub halfway. Burgers, fries, and non-alcoholic beer. Melanie wondered if she should offer to split the check. That would make it *not* a date. But before she could open her mouth, Wayne handed the waitress his credit card without even looking at the bill.

"Thanks for a lovely day. Burgers, fries, and all." Melanie was smiling from ear to ear.

"My pleasure. We should do it again," Wayne said as he signed the dinner check.

"Yes. That would be nice." Melanie decided it really was a date, and another was in the future.

When they arrived at her apartment, she didn't know what to do. One thing was certain—she wasn't inviting him in. She figured a quick getaway would avoid an awkward moment. He'd barely stepped on the brakes when Melanie opened the passenger door. She quickly unbuckled her seat belt and turned toward him. "Thanks again. It was a great day!" She hurriedly grabbed her bag and bolted out of the car. A few steps later, she realized she'd been a bit rude, so she turned and gave him a big wave and a smile. No kiss blowing. Not yet anyway.

The next day, Melanie made certain she stuck to her routine and went to her cubicle. She nodded at her coworkers, but made no special acknowledgement of Wayne. Her personal life was not going to spill into her professional life, or vice versa.

She spent Monday and Tuesday at her desk, only pausing to use the bathroom. She deliberately timed her lunch break after Wayne took his. She knew she was being foolish, but she honestly didn't know what the next move should be. If there was one.

Finally by Wednesday, Wayne approached Melanie at her desk. "Was it something I said?" he asked.

She looked up. "What? No."

"I got the impression you were avoiding me."

"No. Not at all." She lowered her voice. "I have a thing about people knowing my personal business." She finally admitted to herself it had been a date. Not simply two people enjoying an afternoon in a park. Now what?

Wayne screwed up his mouth. "Personal?"

"Well, I mean, it was just the two of us this time." Melanie was referring to the usual group meetings for drinks.

"Right." Wayne seemed to get the message, but wanted clarity. "Does this mean you won't go out with me again, or you won't go out with the gang again?"

Melanie snickered. "I haven't thought it through."

"How about dinner Saturday, and we can talk about it?"

Melanie finally let out the breath she was holding. "Sounds good."

"Pick you up at six?" he asked, and then bent his head down and whispered, "Pick you up at six?" He placed his finger over his lips.

Melanie laughed and then whispered, "Yes."

Beale watched Wayne Howell leave Melanie's cubicle and walk back to his. She was concerned for Melanie. She didn't want to tell her that Wayne had a reputation for breaking hearts. Melanie Drake was surely a paradox. She was one of the brightest candidates to enter the program. She was a quick study, had an exceptional vocabulary, and was an excellent communicator. How she could be so naïve when it came to the opposite sex was a little baffling. *You can't be brilliant at everything,* she thought to herself.

The rest of the week moved at a snail's pace until Saturday finally rolled around. Once again, Melanie was tense about her wardrobe. Black tunic-length silk jacket, with a black camisole, black-and-white-striped pleated pants. Black sling-back kitten heels, and a white peony pinned to her lapel. Her shiny black pageboy haircut danced along her collarbones when she moved her head. She applied slightly more makeup than she wore to work, including black eyeliner that made her steel-blue eyes even more intense. She took a long look in the mirror. Yes, MelDrake was expanding her usual confidence-building technique to include the opposite sex.

Wayne was prompt and fine-looking in a navy-blue blazer, a crisp white shirt buttoned to the top, chino pants, and tan loafers. The two made a very attractive couple. He opened the car door for her and then took his seat. "I never asked where we were going," Melanie said.

"It's a small bistro in the hills near the Prince William Forest Park."

"Sounds lovely." Melanie also thought, *sounds romantic.* Goosebumps.

As promised, it was a tiny restaurant with only a dozen tables and a view of the mountains. The sun was just setting and casting a mystical haze upon the trees. It was spellbinding. Special. *Was it too soon for special?* she wondered. It was only a second date. There it was, that spooky word, *date.*

"It's breathtaking," Melanie said in a hushed voice.

A gentleman dressed in a tuxedo showed them to a table next to the window. Melanie stared at the vista and wondered what Wayne's intentions were. This was quite a snazzy place. A place you would take someone on a special occasion. *Sit back. Enjoy. How bad can it be?*

They talked about the latest films: *Eastern Promises, No Country for Old Men, There Will Be Blood, American Gangster.* Melanie noted, "Excellent films with outstanding acting, but dreadful themes." She took a sip of her wine. Wayne was abstaining. He said he'd rather not drink at all than have to keep track of how many he had and whether he was under the legal limit.

He lifted his glass of tonic water and lime. "Here's to *Ratatouille!*"

It was a pleasant and delicious dinner. Melanie felt the warmth of the wine course through her body, giving her a deep sense of relaxation. Maybe too relaxed. She only had one glass.

Again, when the check came, Wayne handed the waiter his credit card without looking at the bill. Melanie knew it was a very expensive dinner. Maybe he was a couple of pay grades above her.

He helped her out of her seat. She was feeling a bit light-headed, and he gently guided her through the restaurant and to the car. She could barely keep her eyes open. She'd never had a reaction to wine like this before. Maybe she was coming down with something. Wayne strapped her into the seat belt. She could feel his hot breath spreading across her neck. Then it stopped. Melanie kept blinking her eyes to stay awake. Wayne got into the driver's seat and pulled away from the restaurant.

The road seemed very dark to Melanie. It wasn't the same way they'd come. She might be dizzy, but she still had her wits about her. Wayne made a slight turn onto a dirt road. He didn't go far. There wasn't anyone around. He began to stroke Melanie's face, tracing her body with his finger. She thought she was going to pass out. She felt his hand slide between her legs. She'd opened her mouth to scream when a loud knock on the window jolted both of them. A man with a ranger's hat was shining a flashlight into their faces. "Okay, kids. Break it up. Go home or get a room." He tapped the roof. Melanie let out a grunt. The ranger stopped and turned back to the couple. The flashlight was back on their faces. "You alright, miss?"

Wayne pantomimed drinking.

"And you, sir? Have you been drinking?" the ranger asked.

"No, sir. Tonic and lime."

Melanie pulled her strength together and opened her door. She bent over and hurled her wonderful dinner onto the dirt road. The ranger walked over to her. "Miss. Look at me." He could see her pupils were dilated. "Have you taken any medication?"

Melanie blinked and frowned. "No. Nothing."

The ranger handed her a handkerchief and turned the light in Wayne's direction. "May I see some identification?"

Wayne got out of the car and fished for his wallet. The ranger noticed Melanie's purse was on the floor. "Is your ID in your purse, miss?"

Melanie nodded, still bewildered by what was happening. "May I look inside?" he asked.

She nodded again.

Wayne held up his license from the opposite side of the car. "Hang on," the ranger directed. He found Melanie's ID. AFOSI. Air Force Office of Special Investigations. He helped her turn around so her feet were on the ground. He wanted to see if she could walk. "Can you stand up for me?" he asked her.

Wayne was becoming perturbed. "Do you want to see my ID or not?"

That did not sit well with the ranger. "You just hold on a minute. This young woman is in distress." He held his arms out for Melanie to take hold. "Easy does it." He helped her up and looked into her eyes again. "Do you want me to call the paramedics?"

Melanie might have been dizzy, but she wasn't unconscious. "No, thank you. I'll be alright." She didn't want to imagine how a trip to the hospital would play out.

"Come walk with me." He placed his burly arm around her and guided her to where Wayne was standing. She had regained some of her balance and propped herself against the hood. The air was bringing her closer to sobriety. He looked at Wayne's license. "Mr. Howell. What were you and Ms. Drake doing out here in the woods, in the dark?"

He shuffled his feet, feigning innocence. He raised his eyebrows, hoping the ranger would regard it as an "oopsy-daisy"—a young couple caught making out in the forest, instead of what it really was, a rape attempt. "Mr. Howell?" The ranger didn't like not getting a verbal response.

"We had dinner and stopped here for a little, ahem, intimacy."

"Ms. Drake? Is that what happened?"

Melanie had never been a tattletale, although this situation certainly warranted it. No, she would deal with Wayne on her own terms. "It's okay. I think I may be coming down with something." She felt a surge of energy and shot Wayne Howell a look he would never forget. She wanted to punch his face in, and he knew it. He also thought she just might.

The ranger got a bottle of water and some paper towels out of his truck and handed them to Melanie. She thanked him and edged her way back to the passenger side. He waited until she got back in the car and buckled up.

Wayne started the engine and proceeded back to the main road. They sat in silence. Wayne finally spoke. "Look. I'm sorry."

Melanie stared straight ahead.

"I find you attractive." Wayne thought complimenting her would evoke a response. Nothing. He tried again. "Seriously. You're attractive and smart, and interesting." Still nothing.

Melanie sat motionless. *Doesn't this idiot get it? There is nothing you can say. Absolutely nothing.* She wondered when he'd spiked her wine. Then Mr. Cosgrove's words came back like a boomerang. *Be aware.* And so much for dating.

They pulled in front of Melanie's apartment building. Wayne began his litany of apologies. Still not working. Without uttering a word, she turned and gave him her death-ray stare, opened the car door, and got out.

Once she was inside her apartment, she splashed cold water on her face and got undressed. She couldn't even cry.

That's how angry she was. At Wayne Howell, and at herself. Too bad she didn't have a boxer's strength. She would have punched him in the face.

Melanie had all day Sunday to cool her heels and decide how she wanted to handle the matter. She couldn't report him to her boss. She had been warned—they were civilians and consenting adults. Well, one of them was. However, she had some business to discuss with Major Beale and stopped at her door. "Got a minute?" she asked.

"Yes. Come in."

Melanie shut the door behind her, but the blinds were up, so anyone could see who was in the major's office. "I've been thinking about what path I would like to be on. I know the office may have different ideas for me, but I wanted to share my thoughts with you just in case we were on the same page."

Wayne Howell watched from a distance as Major Beale nodded her head. He could only imagine what was being said.

"Continue," the major urged.

"I'd like to pursue psychological profiling. No offense, but electronic trafficking isn't the best use of my talents. Of course, that's my opinion, but you mentioned strengths and weaknesses, and I believe profiling could be a very strong suit for me. For us. For the department."

Beale continued to nod. "You are rather astute, and I agree. I think you would make a very good agent in counterintelligence." She turned to her computer and typed in a few words. "You're to report to the Federal Law Enforcement Training Center in Glynco, Georgia in ten days. Do you know how to handle a firearm?"

Melanie was taken aback. "The only gun I ever handled was at the arcade, shooting at plastic ducks."

Beale chuckled. "You will have to undergo firearm training and a host of other tactical maneuvers."

It hadn't occurred to Melanie that even with a desk job, she had to be able to fire a weapon. She got the heebie-jeebies. "Not thrilled, but willing," Melanie replied.

"Excellent. You will complete a twelve-week course in anti-terrorism, firearms and defensive tactics, interrogation and interviews, military and federal law, and crime scene forensics."

Melanie's head was spinning. She'd really gotten herself into it. Most of it was intriguing; some, not so much.

Beale watched Melanie's facial expressions shift from interest to concern.

"You'll do fine. I have no doubt." Beale gave Melanie another minute for everything to settle in. "You'll get your instructions in a few days."

Melanie was dubious as to the amount of time it would take. A few days could be months in military and government speak. "Thanks, boss." Melanie held out her hand.

Beale gave her a firm shake. "Do us proud."

Melanie walked back to her cubicle as Wayne spied from a distance. The suspense was killing him. What had she told the major? He decided to find out for himself and marched over to Major Beale's office.

"Boss. May I have a word?"

"Yes, of course." She motioned for him to sit down. "What can I do for you?"

"It's Melanie."

"Which one?"

"Drake. MelDrake."

"What about her?" The major was quite curious.

"I think she may have a vivid imagination."

"How so?"

"I think she makes up things about people." Wayne didn't want to dig the hole too deep. He had no idea how much Beale knew.

"Like whom, for instance?"

"Me, maybe." He couldn't sit still.

"She's never said a word about anyone, including you." That was a little fib, but talking trash wasn't part of any conversation she'd ever had with Melanie.

"Oh. Okay."

"Are you alright, Mr. Howell?" She looked at him curiously.

He wiped his palms on his trousers. "Yes." Borrowing a phrase from Melanie, he said, "I think maybe I'm coming down with something." He got up and vanished into his compartment.

Beale wondered what that was all about. Maybe the date went sideways. While she was saddened to lose a top-notch civilian employee, she was excited for Melanie, and also relieved. Wayne Howell would have to find another woman to womanize.

When Melanie got home, she phoned her parents to tell them the good news. Their hope for Melanie was a job in the foreign service, but if this was the way to get there, and Melanie was happy, then they were happy. In three months, she would be transferred to Anacostia, less than a half hour away. They suggested she move back home until she finished her training. At some point, she would be relocated again. No sense to keep writing change-of-address cards. And Melanie would have the company of Bixby, their six-year-old Wheaten Terrier. She missed having a pet.

The next day, she pondered whether or not she should say something to Wayne. Something about his atrocious, vulgar behavior, or that she was leaving. She didn't want him to think he was getting away with anything, so she walked to his cubicle and said loudly enough for a few people to overhear, "Two things, Wayne: Next time you think about taking advantage of someone, punch yourself in the face first." He looked at her curiously. Her stare burned deeper into his skull. "You're lucky you aren't singing soprano right now." He instinctively touched his crotch. She turned on her heel and marched back to her space, feeling very proud of herself.

The remaining two weeks of her stint passed quickly, and then she was on her way to enhanced training. When she arrived at Glynco, once again, she went through a rigorous security check. She was escorted to her new supervisor, given three heavy binders, her residence assignment, and her schedule. It was much more intense than she'd imagined. Especially the firearms part. She had never been a gun enthusiast, but now they were going to be part of her job. Her life.

Chapter Seven

Training
Federal Law Enforcement Training Center
Glynco, Georgia

The rules, regulations, and procedures were pervasive, but her biggest challenge was handling weaponry. She spent whatever extra hours she had on the firing range. As much as it went against her grain, she was going to get her marksman's badge. "Sharpshooter" and "Expert" were much higher rank, but she would be satisfied with marksmanship level. She surely was not interested in becoming a sniper.

Not surprisingly, in twelve weeks, Melanie finished top of her class, and was transferred to Anacostia, which meant relocating back to her parents'. A year ago, she was mortified at the idea of still living at home, but now, it was different. She wouldn't be a freeloader.

Back Home

Her first night home was glorious. Bixby could not contain his excitement at seeing his pal walk in the door and knocked her off balance as he landed both paws on her chest.

She grabbed him by the scruff and nuzzled him. "Oh, Bixby-boo! How I've missed you!" He returned the affection by slobbering all over her face. "Such a good boy," she said as she wiped the dribble from her cheek. Her parents were next in line to show their affection and delight at having their daughter back.

"Let me take that," her dad said as he lugged her duffel bag up the stairs.

Her mother gave her another hug. "I made your favorite dinner." She paused. "Mel, I hope you don't mind, but we painted your room."

Melanie chuckled. "I don't care what color it is, as long as it's not steel gray or army green." She trailed her father up the stairs, with Bixby following at her heels. As soon as she entered her old bedroom, she flung herself on the bed. "There's no place like home." She giggled as Bixby joined her on the comfortable mattress.

"Let us know if you need anything, honey," her father said as he was leaving the room. "We're glad you're back."

Melanie never thought she would have the same sentiment. It wasn't as if she disliked living with her parents. She'd just never thought she would be living in her room again and happy about it. Those few months after graduation were stressful. She didn't have a job at the time and was feeling like a slug. Now, almost a year later, she was on her way to becoming a special investigative agent. Having grown up without guns around, she debated whether she should tell her parents she was a "marksman." She decided against it. It would make her mother fret, knowing her daughter was packing a weapon. Yes, it was in a locked case, and, yes, she would keep it in a safe place. But still. Having a gun in the house was never a thing for her family.

She peeled off her traveling clothes, took a shower, and put on a pair of comfortable black jogging pants and a matching sweatshirt with the letters O S I on the front in three-inch block letters. Her hair framed her face, emphasizing her deep blue eyes. She gazed in the mirror, checking for any lines or signs of stress. She'd packed a lot in over the past year. It was rigorous training on many levels: physical, mental, emotional, and well, she wasn't going to give the dating debacle another thought. She stood silently, closed her eyes, and practiced one of the stress relievers she'd learned many years ago. *A slow deep inhale through the nose. Let the air flow through your body, your arms, and your legs. Hold for one second and slowly release the air through slightly parted lips, as it cleanses the tension from your body, mind, and spirit.* She did it three times, feeling the layers of stress lift from her psyche. There was a lot for her to mentally unpack. Much more than what was in her duffel bag.

She heard her mother's voice calling her for dinner, her words floating on the aroma of short ribs that had been cooking for over eight hours. Melanie envisioned the juicy, tender meat and her mom's smashed potatoes. Her stomach growled, prodding her to slap on her sneakers and bound down the stairs.

Bixby hadn't left her side, and both went racing into the dining room. "Smells fantastic!" Melanie hooted. Bixby's tail was beating like a drumstick against her leg. Dinnertime was generally a good occasion for the family. Whether it was a holiday or any night of the week, it was an opportunity for them to talk about their day or discuss important or not-so-important matters. They rarely argued, and if they did, no one went to bed without reconciling. Maybe that was another reason Melanie thought a career in diplomacy would be a good fit for her. It was how she was raised. However, Major Beale had aptly pointed out that reality and ideals don't match up very often.

As they were about to sit, Melanie noticed an extra place setting. "Dinner guests?" Bixby answered by running and yapping at the kitchen door, and she heard the familiar voice of her brother Justin. "Jus!" She dashed toward his wide-open arms.

"Mel!" He picked her up and swung her around, careful not to knock over one of the many potted plants their mother cherished. He set her back down. "Look at you, all grown up."

It had been two years since they'd seen each other. Justin was deployed and constantly on the move to parts unknown. He wasn't at liberty to discuss his whereabouts. If his family wanted to get in touch with him, they had to send letters to a special military post office box where communications would be forwarded to him. If they wanted to talk to him, they had to go through a secure line with the permission and cooperation of his wing commander.

They took their usual seats, said grace, and began to pass the serving bowls. Dorothy looked at both of her adult children. "Who would have thought we'd be sitting here one day with both of you doing secret spy stuff."

Justin was the first to break in. He cleared his throat. "Mom, we are not spies."

"Yes, we do secret stuff, so the bad guys don't know what we're up to," Melanie quickly added.

Dorothy raised an eyebrow. "If you say so." She knew there was a tremendous amount of secrecy involved in the work both were doing. It worried her from time to time. She had no idea if they were in danger or not. "I can't help being concerned about your well-being. I am your mother, after all."

"Remember what you once told me?" Melanie asked, and then repeated it. " 'Worry is like paying a debt you don't owe.' You can try to be prepared for the obvious things when you are driving, cooking, working."

Justin took it from there. "Mel is right. There are things that are totally out of your control. Dwelling on the *what ifs* is a waste of time."

Peter chimed in. "Seriously, Dorothy. You could worry yourself to death if you let every possible negative scenario into your head."

Dorothy was never one for being soppy, but having both her children working in high-risk careers wasn't ideal. *Why couldn't Justin have become a real estate lawyer? Or Melanie a college professor? Or vice versa? It doesn't seem right.* "Well, I don't think it's crazy for me to be uneasy."

Peter reached over and took her hand. "Be proud. They are doing good work for our democracy. We raised two very smart, educated kids. Adult kids." He winced. "Is that an oxymoron?"

"We'll always be your kids." Melanie clucked.

"Thank you for the clarification." Peter smiled. "My point is, neither of you are reckless. You're bright. Sharp. I don't recall anything ever getting past either of you." He said thoughtfully, "I have complete confidence you will be cautious, wary, and mindful."

"Thanks, Pops!" Justin grinned. "See, Mom? That's the way to think about it."

Dorothy smiled. "I know you're right. Must be something in my DNA."

"Like you said, you're a mother." Melanie chuckled, as did everyone else, including Dorothy.

With Justin in special ops, he couldn't discuss what he was working on or where. Anyone could find out where the Air Force bases were located, but not everyone in the Air Force worked specifically at the base. Operatives could be in a safe house hundreds of miles away, depending on the mission. But he could talk about layover cities he had visited, as long as they weren't in chronological order. He'd enjoyed Amsterdam and England and talked about the tourist-type things he'd experienced.

"But the most incredible thing was Stonehenge. A testament to human ingenuity." He went on to describe the prehistoric monument on Salisbury Plain. It was an outer ring of vertical stones standing about thirteen feet high and seven feet wide, with several connected by horizontal stones.

"It dates back to four or five thousand years ago. We took a VIP tour called the Stone Circle Experience. It's a small group of about thirty people, and you get to wander around through the pillars and walk on the same path as people who lived thousands of years ago."

"Many connect the Druids with Stonehenge," Melanie added. It was on her bucket list. "Historians believe it was a place of worship."

Justin broke in. "I can believe it. The sunset was spectacular. It was a very humbling experience."

"You? Humble? That is to laugh." Melanie shot him a devilish grin.

"London was a different story."

"How so?" Dorothy asked.

"Pubs. Everywhere you turned there was a pub. Or so it seemed."

"That's because you were probably looking for them." Melanie shot another jab.

"It's so nice to have both of you home." Peter laughed and leaned back in his chair.

For Melanie, there wasn't much glamor to share. Actually there was none except her visits to the Arboretum, which she'd visited often before her afternoon with a sociopath. If only she had punched him in the face.

They sat and talked for over two hours. It was after ten p.m. when the conversation began winding down.

Once the kitchen was cleared of any evidence of a delicious home-cooked meal, they said their goodnights with hugs and kisses. Bixby followed Melanie up to her room and made himself comfortable right in the middle of the bed. She scooted him over as she pulled the comforter down and wriggled into her warm, cozy bed. She let her body settle into the familiar cocoon and easily drifted into a deep sleep.

The next morning, she awoke with a start. For a second, she didn't know where she was or what day it was. The big lump of fur next to her moved and stretched. She immediately recognized her surroundings. She snapped to. Being in that semi-lucid state could cost her. It almost did the night of the never-date-again incident. She also realized she hadn't slept so deeply since she'd joined OSI. She wondered if she ever would once she went back to work. She didn't want to think about it. As she scanned her bedroom, many things reminded her of the time when she was innocent. Naïve. She sure could talk about many things. It was the experiential part of life she needed to get under her belt. She supposed that was what life was really all about. Experiencing it. Bixby nudged her arm. "You are correct. There is plenty of time to be serious. Pancakes are a priority right now." Bixby leaped off the bed at the mention of pancakes.

Melanie and Bixby made their way into the kitchen. They were the first up. She put on a pot of coffee, dug out the eggs, pancake mix, butter, maple syrup, and table cream. Bixby tilted his head and gave a funny yowl.

"What?" He got in a downward dog position facing the refrigerator. She opened the door and spotted the package of bacon. A quart of blueberries sat on the middle shelf, along with many of Melanie's favorite foods. She smiled. "Yes, definitely a mom."

Once Melanie started frying the bacon, it didn't take long for the others to appear. Justin was first. "Morning. Mmm. Smells good." He kissed her on the top of her head. Even though Melanie was tall, Justin was five inches taller. He poured himself a mug. "Refill?" He glanced at her mug sitting on the counter.

"Not yet, thanks." She wondered if she should share her

concerns about future nights' sleep. Why not? She'd never pulled her punches before. "Jus? How do you sleep at night?"

He tilted his head. "How do I sleep at night? Or how can I sleep at night?" He thought she might be alluding to what he did for the Air Force.

She flipped the bacon. "Make the batter, please." She gestured to the ingredients. "Last night was the best sleep I've had since I started this adventure. When I woke up this morning, I was disoriented. Only for a few moments."

"That's not unusual. You've moved a couple times in the past year. What I find helpful is to tell yourself where you are just before you fall asleep. When you feel yourself coming awake, tell yourself where you are. If you're not sure, remember the last thing you told yourself."

"Thanks." She put that bit of advice in her vault. She was about to talk to her brother about her newly acquired skill as marksman, when Dorothy and Peter breezed into the kitchen.

"What have we here?" Peter took a big inhale of the bacon aroma that was filling the room.

"Breakfast!" Melanie grinned. "It's been a long time since I was let loose in a kitchen. Mostly takeout or institutional food."

Justin fired up the griddle. Dorothy and Peter set the table, and Bixby sat in the middle of the kitchen to be sure he didn't miss anything. It was such a normal occurrence that everyone was accustomed to stepping over or around him. Only once had his tail been caught under a foot. Since then, he kept it tucked between his legs. He was no dummy.

As they passed the plates, the conversation turned to what they were going to do over the weekend. When Dorothy suggested the National Arboretum, coffee flew from Melanie's mouth and nose. She vigorously wiped her face between coughs.

"Are you okay?" everyone asked.

"Yes. I'm fine. Went down the wrong pipe." Melanie was telling a half-truth. Should she tell them about her adventure in horny young men? *Men who have to drug their dates to get into their pants?* That was something Melanie couldn't wrap her head around. Why would he do that? He was charming and good-looking. Then, she remembered, so was Ted Bundy. A chill went up her spine. Her jaw dropped.

Dorothy leaned closer. "Honey, are you sure you're alright?"

Melanie shook it off. "I'm okay. Really. Now pass me some bacon before Justin eats it all." Melanie tried not to go back to the thought of Wayne being a sociopath, or psychopath. But what if he was? She checked herself. *Think about it when the weekend is over.* Psychological profiling seemed even more important now.

Rushing to change the subject, she said, "I hadn't given our weekend plans much thought. I just want to sit on the patio. Have Dad grill some chops. A nice bottle of wine. We don't have to go anywhere or do anything."

"I'm all about that, too," Justin added. "It's been a long time since we've been together."

"Okay, but if we start getting on each other's nerves, someone is going to have to find something else to do," Dorothy insisted.

"Deal," Melanie replied.

"Works for me," Peter added. "Happy to grill some steaks."

"No argument here," Justin responded.

"Yeah, you'll save it for later," Melanie teased.

After they cleared the table and restored the kitchen to pre-breakfast status, they moved outside.

Normally Dorothy would be showing houses or condominiums, and Peter would be doing the filings, but they'd handed off potential clients to their colleagues that weekend. Spending time with the family was worth more than a commission.

The patio was made of paving stones and decorated with large ceramic pots filled with million bells, cascading petunias, and vinca vines. The patio ran the entire length of the house, extending out fifteen feet where it met with the rest of their yard. The roofline of the house created an awning effect over part of the patio, shielding them from direct sunlight. It was the perfect spot for an outdoor dining area and had enough space to accommodate Peter's Napoleon Prestige 500 grill.

The same stones had been used to create walking paths throughout the landscaping. There was no traditional lawn, but there were lots of trees and plants. On one side was a putting green. The other held a horseshoe pit. The yard was its own vacation spot. A place where the family could congregate, entertain, and relax. Peter and Dorothy had bought the home thirty years before and made renovations over the years. They'd learned that people with high-pressure jobs and an unpredictable commute wanted more space for the family to entertain. Having an inviting backyard was a plus. It was an outdoor living space.

Like everywhere else, the more money you had, the bigger and nicer your house, and the better your neighborhood. The richest people in Washington DC lived within twenty miles of the Capitol, either in Georgetown, Lincoln Park, Observatory Circle, or a few other neighborhoods where properties fetched double-digit millions. The Drakes could probably get a million for their place, but no one was in a hurry to go anywhere, and they didn't know where Melanie or Justin would end up or with whom.

Dorothy looked at her daughter, who was soaking up some vitamin D in a cushioned chaise lounge. Her hair was wrapped in a scarf. Dorothy was glad they'd decided to stay home. Peter brought the newspaper and handed half of it to Dorothy, who was already sitting at the glass dining table.

Justin sat in a lounge chair next to Melanie. Dorothy looked up at Peter and smiled. They didn't have to speak. The joy of being together spoke for itself.

Melanie was anxious to talk to Justin about the gun thing, but her parents were still within earshot. Maybe later she could coax him into helping her make margaritas, and they'd have some privacy. He broke the silence. "So how are you liking OSI?" It was the first time anyone had addressed the elephant in the room, in spite of the logo on Melanie's hoodie.

"I thought we weren't supposed to talk about it." She sat up, her sunglasses dangling from their cord.

"I didn't ask you to go into any detail. I only asked if you liked it." He shook his head. "Some things don't change."

"What's that supposed to mean?" she huffed.

"Your blockheadedness."

"Huh. Says you." She pulled her sunglasses over her eyes and folded her arms across her chest.

Justin chuckled. "Good thing."

"What's a good thing, Mr. Smarty Pants?"

"That some things don't change."

Without looking, she took a blind swipe at him.

It had been a lazy kind of day. Exactly what Melanie was hoping for. So much had happened in the past year since she'd graduated from college. Six months of waiting, three months of intense technology training, then three months of enhanced tactics. It was a lot to cram into one's head. The waiting part took up none of her gray matter. The last six months of preparation made up for it.

The morning drifted into lunchtime. "Anybody hungry?" Dorothy asked.

"What do you have in mind, Mom?" Justin asked. He was always up for food, especially his mother's. Real, delicious meals were a luxury.

"I'm going to grill some steaks for dinner," Peter reminded them.

"Yeah, but that's hours away." Justin got up from his chaise and walked over to where his mother was standing.

"I have fresh crabmeat." Dorothy raised her eyebrows.

"And avocados," Melanie called from across the patio and jumped up from where she was lounging. "I'll help." As she approached the two, she said, "Mom, why don't you let Justin and me make lunch."

"Dear, you already made breakfast."

"I know, but I don't get to have fun in the kitchen very often."

"Oh, alright. You know where everything is?"

"Of course," Melanie answered with a grin. "I did an inventory of the fridge this morning." Then she looked over at her brother. "Unless the bottomless pit cleared it out."

"Ha. Ha." Justin flicked his finger at the back of her head.

"Creep," Melanie scolded.

Peter was standing at the putting green. "Yep. Great having them back." And he took a slow, deliberate swing.

Melanie linked arms with Justin and pretended to drag him inside. When they were far enough into the kitchen, she whispered. "I need to talk to you."

Justin looked alarmed. "Everything okay?"

"Yes."

"But?"

"It's the gun thing," Melanie whispered.

Justin let out a loud guffaw. "It hadn't occurred to you?"

"You know something? I am not as smart as I think I am." Melanie put her hands on her hips. "I wasn't really thinking what I was getting myself into."

"The dichotomy of Melanie." Justin leaned against the kitchen counter. Melanie handed him the crabmeat, red onion, celery, and mayo.

"Here. Get busy." She washed the avocados, split them in half, and removed the pits. She squeezed some lemon juice on them so they wouldn't turn brown too quickly. "Dichotomy. Using four-syllable words now, eh?"

"Just because I wasn't a straight-A student doesn't mean I don't know words." He chuckled. "You always looked at the big picture, but I guess you weren't focusing on the details." He pulled a clean fork from the drawer and took a taste of his shellfish concoction. "I don't believe I am saying this, but don't be too hard on yourself." He snickered. "You had zip adult experience. Everything was theoretical."

She directed the knife she was holding at her brother. Not as a threat, but to make a point. "Exactly!" Her eyes widened. "Remember Mr. Cosgrove? The economics teacher?"

"Sure. He made us read the newspaper."

"Yes. And you know what he emphasized? Be aware." She scooped out some of the avocado flesh and put it in a bowl. "How did I not see that coming?"

"Didn't you ever watch NCIS? Or any of those other military shows?"

"Not really." Melanie was not a habitual television watcher.

"So what you're telling me is that you had no idea you would have to have firearm training?"

"I thought I was training to be an intelligence specialist. You know, one of those people who sits at a desk and analyzes stuff."

Justin laughed. "Oh, that will come, too. But you may be called to do surveillance. You'll need to be able to defend yourself."

"I thought that was what you guys were for."

Justin could not contain his amusement over his sister's inexperience and expectations. "Things sure are different in the real world, aren't they?"

"You're not kidding."

"So what's the problem? Did you fail?"

"Certainly not! I may not have enjoyed it, but I was going to be good at it." She pouted.

"Don't worry, sis. You will probably never be in the situation to have to use that training. There are other people around who are firearms experts, but you need to know how to defend yourself should something go wrong."

"I get it." She wiped her hands and began to make guacamole with the leftover avocado. "I didn't tell Mom and Dad."

"Good thinkin'. We already went through the 'talk Mom off the ledge' exercise last night."

"True." She smirked.

Justin put his arm around her. "Don't think about it. They'll let you know if and when you will need your gun, and in any case, you'll know when to use it. You won't be out in the field right away, so take your own advice. Don't worry about it."

The rest of the day and the day after were exactly what everyone needed, some R&R. Come Monday, Justin would be reporting to an undisclosed location, and Melanie would be reporting for duty at Anacostia. As they said their affectionate goodbyes, Dorothy blotted the tears from her cheeks.

Anacostia was less than thirty minutes away, but Melanie planned on giving herself plenty of time, knowing how congested the beltway would be. There were alternate routes, but one wasn't necessarily any less crowded than another. The once little-known back roads were no longer little-known. *Where did all these people come from?*

Chapter Eight

Moving On

When she arrived at the gate, she went through the usual clearance process, showing ID, having her photo taken, the phone call to her immediate supervisor, and the directions to a specific parking spot for her car. Once on base, everything was noted and tracked. No one was getting in or out without being under surveillance. She walked through another security area and handed over the safety case that contained her Glock 9mm pistol. "We'll keep this until you're ready to leave the base," the guard explained and gave her a chip, as if it were a coat check.

An Air Force officer greeted her while her personal tote and go-bag were sent through the conveyor belt security check. Everyone was required to have a go-bag in case of an emergency. It held a small bag of toiletries, a change of clothes, a pre-paid debit card with 1000 dollars, 200 dollars cash in small bills, and a burner phone. Operatives were not allowed to activate the phone unless it truly was an emergency. Any attempt to break that rule would be picked up by the audio surveillance in place.

"Ms. Drake?" he called.

"Yes, sir." She held out her hand. The young man appeared to be close to her age.

"Welcome to Anacostia. I'm Airman Gonzalez. Follow me, please." She walked down a hallway lined with photos of military leaders that dated back to World War II. At the end of the hall was a door with an electronic keypad and a camera. Gonzalez swiped his badge and looked into the camera. He turned to Melanie. "Please." Indicating she was required to have her face in the surveillance footage.

He escorted her to a processing room, where she was introduced to a female also wearing civilian clothes, except her badge was a different color from Mel's. She began the process by fingerprinting Melanie. It was important her fingerprints matched those on record for Melanie Drake. Another photograph was taken for her new ID. Melanie was wearing a VISITOR badge that was about to be turned in for one that read:

OSI
USAF

She noticed the badges were color-coded. Probably had something to do with rank or levels of clearance. She'd find out soon enough. Within minutes, her lanyard was handed to her.

"Wear this at all times. Do not lose it," a woman in a uniform instructed. Then she handed her a Blackberry, the DOD communication of choice at the time. It was considered the most secure piece of handheld communication technology. "It's already programmed with the speed-dial numbers for security and your immediate supervisor. Welcome to Anacostia." She paused. "And don't let them fool you by asking you to find a left-handed monkey wrench."

Melanie laughed. She knew that was an old prank people played. There was no such thing. "I have an older brother.

But I'll be sure to ask someone for a bucket of steam!" She grinned and made the woman chuckle. Melanie thanked the woman and placed the cord with her dangling ID over her head. Airman Gonzalez escorted her down another hallway to another door with an electronic pad and camera. He motioned for her to swipe her lanyard. Up popped her name and ID number on the panel, and there was a click to indicate the door was now unlocked.

The room was massive with dozens of cubicles, monitors, and personnel. An open staircase was on one side of the space with a sign that read:

RESTRICTED AREA.
AUTHORIZED PERSONNEL ONLY

Of course, there were many levels of authorization. He walked her to a cubicle similar to those she'd sat at in Quantico and Glynco. "I'll give you a few minutes to get settled and then take you to the Education Complex."

"Thanks." Melanie checked around her desk. Nothing different from what she had seen before, except this time she was able to bring a tote, but no cellphone. As she was walking to her cubby, she noticed most of the others had their go-bag stashed under their desk. She did the same and dropped her personal tote into one of the drawers, locked it. Not that anyone was going to steal her lip balm. But you never know. She clipped the key to the cord around her neck, and then stood waiting for Gonzalez to return. Minutes later, he appeared.

"Follow me, please."

Melanie observed that no one looked up from their workspace. No one seemed to notice a new arrival. People were engrossed in whatever they were doing. She quietly followed the airman out a door, through a small quad atrium, and then to another highly secured entrance. "This is the education complex. You'll get your materials and assignments here."

They entered an empty classroom. There were long tables set with chairs facing the front of the room. No computers except for the large screen ahead and a very large binder in front of one of the chairs. "Please take a seat. Captain Chen will be with you shortly."

Melanie took the seat with the binder while Airman Gonzalez stood at attention by the door. Ten minutes passed on the clock on the wall. Another "hurry up and wait" situation. Then the door opened abruptly, startling Melanie from her seat. Airman Gonzalez saluted Captain Chen. "As you were," Chen ordered.

Melanie stood and faced the captain.

"You are Melanie Drake." He said it as a statement, not a question. "Welcome aboard. You've come with excellent recommendations."

"Thank you, sir," Melanie replied.

"Do not disappoint me," the captain said in a very stern tone.

"I will try not to," Melanie answered.

"Trying does not count. Only results." Captain Chen made his way to the front of the room. "Please take a seat."

Melanie knew he was a no-nonsense kind of guy. Naturally all military personnel were no-nonsense, but this man seemed particularly buttoned up. Not a smile on his face. Not even when he'd made his first complimentary statement to her. She thought he must have seen a lot of people come and go over the years. Mostly go, she guessed.

"You will be studying the area of criminal profiling. Also known as psychological profiling. You'll read about the history of the science and procedures, and then after a period of time, you will be given a mock scenario where you will review the evidence and make your own assessment. We have a library that is available twenty-four-seven. I suggest you spend as much time there as possible."

"Yes, sir."

"The binder in front of you outlines this course of training and all details that pertain to your level, security, etcetera. Any questions?"

Melanie didn't have any at the moment. "Not right now, sir."

"I'm sure you will. If not, you're not doing the job. Questioning everything is how you get to the conclusions. Am I clear?"

"Yes, sir." She stopped herself from saying "crystal."

"Good. Airman, please give Drake some time to peruse the binder and then show her to the library."

"Yes, sir." He saluted as the captain left the room.

Melanie resisted the temptation to utter the word *chilly* to Gonzalez, who remained standing, but her expression didn't lie.

"Are you allowed to sit?" she asked innocently.

"No, ma'am. Not as long as you are in my custody."

"Custody? Well. I suppose I should get busy." She opened the binder, scanned the table of contents, and flipped through the pages. The rules and regulations were exactly the same as those at Glynco. The binder was also divided into three sections denoting the levels of organization. As of now, she was at the bottom, but she was determined to get through this part of her training so she could begin to do something important. Something worthwhile. She knew her work was cut out for her, but she was also used to being a bookworm study sponge. She spent a half hour with the binder, then decided it was time to get on to the next thing. She looked up at Gonzalez. "I think I'm ready."

"Follow me, please." He opened the door but immediately got in front of her as soon as she exited. They walked through the quad that led to the library. It was massive, re-

sembling those she was used to in college. The only difference was the people. Everyone was in one type of uniform or
another. Since enrolling in the program, she'd learned to dif-
ferentiate between the ranks and the civilians. There was a
mixture of both here.

Gonzalez brought her over to the librarian. "Major Gunther, this is Melanie Drake, our new profiling apprentice.
Please see that she is furnished with the necessary materials
to begin her studies."

"Good morning, Melanie. We normally call people by
their last name, but there are several Drakes here."

"Can we use a moniker? I've been referred to as MelDrake
to avoid confusion."

Major Gunther smiled. "I think that should be fine. You're
civvy," meaning a civilian. "Airman, please show MelDrake
to the research area of her field."

"Yes, ma'am." Gonzalez gave the librarian a short salute.
"Follow me." Melanie obeyed as they made their way to an
escalator that brought them to another floor filled with
books, tables, and personnel. "One more." He gestured to
another escalator.

When they arrived on the third floor, Melanie noticed that
every volume looked identical. Gonzalez spoke. "These are
all reference files. They are in chronological order. The main
directory will indicate which volume coincides with your investigation."

"Thank you, Airman Gonzalez."

"You're welcome. I'll be back at twelve-hundred-hours to
escort you to the cafeteria." He turned and walked away.

Melanie stared at the hundreds upon hundreds of volumes. Figuring out where to start was part of her orientation.
She decided to start at the beginning.

She looked up the first, most infamous serial killer, Jack
the Ripper. He had lived during the nineteenth century, when

Scotland Yard was burdened with the murder and mutilation of five female prostitutes in the Whitechapel area on the East Side of London, between August and November in 1888. The assailant would kill his victims, remove their internal organs, and slit their throats. Dr. Thomas Bond, a police surgeon, investigated the case and drew several conclusions. The perpetrator, most likely male, had to be physically strong. Cool-headed, as well as daring. The fact that his victims were prostitutes led Bond to believe the perpetrator had erotic tendencies coupled with a homicidal mania. Though he was never apprehended, the five cases were identical in nature. There were several other murders in London at that time, but none had the same characteristics.

This new way of looking at crime began a movement among forensically inclined psychologists and psychiatrists, who began publishing articles and case studies on the subject, including a psychological assessment of Adolf Hitler.

Between 1940 and 1956, New York was plagued by a madman who detonated over 37 bombs in public places such as subways, theatres, bus depots, and a library. For sixteen years, the city of New York was terrorized by this mastermind of destruction appropriately named "The Mad Bomber." He confounded the largest police department in the world, with his homemade bombs and cryptic notes.

Out of utter desperation, the police contacted Dr. James Brussel, a New York psychiatrist who worked with the New York City Department of Health and Mental Hygiene and specialized in criminal behavior. Initially, Brussel was hesitant to take part in such a high-profile case, but was ultimately encouraged to do his civic duty. His approach was to work backward, in what he called reverse psychology. Today it's referred to as criminal profiling.

Brussel studied the crime scene photos and the notes left by the bomber. The psychiatrist had an uncanny ability to connect clues and concluded the offender suffered from paranoid schizophrenia. Brussel explained that people with this disorder suffered from the belief that people were plotting against them. They were usually antisocial and reclusive but could function within the main populus for short periods of time. Brussel believed the condition didn't fully manifest and become completely symptomatic in most patients until the age of thirty-five. Given the sixteen-year span of the bombings, he surmised the perpetrator was in his fifties, unmarried, and self-educated. His rudimentary bomb making supported that conclusion. In addition, Brussel offered the theory that this person had a very high regard for himself, and felt the need to exhibit his superiority. He did so by sending handwritten letters to local newspapers, signing them F.P. Another characteristic Brussel observed was the way they were neatly printed in block letters, and erratically spaced with outdated phrases, suggesting English was not his first language.

After Brussel concluded his findings, he urged the police to have them written up in *The New York Times* on Christmas Day. If Brussel was right, F.P. would make his presence known. Brussel lived in a residence at Creedmoor, a psychiatric hospital where the switchboard was instructed to loop in the police department should Dr. Brussel receive any odd or suspicious phone calls. As predicted, two days later, Brussel received a call in the middle of the night. The caller identified himself as F.P. and threatened the doctor. Several weeks later, George Metesky was arrested in his home in Westchester, establishing Brussel as a folk hero. This widely publicized case united the fields of psychiatry and police work, now known as "profiling."

Melanie slumped in her chair. That was a lot of heavy reading she'd just ingested. Speaking of digestion, she glanced at the clock. Gonzalez should be arriving any minute to escort her to lunch. She stretched, stood, and stretched again.

She thought about what she'd read. Gathering clues. Connecting clues. It was a mental jigsaw puzzle. For the first time since she'd joined OSI, she had a good feeling about her pursuits. Having been an avid reader of mysteries, she believed this could be the path she was meant to follow. Gonzalez appeared and invited her to join him for lunch. "First day is on me." He smiled. It was the first time he'd broken the formality of strict military conduct. She was, after all, a civilian.

"Thank you. That's very kind." Melanie smiled.

"Don't thank me yet. You haven't had our installation food." He chuckled.

"I'm sure I've had worse," Melanie replied. She followed him down the two escalators, out the door, through the quad, and then down another hall to another quad that led to a cafeteria adjacent to the commissary.

He handed her a plastic tray as they made their way down the selection of hot food. "I know it may all look the same, but there's a difference." He pointed to one tray. "That is chicken with brown sauce." He turned to another one. "That is pork with brown sauce. Yes, the same brown sauce."

Melanie noticed everything seemed to be covered in brown sauce. "Can we bring our own lunch?"

"Told ya." Gonzalez handed several bills to the cashier. "Newbie. On me."

"Welcome." The petite woman nodded.

"Thanks." Melanie picked up her tray and followed the airman to a table where several other people were sitting. "Gang, this is Melanie Drake."

Greetings were mumbled through half-chewed food.

"Call me MelDrake."

The usual questions made their way around the table. "Where are you from?" "Where did you go to school?" Small talk.

Melanie sensed a different sort of camaraderie here. Everyone seated had been at Anacostia for a few years. Quantico and Glynco had a lot of transitional people. It was hard to get close to people, especially knowing you weren't going to be there very long. She thought back to her second and final date with Wayne Howell. Maybe that was his M.O. He knew women would be leaving at some point, and he'd gladly fill in the gap of affection, wanted or otherwise. She thanked her lucky stars again. *What if that ranger hadn't shown up when he did?* She flashed herself forward to the here and now. Gonzalez was the first to get up. "Come on." He signaled to Melanie. They returned the trays and walked back to the library.

Riding up the escalator, Melanie turned to Gonzalez. "So what happens next?"

"What do you mean?" he asked.

"Do I spend the rest of the day in the library? Is there a class I'm supposed to attend?"

"Yes. And yes. Keep doing your own research. It's forensics, remember?"

Melanie chuckled. "I see. I'm supposed to come up with a procedure. Then I'll be given an assignment."

"Correct. You *are* pretty smart." He remembered what the Captain had said about her high recommendations. "You can stay as long as you want to or need to. But tomorrow, you'll report to the classroom at oh-eight-hundred-hours."

"Got it." She gave him a thumbs-up.

He turned to leave, and Melanie spoke again. "Airman?"

He swiveled. "Yes?"

"Thank you. Really. It was nice of you to be so hospitable."

"Yes, ma'am. Just doing my job."

Melanie knew he'd done a little more than that. He'd showed her kindness. He could have operated strictly by the book. There would be no "getting to know you" stuff. Simple, mundane conversation. No, Gonzalez was a good egg.

Melanie gave him a big smile, her blue eyes wide. "I think

I'm going to like it here." She bit her lip. "Except for maybe the brown food."

Gonzalez gave her a two-finger wave. "Oh-eight-hundred."

"Roger that."

Melanie decided the next case would be Ted Bundy. After her encounter with Wayne, she wanted to test out her theory that he could be a psychopath. *They are very good at being psychopathic. Probably why they're called psychopaths.* She chuckled to herself. She saw there was a copy of *The Stranger Beside Me* by true-crime writer Ann Rule. It was bound into a larger binder. An autobiographical account of her friendship with Ted Bundy, it demonstrated how a person could be in the company of a monster and never know who they were really dealing with. Her story described a sensitive coworker at a crisis hotline. A man who walked her to her car at the end of a shift. A man she trusted with her children. It was the summer of 1973 in Seattle. Ted had quit his job at the hotline when women began to be brutally murdered at the rate of one a month. A few eyewitnesses gave the police a good description that gave Ann the chills. She couldn't believe it could be Ted. He moved to Utah, and suddenly the murders stopped. They stopped in Seattle, but Bundy was continuing to kill in other parts of the country. When he was finally arrested, he confessed to the murders of thirty-four women across seven states.

Melanie had read enough. She checked the clock. It was past six. No wonder her stomach was grumbling. Or was it churning? She gathered her notes, went back to her cubby, grabbed her tote, and headed home. The traffic was a bear. She phoned her mother to let her know she would be late for dinner, something that would become a regular occurrence.

"Don't worry, dear. You can pop it in the microwave," her mother reassured her.

"You still use that thing?" Melanie asked. She was not a fan of a device that could generate intermolecular friction.

Even though the machines themselves were safe, who knew what they were really doing to your broccoli? And by the time scientists found out, it would be too late. She'd rather wait an additional ten minutes and use the stove.

She finally pulled into the driveway at seven o'clock. Bixby greeted her with his tail smashing against the door. "Hey, pal!" She bent down to give him a hug. Her reading assignment that day had been a lot more disturbing than she'd thought it might be. The idea that there might be between twenty-five and fifty serial killers still walking the earth was unnerving. On second thought, maybe profiling wasn't the best idea.

She bounded up the stairs to shake off the day. It was good to be home. The aroma of chicken parmesan still lingered in the air. It was a salve for her soul. After washing her face and changing her clothes, she joined her mother in the kitchen.

"Where's Dad?"

"Playing cards with his buddies."

"Right. Every Monday and Thursday." Melanie checked the ovenproof dish that contained her salvation. "Yum. It's still warm." She dished out a large portion and pulled off a piece of semolina bread. "Where did you learn to cook like this?" she mumbled as she dipped the bread into the red sauce.

"I've always cooked like this," her mother answered, pouring both of them a glass of Chianti.

Melanie looked at the bottle. "Chianti." She sighed.

"You always enjoyed a glass. What's wrong?"

"Serial killers."

"Oh, you mean Hannibal Lecter?" her mother answered with a bit of amusement.

"Not him specifically. Just his type. You know, cray-cray." She made a circular motion around the side of her head. "It was the theme of the day."

"I don't understand."

Melanie wondered if it was a good idea to tell her mother about her research. It might alarm her, and repeating what she'd learned would only reinforce Melanie's uncertainty about her career choice.

Her mother took the seat next to her. "You seem a little distracted."

Melanie never held anything back, so why start now? She would be careful not to divulge anything that could be considered top secret, but all the cases she'd read about that day were public knowledge. Huge public knowledge.

"I had to do research today on serial killers."

Her mother looked horrified. "What? Serial killers? What does that have to do with OSI?"

"It's called profiling, Mom. I had to read about the history of criminal profiling from Jack the Ripper to The Mad Bomber, Ted Bundy, and Son of Sam." She decided to leave out the part about serial killers still on the loose.

"How gruesome!" Her mother's mouth was agape.

"True. But I was learning about how to piece together clues. It's fascinating but, you're right, can be gruesome." She savored the mozzarella, which was still gooey.

"Do you mean you are going to have to find serial killers?"

Melanie thought for a moment. "Not necessarily. Profiling isn't just about murderers. I could be tracking any number of illegal things people do out of obsession."

"I don't understand."

"There are people who simply like to create disruptions." She took another bite and wiped her chin. "People get off on spreading disinformation, just for kicks."

"What has the world come to?" her mother asked rhetorically.

"It's a big, hot mess." Melanie continued to enjoy her meal in spite of the subject. She was going to have to get used to it if she planned on staying with OSI.

"Well, honey, I hope this kind of thing doesn't upset you."

"Not too much." She raised her glass and clinked it against her mother's.

The following day, she reported to the classroom where Airman Gonzalez was waiting. "Good morning, MelDrake," he said cheerfully.

"Good morning to you, Airman," she replied.

"You can call me Leo when no one else is around. I meant to tell you yesterday during lunch, but everyone was monopolizing your attention."

"Really? I hadn't noticed." She remembered her motto. *Be aware.* "There was a lot for me to process yesterday."

"I understand. How did you make out in the stacks?" Leo was referring to the massive binders at the library.

"I learned a lot about serial killers."

"Ew. Gruesome."

"That's exactly what my mother said."

He gave her a suspicious look.

"Don't worry—I didn't divulge anything that wasn't already public knowledge." She pulled her chair out. "I simply mentioned Jack the Ripper, Ted Bundy, and a few other evil beings. Not great dinner conversation, I can assure you."

Gonzalez grunted and replied, "True dat." He looked at the clock. Exactly eight o'clock. "Captain Chen should be here . . ." His voice trailed off as the door swung open. Gonzalez snapped to attention.

"At ease," Chen directed. "Good morning, Drake. I take it you examined our data?" She noticed he had a thick file under his arm.

"I did, sir. Question. Isn't this information in an electronic database?"

"It is."

Melanie was puzzled. Then why have her comb through binders?

He moved toward the front of the room. "Everything is in

a database. Everything we already know. But you will be working on new cases with new information. I wanted you to get a feel for digging into the subject. Having access to a database can make a researcher lazy. It also doesn't promote the detective's coming to their own conclusions."

Melanie thought he made a good point. She felt the same way about writing something down. She processed the information better.

"Yes, I see what you are driving at. Personally, I still embrace the art of taking physical notes."

For the first time, Chen smiled. "Good. I'm a pencil and paper man myself."

Good. Something in common, Melanie thought.

"Today I am going to give you a hypothetical case. There will be photos and evidence. I want you to give me your best evaluation of the perpetrator."

Melanie nodded. She hoped the photos weren't too gory.

He continued. "You will have the entire day to answer the questions and then write up a summary. I want it on my desk by seventeen hundred hours." Before she had a chance to ask, he added, "Airman Gonzalez will bring your lunch, and you can use the bathroom facilities outside the door. You are not to discuss this with anyone. Am I clear?"

"Yes, sir." Boy, did she wish she could use the word "crystal."

He tossed the file on the table in front of him. "Have at it." He saluted the airman and left the room.

Melanie let out the air she had been holding in for what seemed like an eternity. She didn't know if she should speak to Gonzalez, but he beat her to it. "I'll be on my way. If you are in dire need of anything, please hit three-one-one on the speed dial. If there's nothing else, I'll be back around eleven hundred to take your lunch order." He smiled. "I'd go with the club sandwich if I were you."

"Roger that. Make it a club sandwich." Melanie smiled. "Thanks. I appreciate it."

Gonzalez left the room. Melanie stared at the three-inch-thick folder in front of her. She began to spread the documents across the long table. They were in no particular order, which she assumed was part of the process. *Figure it out. All of it.*

She checked the questions first, so she would know exactly what she had to look for. Good move. Then she began to sort the reports by incident and laid the evidence out in chronological order. Locations of death were different in every case. Different towns, different states, but the MO was similar. All the women were found on the side of interstate highways, which gave her the idea the perp was a truck driver. All the women were also waitresses at low-end eateries, but not at truck stops. Still, that didn't eliminate her theory of a driver. He could have parked his vehicle elsewhere. All the crimes were committed in the late hours of the night, and none of the victims were married. She looked over at one of the walls, where there was a map of the United States. She took a washable marker and pinpointed the locations where the murders occurred. It appeared the killer was someone traveling across the southwest section of the country.

Several hours passed as she went through records of cross-country haulers. She eventually came to the conclusion the killer was not an eighteen-wheeler driver, but someone driving a box truck. A truck that could get in and out of places easily, as opposed to a big rig. By noon, she was ready for her sandwich, and like clockwork, Gonzalez entered the room with a tray. "Chocolate milk?" he asked.

"How did you know?" Melanie was a chocoholic but had made no mention of it. At least she didn't think she had.

"You got a mocha latte from the machine. After you took your first sip, you frowned and said, 'Not enough cocoa.' "

So I did drop a hint. Better stay on top of that.

"You are quite observant, Airman Gonzalez."

"Thank you. I, too, am training for profiling." He gave her a friendly wink.

"You devil." Melanie grinned. "And you said nothing yesterday."

"Correct. Part of being a good agent often requires listening. Observing."

"Well, you're doing a good job of it." Melanie walked over to a table that wasn't cluttered with documents. She unwrapped her sandwich and asked Gonzalez to sit.

"No can do. You're on your own. I'll see you at seventeen hundred hours." He turned and left the room.

She chomped through her sandwich lickety-split. She didn't realize how hungry she was until the salt of the bacon hit her lips. She opened the carton of chocolate milk. This would be a lesson for her. She had to pay better attention to herself and others.

As the afternoon wound down, Melanie surmised the trucker was carrying something perishable, because traces of wood fragments were found in some of the clothing of the victims. The fragments came from the same type of wood used to make crates for citrus. She checked the clock. She had an hour left to write up her summary. It was like being back in college when she had to finish a test before the buzzer rang.

She finished her analysis, certain the criminal was a truck driver who went from state to state doing what they called "short runs." He'd show up at a distribution center somewhere and do a local run. Then he would travel to a different state and do the same.

Captain Chen entered the room at the stroke of five o'clock, or seventeen hundred hours. Melanie stood and read her notes out loud. Chen stood with his hands folded. He had absolutely no facial expression whatsoever. She didn't know if she was going down the right path or boring her supervisor to death. When she finished, he said, "Congratulations. You solved your first case."

Melanie was stunned. *So soon?* "Thank you, sir." Melanie was accustomed to doing research and compiling data. This was similar to doing a term paper, except she only had one day to finish.

"Were you considered studious in school?" he asked.

"I suppose so," she answered.

"Never *suppose*. It's either *yes* or *no*."

"Understood," she replied in an even tone. "But sir, doesn't this process utilize suppositions?" She wondered if she had overstepped.

"Very good point," he said. "So were you or were you not studious?" He knew she had to have been in order to advance this far in the organization. He was also very impressed with how quickly she could process information.

"Yes, sir. Studious." Melanie didn't want to get into how she got engrossed in books. She also didn't think it was a good idea to tell him she had a few magic tricks up her sleeve.

"Very good," Chen continued. "You will be trained in the prescribed program under my tutelage and be given intermittent exams. Upon passing said exams, you will move to the next level until you become classified as a special agent."

Melanie didn't dare ask how long that was going to take.

He answered her. "The speed with which you complete the courses will determine how quickly you get to do field work. Understood?"

"Understood, sir."

For the next two years, Melanie worked on kidnapping cold cases, reviewing old data and looking for new evidence. She felt it was important work. People needed to know what had happened to a family member who'd been taken. She knew the older the case was, the less the chance of recovering anything. But she had to try. Not just because it was her job, but because she felt the need to help if she could.

Most of the cases remained cold, with no more insight than in the past. Only two of them had resolution, but not the kind she'd hoped for. One body was found as a result of digging at a new construction site; the other, by hikers who were digging a shallow depression in the soil in order to build a campfire.

There was no satisfaction in shutting those cases. At least the family would have some closure. But not Melanie. She was never able to shake the fact that someone had gotten away with murder. It disturbed her deeply.

By the third year, Melanie was sent to the Special Issuance Agency, where she was issued a maroon passport. It was the color for U.S. Government employees who would be traveling for official duty. Often, they were called to assist other agencies across the globe. The travel was draining. There was no commercial flying unless absolutely necessary, and agents were expected to travel in Air Force cargo planes. She had to leave on *their* schedule, which sometimes meant getting up in the middle of the night.

Accommodations were often hostels, the food was whatever was available, and a hot shower was a luxury. Most of her work involved tracking terrorists and developing profiles on them. She would travel to the country where the chatter was coming from, so she could get a feel for the type of environment the offender was living in. After several weeks, she would return stateside and enter her data, analyze her data, and share her data. She wondered how long she could keep this up. She hated it. So much for diplomacy. Beale was right. It was a matter of thwarting disasters.

By her tenth year, she requested a posting stateside. She had no personal life, but at least she could count on a hot shower and decent food if she remained in Virginia. She had lived with her parents for too long. Not that she spent much time with them. She was away more than she was home. Living at home was convenient, and she enjoyed her parents' company, but she wanted to have her own space. Her own base. Her own slice of peace and sanity.

Because of her excellent record, she was promoted to a desk job. Most of her coworkers would have considered it a demotion, but they were also in their first couple of years of international hijinks. *Give them a decade of doing this.*

When her fifteenth anniversary was on the horizon, she knew she had to get out sooner rather than later and finally began to look into programs where she could get her master's degree through her job. It occurred to her that thwarting disasters should begin at the beginning. In elementary school. Don't wait until the person is an adult with all sorts of behavioral problems that were now ingrained. Catch them while they're young. She had no interest in teaching, but guidance counseling would be a good place to start; a good place to start guiding little humans toward the right way to behave. Even if she could influence one person to become a better human being, it would all be worth it. The idealistic side of Melanie was coming out.

She made an appointment to speak to her current supervisor, Richard Patterson, and he agreed to sign off on her forms to take graduate classes in psychology.

"Only one request," he said. "I want you to look into a case of five women who went missing. Their bodies were eventually discovered, and the murders have all the markings of a serial killer."

"Is it a cold case?"

"Essentially, though the bodies have been recently discovered. They were all within a ten-mile radius of each other. According to forensics, the women were murdered two years apart, spanning the past ten years."

"Where was this?" Melanie asked.

"Outside Quantico."

Melanie's blood turned cold. "Where, exactly?" She already knew the answer.

"Price William Forest Park."

The color left her face. She thought she might faint.

"Are you alright?" he asked.

"I think I know who the killer is."

"What?" he asked in disbelief.

"I know that sounds crazy, but I have a gut feeling about this." She knew if she used the word *gut* instead of *intuition*, Rich would be more inclined to listen.

"Really?" He sounded unconvinced.

"Were the women in their early twenties?"

"Yes."

"Were they sexually assaulted?"

"Yes."

"Did they find any traces of drugs?"

"Yes." Patterson was beginning to believe she might have a clue, even though those questions and answers were not unusual.

"Let me look at the file. Please, sir." Melanie could not wait to review this case.

"How do you know about this?" he asked curiously.

"Let's just say if I'm right, then you are looking at someone who could have been victim number six."

"Wait! What?" Again he was baffled.

"When I was at Quantico, I went on a date with one of my coworkers. I know. I know." She waved away the lecture.

"At some point during dinner, he slipped something into my drink. As we were leaving the restaurant, I felt a little dizzy, but I'd only had one glass of wine." She closed her eyes for a moment as she remembered as much as she could. "I was nodding off in the car and realized we were not going in the direction of my apartment. We were on a dirt road in the dark."

Patterson was leaning forward. His elbows were on his desk and his chin propped up by his fists. He was totally engrossed in her story.

"I felt his hands on me, but I couldn't stop him. Thank heavens, a park ranger did."

"What do you mean?"

"A park ranger came up to the window and shined his flashlight into the car. He must have thought what was going on was consensual, but then he saw I was woozy. Oh, and I threw up. He asked for identification. Wayne Howell— remember that name—pulled out his wallet, and the ranger helped me with mine. Once I was a bit steadier, he let us go."

"What did you do about it?"

"Nothing. I did not want Wayne to see I was upset. That would have given him more of an upper hand. We drove to my apartment in silence."

"And you didn't report it?"

"What was there to report?" Melanie shrugged. "I could have told the ranger that the man was trying to take advantage of me, but I didn't want repercussions at work."

"You said nothing?"

"Not until today. You are the first person I ever discussed this with."

"But why?" He looked confused.

"Several reasons. As I said, I didn't want trouble at work, and I couldn't prove anything. I didn't get a drug test, which in hindsight I should have. I felt a mix of humiliation and relief. How could I have been so stupid? And thank God I'm alive." She cleared her throat. "I did speak to Wayne a few days later."

"Seriously? What did you say?"

"I told him he was lucky he wasn't singing soprano."

Patterson burst out laughing, getting her reference to being hit in the scrotum. "That was pretty risky. And funny."

"True. But it hadn't occurred to me at the time that he could be worse than a horny dude wanting easy access." She shook her head. "Dating. Not my strong suit."

Patterson thought a moment. "So you think this is the guy?"

"Well, he fits the profile. He's attractive, attentive, intelligent."

"That covers a lot of men." He smiled. "Let me check and see if he's still at the base." He turned to his computer and powered up the contact list of all OSI agents. "You said his name is Wayne Howell?"

"Correct."

"He was at Quantico until three years ago."

"When were the bodies found?" Melanie asked.

Patterson checked the file. "Huh. A little over a year ago."

Melanie paged through the documents. "Last one was determined to have died two years prior, which means Howell was still in the area at the time of the last victim's death. He must have moved after killing his latest victim. The time frame fits."

She looked further. "They found traces of Ambien in the most recent body. It doesn't look like they checked on the earlier victims."

Patterson was still stunned about Melanie's connection to a suspect.

"Let's see," she said to herself. "Skin samples were taken from under one of the victim's nails." She looked up. "We have DNA." Her eyes glistened.

"Yes, but we don't have his," Patterson reminded her.

"What if we can get his?" Melanie stared straight at her boss.

"How?" Patterson furrowed his brow.

"Do we know where he lives?" Melanie asked.

Patterson turned back to his computer. "He works in the contracts division at one of the DC offices."

"That's an odd career move, don't you think?" Melanie wondered. "Did he request the transfer?"

Patterson looked again. "Yes. According to his record, he was transferred by request for personal reasons."

"Does it list the personal reason?"

"That's confidential, I'm afraid." Patterson frowned.

"How close would I be if I said it was to be closer to his ailing mother?"

"You really have been doing a lot of profile research." He snickered.

What is it about serial killers and their mothers?

"Let me think about this. People like him have strict routines. They have to be in control." Melanie ruminated. "Can you give me his location?"

"Excuse me a minute." He got up from his chair and swiveled his monitor slightly in Melanie's direction. He walked out of the room for ten seconds, giving Melanie a chance to glance at the screen, snap a photo of Wayne's most current ID, and scribble down his work and home addresses.

Patterson cleared his throat as he returned. "Remember, *burn-bag.*"

"Roger that." Melanie knew he was referring to placing written information in a bag and burning it. Most people would be surprised at how much information is exchanged via paper. No electronic fingerprints. She thought of Major Beale. That was her specialty. As long as people were stupid enough to leave a cyber trail, Major Beale would have a job. It was astonishing how reckless people were. It made catching the lawless a little easier, but the number of crimes was growing exponentially.

Melanie drove home that evening with a new sense of purpose. Two, actually. She was getting out of the crime business and moving on to a new career. But before she turned in her badge, she was going to settle an old score.

She took a few days off work to formulate and execute her plan. She was familiar with the neighborhood where Wayne Howell worked. It would be easy enough to set up a stakeout. She'd arrive an hour before the building opened to ensure she had a good perch. Close enough to see who came and went, but far enough so she would not be spotted. She scoped out the neighborhood and found a parking place near a café. She went inside to survey the place, check the location of the restroom, and purchase a mocha latte, then returned to her car.

She knew once Howell was in the building, he wouldn't leave until after his shift ended. She had an official parking badge she could flash if any traffic officers questioned her. "Official business," was all she had to say.

By seven thirty, people were bustling to their places of employment. She checked her phone again to be sure she had a clear image of what Wayne looked like now. He had some gray at the temples and was now wearing glasses. His face was thinner, but she recognized those engaging eyes. After all these years, she still didn't know who she was angrier with, him or herself.

She spotted him among three other people. Two were women. He must have said something to make them laugh. She wondered if he had stopped his heinous deeds or if he was grooming new victims. She noted the direction from which he came and which door he entered. There was a municipal underground parking garage nearby. Most people who worked in the area parked there. They got a special government discount.

An hour later, she got out of the car, making sure her hat and sunglasses were in place. She stretched her long legs and leaned against the side of the vehicle.

Melanie looked at the well-kept townhouses and the immaculate streets. Washington DC was a contradiction. It was a power playing field, filled with thousands of agendas, most of which were not necessarily in the voters' best interest.

It troubled her that the people of the country were not well represented. Politics was a career, and not an act of civic duty. She wanted to get a bullhorn and yell, "Term limits! No more lobbyists!" That outburst would get her fired and arrested, but she knew almost every American would agree with her. She could probably raise bail money easily. She chuckled at her fantasy. *But, dang. Someone really should do it.*

It was getting close to lunch, and people were milling about. She noticed one of the women who had been walking with Howell earlier. She quickly ran toward a man close to her age. They kissed. *Not a target for Howell.*

Melanie got comfortable in her car and waited. As predicted, Howell didn't leave the building until four thirty. Her eyes followed him across the large patio area, and then he disappeared behind the hedges that led to the garage. *Routine.* Her plan for the next day was to go to the cafeteria during lunch. She would be incognito and keep a good distance away. She wanted to observe him with other people.

Melanie knew she was onto something. She'd had a weird vibe when she'd first seen him that morning. She'd convinced herself it wasn't a visceral reaction. But she had witnessed many demons in her career. She could feel that he was one of them.

She made her way back to her apartment and heated up some leftover chicken her mother had dropped off the day before. She was glad she was close enough to home to get a good meal, but far enough for the quiet space she needed. She missed cuddling with her favorite doggie, but she made an effort to spend time with him on the weekends. Having a desk job had its perks.

Melanie scrutinized the schools that offered degrees in psychology that would also be eligible for government reimbursement. There was one hitch. If you didn't get your degree, you had to pay all the tuition back. Melanie knew that wouldn't be a problem for her. The sooner she got her degree, the sooner she could get out. She imagined buying a modest cottage in a small town, getting a couple of dogs, and working at an elementary school. She would have her mother help plan her gardens. She was jostled from her musing by the phone. It was Patterson.

"What's up, boss?" She knew it had to be important for him to be calling her at home.

"They found another body."

Chapter Nine

The Pursuit

Melanie postponed her stakeout and went directly to the office the next day. The team was meeting in a conference room.

Patterson had the large media screens on the walls lit up with a map. There was a round dot on the map where the body had been found. Outside the National Arboretum. It took Melanie's breath away.

Patterson pulled up the information about the other victims. "Same M.O."

One of the agents raised his hand. "But it's almost two hours away from where the others were found."

"We have reason to believe the perpetrator is in our area."

"Oh?" one asked.

"We got a lead."

Chatter filled the room. "From who?"

"Whom," Patterson corrected them.

"A witness?"

The questions were flying at him.

"We have a person who believes she encountered the perp

several years ago." Patterson was careful not to divulge Melanie's connection.

More questions.

"How did she know to come forward?"

"Did he assault her?"

"In a manner of speaking," Patterson responded.

"When did this happen?"

"Several years ago, a woman was on a date and was drugged. She was fortunate enough that someone interceded and ruined the perp's plan."

"Who interceded?"

"I'm only at liberty to share a few of the details until we have more information from the coroner's office. Right now, what we do know is that the body was buried outside the park with the same M.O. Based on the condition of the body, it's been there between twelve to fifteen months."

He proceeded to project the information on the five previous victims onto the big screen. Melanie pretended she was taking notes. She already had the information from her meeting with Patterson two days before. She showed no sign she had any prior knowledge of the murders, or her close proximity to the killer. "I want each of you to take a partner and work the info together." He looked in Melanie's direction. He knew her well enough to realize she was going to go above and beyond to catch the guy, and he wanted her working with someone who was equally as experienced as she was, and also a bit bigger and brawnier. He chose Gregory Gilmour, a seasoned agent. He was six feet tall and tipped the scales at two hundred pounds of solid muscle. "Gilmour. Drake. With me. The rest of you double up. We'll recon as soon as I get the autopsy results."

Gilmour and Melanie walked with Patterson to his office. He motioned for them to have a seat as he shut the door.

"Drake, I don't want you to be a lone wolf on this one."

Gilmour looked perplexed. "Aren't we doubling up?"

"Yes, but Drake has some inside information that might prove useful."

Gilmour glanced at her. "Seriously? How?"

Melanie looked at Patterson for direction. "Tell him."

She recounted the story as Gilmour stared in disbelief. "You really think he's the guy?"

"It fits. I don't think it's a coincidence another body turns up exactly two years after the last one, which was two years after the previous one."

"Some kind of anniversary?" Gilmour put forward.

"That's what I'm thinking," Melanie said. She cleared her throat. "I know where he works." She stopped. She did not reveal how she'd acquired the information, but upper-level officers had access to the personnel database.

"You do? But how?" Gilmour was completely absorbed.

Patterson nodded for Melanie to continue, but she knew not to reveal that her source was their boss. "I spotted him outside one of the DOD offices." When she finished detailing her story and her theory, Gilmour was baffled. "He's one of us?"

"Looks that way." Melanie nodded. She wanted to be as transparent as possible, but she tilted the story to protect her informant, so to speak. "I had the day off. I was in a café getting a coffee. After I spotted him, I decided to spend the rest of the day staking out his office just to be sure it was him."

"And you believe it's the guy," Gilmour commented.

"Absolutely. I'd recognize that slightly cocky walk from a mile away."

"So, what's the plan?" Gilmour asked.

"We need to get his DNA," Melanie answered. Patterson was letting her run the meeting. She certainly knew more than he did.

"That's going to be tricky," Gilmour said.

"Not if I have help." She gave him one of her intense stares that said, *It's you, buddy.*

Melanie laid out her strategy.

Gilmour and Melanie would go to the cafeteria the next day. They would enter a few minutes apart and go in different directions, ultimately arriving at the cafeteria. They would not show any signs of familiarity and would keep their distance from each other. Gilmour would insinuate himself at Howell's lunch table, pretending he knew him from the past. He'd mention the Bugle Pub near Quantico, where Howell and his colleagues used to hang out after work. Melanie would take a seat far enough away not to be spotted, but close enough to watch Howell's moves and what he ate. When finished, Gilmour would walk Howell out of the cafeteria. Once out of their line of sight, Melanie would fish his lunch debris from the trash. If anyone asked what she was doing, she would claim her bracelet had fallen off when she put her scraps in the bin. She would have to act quickly, before his refuse was covered by someone else's. If he hadn't changed his preference for beverages, there would be a can of ginger ale.

Patterson finally spoke. "When you enter the building, tell security you are there to visit Mr. George Remedy."

Melanie tilted her head. "George Remedy?"

Patterson smirked. "Code word. How long have you been working here? It's a name that's used to gain entry into other departmental buildings. As far as anyone is concerned, George Remedy has an office on the fifth floor." He folded his arms across his chest. "Do what you would normally do if you had an appointment with Mr. Remedy. You go to the fifth floor, tell the receptionist who you are there to see, and she will show you down a hallway with a secured exit to the stairwell. She'll buzz the door, and then you can proceed to the fourth floor. Once you get to the fourth floor, exit the stairwell, and take the elevator to the lower level. The cafeteria doors will be to the right. Remember to enter the building several minutes apart. I suggest whoever gets there first wait on the fifth floor to be sure both of you are in the building."

Melanie was taking copious notes, not that she needed them. She had the instructions rooted in her mind.

"Gilmour, after lunch, you'll walk Howell to the elevator and get in with him. He should hit the button for the third floor. You'll get out in the lobby and exit the building. Mel, once you retrieve the evidence, get out of the building as quickly as possible and meet Gilmour at your designated spot."

"Question." Melanie raised her pen. "If I can't locate the soda can, should I take the entire bag? Or find a place to dump it out?"

Patterson looked at Melanie. "I am sure you can convince someone to find a place for you to sift through it. I don't think they want anyone traipsing around a government office building carrying a bag of cafeteria trash."

"I have a cheap bangle bracelet I will gladly sacrifice to toss in the can." She pinched her lips. "Gloves. I'll play it by ear once I see how many people are around. If it looks like I can grab something without attracting any attention, I'll use my own. If not, I'll ask one of the staff for a pair and do my lost bracelet routine."

Patterson slapped his hand on his desk. "Sounds like you have this buttoned up. Any questions?"

Gilmour looked at Melanie with admiration and amazement. "Not me. Drake's got it under control."

Patterson had a few last words. "Be careful. If he's our guy, we want to nail him. But if he gets wind we're on to him, he'll be a Gone Elvis." Patterson was referring to the term for people who disappear.

"Roger that," Gilmour and Melanie chimed in together. They left Patterson's office and continued to make their plan for the next day. Melanie knew she couldn't use a disguise, or she would never get past any of the security guards. She had to be stealthy.

The following morning, Gilmour and Melanie met in front of the café near Howell's building. Howell arrived right on time, walking and talking with the same two women from the day before. She surmised the woman without the boyfriend was most likely his next target. This would be within his kill window; the "anniversary" was looming. They waited until eleven to enter the building, with Gilmour leading. Melanie checked her watch. Ten minutes later, she was at the security desk asking for Mr. Remedy. The security guard had her face a security camera, took her photo, and scanned her lanyard. Not a hiccup. When she got off the elevator, there was a single desk with a woman sitting in front of a monitor. There were no other chairs or people.

It was a bit eerie.

"Good morning. I have an appointment with Mr. Remedy." Melanie smiled.

"Yes." The woman pressed a button that electronically locked the main entrance to the reception area. She stood, expressionless. "This way, please."

Melanie obediently followed her down a long corridor. The hallway was stark. No artwork, no awards, no photos, no signs. Not even doors. At the end of the hallway, they turned the corner to another bleak corridor with only one door. Gilmour was waiting for her.

The receptionist said nothing. She pulled out a magnetic card, swiped it over the lock, and punched in a security code. The code was changed every day to ensure the highest security in the back halls of the building.

Gilmour and Melanie took the stairs to the fourth floor, where Melanie waited inside the stairwell. Gilmour took the first elevator down to the cafeteria. She checked her watch and set it to vibrate in fifteen minutes. It was the longest fifteen minutes of her life. As soon as it signaled, she moved to the hallway and toward the elevator. If an elevator stopped on her floor with people in it, or if someone approached the elevator bank while she was waiting, she'd fake forgetting something. It was crucial she keep as low a profile as possible. If anything went sideways, the fewer people who could identify her, the better. Not that she expected trouble, but better to be incognito than obvious.

While she was waiting, one person approached the elevator bank. He nodded. She smiled. When the elevator arrived, she said, "Dang. Go ahead. I forgot something."

The man seemed to think nothing of it and took the car. Melanie checked her watch again. Finally the soft ding of the elevator accompanied the light above the door. She got in and pressed the button for the lower level. Her heart was beating much faster than usual. She had been on many cases over the course of her career, but this one was personal. She peered into the massive room. There was a pillar just ahead where she could scope out where Howell and Gilmour were sitting. She saw Howell look in her direction and darted behind the pillar. She couldn't tell if he'd seen her or not. She'd have to wait. But for how long? What if he recognized her? Would he remember her?

She shook off her fears. She was a champion of karma. And luck. She'd also learned that luck often meant being prepared for when an opportunity presented itself. Here was her opportunity. And she was prepared. For anything.

At the moment, the big question was how was she to keep an eye on Howell when he was facing her? She glanced in both directions. The only way to get to the other side of the cafeteria was through the kitchen. Even though the swinging door said EXIT, she was going to change its purpose for a few seconds. She looked over at the food counter. The protective plexiglass in front of the stainless-steel trays of food proved to be a valuable tool, and she was able to spot Howell's reflection. She hoped he wasn't able to see hers. She held her breath as she watched him get up and walk in her direction. He stopped in front of the vending machine and purchased a can of soda. She couldn't make out what brand it was but would bet it was the same ginger ale he used to drink years ago. As soon as he turned to go back to his table, she darted into the kitchen, practically knocking over a busboy.

"Hey! Watch it, lady," the scrawny adolescent cried out.

She flashed her OSI badge long enough for him to see what it was but too quickly to see who it was. She excused herself and moved quickly past the rows of pots and pans. The half-hour lunch break was almost over. She had to get to the other side of the room posthaste if she was to have any chance of retrieving anything that might have his DNA.

Melanie watched from several yards away, with another column blocking her from view. Gilmour stood. He spotted her. Then Howell got up. Gilmour placed his arm on Howell's shoulder and gave him a "good buddy" pat on the back. From where Melanie stood, it appeared the ruse was successful. She pulled on a pair of clear plastic gloves. Once Gilmour and Howell were out of sight, she hurried to the recycling container, where he'd deposited his empty can of soda. She checked around the room. No one was paying any attention to her. She peered inside the bin. There were two cans of ginger ale. She picked them out and placed them in the plastic ziplock bag she carried in her pocket and quickly put them in her tote bag. She took her time exiting the cafeteria, thinking Howell and Gilmour might still be in the hallway chatting, even though that wasn't part of the plan. Gilmour was to follow Howell to the elevator, but she didn't want to take any chances. Not now. She listened for voices. The hallway was quiet except for the clamoring of the janitorial crew in the cafeteria. She hit the elevator button. It was empty. She let out a sigh of relief. Just a few more doors and a few hundred yards, and she was home free.

She hustled through the lobby and bounded down the steps of the large quadrangle. Gilmour was leaning against his car. "Bingo!" She pulled the bag from her tote. "Let's get this over to the lab ASAP."

Melanie got in her car and began to drive in the direction of Interstate 695 to Anacostia. As she passed the parking garage, she didn't notice a car exiting behind her. She also didn't notice the car was following her. She drove for several miles, turned on her directional signal, and got on the exit ramp to a quiet intersection. As she was rolling to a stop, she felt a strong bump against the back of her car. "Oh, not now. Please," she muttered. She looked in the side-view mirror and saw a man running toward her. She leaned over to the compartment where she kept her gun. It was always locked unless she was in a perilous situation, and this could be one. But by the time she'd unlocked her seat belt, the man was yanking her door open and dragging her out of the car. Melanie began to kick and scream, but Howell placed a bag over her head, forced her arms behind her, swiftly shoved her onto the floor of the back seat of his car, and then cuffed her wrists. There was no one to save her this time.

Howell got back into the driver's seat and pulled away, leaving her unattended, slightly crumpled automobile on the side of the road. Police would eventually identify it, but by then, it could be too late.

He began to speak. "You know, MelDrake, you always thought you were a notch above the rest of us. Such a clever girl. Did you really think you were going to get away with that pathetic play you and your cohort devised?" He was waiting for a reply.

Melanie didn't answer him. Let him keep talking while she focused on what her next move should be.

"How did I know? You might ask. I spotted you the minute you walked in. My eyes always go to the ladies. You never know when you will meet someone interesting." He cleared his throat and spat out the window. "Then I realized you looked familiar. But your pal? He needs to take acting lessons. I knew something was up."

Melanie listened. He was not the same Wayne from years ago. His voice had much more of a chill to it now. He'd become desensitized. She knew trying to reason with him would be futile. Arguing would make him more aggressive. She had to appeal to his ego without his realizing it.

"How so?" she asked.

"He was too friendly. Too handsy." Howell chuckled. "He thought he gave me the slip, but I got out of the elevator and followed him. I figured the two of you were watching me and would meet up at some point. I went straight to my car and waited. And bingo. There you were." He glanced at the rearview again. He could barely see the top of the bag on her head. "And bingo, here you are now."

Melanie wondered if he knew about the ginger ale. If she wasn't able to escape, at least there would be evidence in her car. She knew she needed all the psychological tricks she could pull out of her bag. Then she remembered Uncle Leo. He'd taught her how to pick her way out of a pair of handcuffs with a small paper clip. But where would she find one at that moment? Her lanyard. The bobby pins. She always had two clipped on it in case she had to get her hair out of her face. She figured it was close enough and her only option. She struggled to move the lanyard around her body.

"Getting cozy back there?" Howell asked sarcastically.

"Wayne?" She knew addressing him by name would help humanize her, make her a bit less of a victim in his eyes.

"Yes. MelDrake."

"Do you think you could take the bag off my head?" Her words were muffled. "I promise I won't scream, and even if I did, no one would hear me. Please? I'd rather not have an asthma attack." Melanie's voice was calm as her muted words reached the front seat. "And my arm is asleep." Still calm, but she was lying. Lying about the asthma and her arm.

"We'll wake it up soon enough. In about an hour. So relax and enjoy the ride." That was the end of the chatter.

Melanie knew she had less than sixty minutes to untangle herself. She rolled up into a crouching position. She pressed her cheek against her shoulder, inching the cord away from her body. She just needed enough room to get the lanyard over her head. But the bag. It would be in the way.

"Wayne? Please." She was being submissive, just short of begging. She knew he would like that.

Without turning around, he reached one arm over the seat and yanked the bag off her head.

"Happy?" he asked.

"Yes. Very. Thank you." She crouched farther, bent her head, and wriggled a little more, letting the lanyard drop to the floor. She rolled and lay on her side with the lanyard behind her.

Wayne looked into the rearview mirror again. Mostly to check whether there were any police following them. He was crafty but also paranoid. "Do you know where we're going?"

"No." She thought he might be taking her back to the original scene of his failed attempt at molesting her, and who knew what else.

"I don't think there'll be any park rangers around, do you?"

Melanie didn't answer. She knew he was probably right but prayed he was wrong.

"I heard they do most of their patrolling between eleven p.m. and three a.m. To scare out the vagrants."

She strained her arm to get hold of the cord. She was inches away. She wiggled again.

"Getting excited?" he said viciously. "I know I am."

Melanie sighed but said nothing. She had to focus on un-hitching herself without his finding out. She could feel the plastic badge. Directly above it, there were two bobby pins attached to the cord. She closed her eyes and remembered a technique she'd been taught called remote viewing: the abil-ity to view things that couldn't be seen from one's current lo-cation; the ability to "see" something from a different vantage point. Some took it much further with the idea of as-tral projection, an out-of-body experience, but that was a metaphysical concept many considered "fringe." No time to contemplate that idea. At the moment, she had to get out of those handcuffs.

She began to imagine herself as a passenger in the back seat. What would she be able to see? She visualized herself curled in a ball on the floor of the car. Locked wrists, a cord with a laminated badge near the small of her back. Two bobby pins attached to the cord. She walked her fingers up slowly, inching closer to the target. Using a fingernail, she carefully pulled one of the pins from the cord. Then she real-ized she might make suspicious noises while working on the handcuffs. "Hey, Wayne?"

"She speaks!" he roared.

"Yes." She replied loudly enough so he wouldn't have to lean back. "Do you think you might be in the mood for some music?" That was risky. It could infuriate him. He'd think she was being bossy. Taking control. But she'd used the word *you* twice, placing emphasis on him.

"Your wish is my command."

If only, she thought. She could think of many wishes right about now.

He cranked up the dial and blasted explosive-sounding music though the car, hammering his fists on the steering wheel to the beat of the deafening sound. He actually started to growl along with whoever the singer was, if you could call it singing. It sounded more like the devil screaming words of annihilation. The only solace was that it was loud, and Melanie could maneuver without disturbing Wayne as she jiggled the cuffs.

He screamed over the noise. "How do you like this?"

She screamed back. "I've never heard this before. Who's the artist?" She hoped to distract him with conversation.

"You never heard of Rage Against the Machine? Heavy metal, punk, and rap. They melded the genres together." Wayne was clearly a fan.

Keep him talking, she thought. "Oh, yes. I've heard of them. What's the lead vocalist's name again?" she shouted above the noise.

"Zack de la Rocha. Then there's Tom Morello on guitar, and Brad Wilk on drums. Greatest alternative band ever." There was true admiration in his voice.

Melanie thought the music was horrible, but she pretended she was interested. "What was their big hit?"

"Oh, come on, MelDrake. It was 'Killing in the Name'."

Perfect, she mused.

"Can you believe they were nominated for the Rock and Roll Hall of Fame four times and their bids failed? Talk about politics!"

"Isn't that the way with most things?" She sounded genuine. Melanie bent the bobby pin and carefully slid it into the handcuff keyhole. It was physically awkward, but she was determined to become a contortionist if it was going to save her life. And that of others.

She closed her eyes and imagined the bobby pin dislodging the mechanism. She was grateful it was handcuffs and not zip ties. Unless you had a blade, they were impossible to escape from. She felt the click and then the release. She twisted one wrist slowly, the way Uncle Leo taught her. If she moved too quickly, the lock could jam with the pin still in it. The music continued to reverberate off the interior of the car.

With the decibel level cranked as high as he had it, he

couldn't hear her motions at all. Now she had to figure out what to do next. She could reach over and put him in a choke hold with the cuffs, but he was driving too fast, and when he lost control, both of them could be killed. No. She would have to wait until he stopped the car. She knew there would be a few traffic lights once they exited the interstate. Timing was everything. Whatever she decided, she knew she had to be fast. Lightning fast.

The car came to a slow roll. She interlaced her fingers and positioned her arms as if they were a baseball bat and took a major swing at his temple, putting all her weight behind it. He cried out, but before he could react, Melanie grabbed a cuff in each hand, slipped them over his head, and pulled them back against his throat. He sagged forward, and his foot came off the brake, as the car careened through the intersection. She leaned halfway over the seat and yanked on the steering wheel, forcing the car to jump the curb and crash into a mailbox. Melanie was propelled forward, taking a glancing blow to the side of her head from the steering wheel. Both of them were now in the front seat. Wayne was coming around, but he was still strapped into his seat belt. Then his eyes flew open, and they were filled with rage. He grabbed her hair and slammed her head against the dashboard. She elbowed him in the chest and then the ultimate target, his groin. He was alternating between screams and gasps. He grabbed her by her hair again. She swiveled and punched him in the throat. She continued to pummel him in the face, neck, stomach, and again in the groin for good measure. He would be singing coloratura by the time the police arrived. She pounded her knuckles raw, repeatedly smashing him in the face, drawing blood from his nose and mouth. He was gagging as people began to gather around the car.

"Someone call 911!" she yelled.

*   *   *

When Melanie didn't show up at the office after procuring the evidence, Patterson and Gilmour began calling her cell. After an hour, they were able to get a location from the cell tower where the last signal pinged. Gilmour knew Melanie had taken the local roads and drove in the direction where her car might possibly be. By the time he arrived, a police car and a tow truck were on the scene.

He got out of his car and approached the officer. He showed him his badge. "This belongs to one of my coworkers. Do you know where she is?" Gilmour looked around for signs of Melanie. Her tote bag and phone were in the front passenger seat. Melanie would never walk away from her personal belongings. Nor would she walk away from an accident.

"No. We got a call saying there was a car blocking the road and there was nobody in it."

"So you didn't get the call?"

"Nope. Went to the main board. I was around the corner, so they sent me to respond." The officer took note that there were personal belongings in the front seat. "Do you recognize those items?"

"Yes. They're Melanie's." He kept looking around for any sign of her or somebody who might have seen her. "Any witnesses?"

The officer pointed to a camera on the light pole. "Waiting for techs to run through the video. Should be another minute." His phone chimed with a link to the video. Gilmour leaned over the officer's shoulder and watched in horror as Howell snatched Melanie and shoved her in his car. "Run those plates, would ya?" Gilmour was certain the car belonged to Howell. He made a phone call. "We need an APB for a silver Chrysler minivan. License plate three-five-eight, one-seven-one. Driver may be armed and dangerous, OSI agent Wayne Howell. Suspected abduction of OSI agent, Melanie Drake. Last seen entering entrance of three-sixty-five. May be headed to Prince William Forest area."

"Copy that."

Seconds later, he heard the call come over the other officer's radio. They were on it.

Wayne Howell was slumped over, a half-conscious bloody heap. By now, the car was surrounded by onlookers and Good Samaritans who were desperately trying to open the car doors. Melanie knew she'd come close to killing him. But then there would be two hearings, one for her and one for him. Killing someone, even in the line of duty, required deep scrutiny during an inquiry. It would go on her record. She looked at the rumpled pile of the impaired psychopath. *One knee to the throat would end him.* It was tempting, but she didn't want to be the subject of the investigation. She'd be called to testify, but as a victim. He'd be the criminal justice system's problem now.

She pulled on the passenger handle, slowly opened the door, and crawled out. Two people helped her stand upright. "Do not let that man get away."

Two police cruisers pulled up, blocking the car on each side. Questions were bouncing off the sidewalk.

She thanked the people who'd come to her aid. "OSI. Badge is in the back seat." She was huffing.

One officer wrapped a blanket around her and escorted her to his vehicle. Another officer checked Howell's pulse. "We're gonna need a bus," he shouted to his partner and held up two fingers. He felt Howell's pulse. It was weak, but steady. He cuffed Howell to the steering wheel just in case.

The first officer handed Melanie a bottle of water. "Are you okay?"

Melanie was shaking. She'd never been in a real fistfight before. She'd learned basic evasive tactics as part of the program, but she'd never expected she would have to use those particular skills. "I will be." That was one thing she was certain of. She'd finished the water by the time two ambulances arrived.

Melanie told the officer to bag her hands so they could collect Howell's DNA. His blood would surely give them an excellent sample. She proceeded to give the officer the basic outline of what had happened. He'd abducted her, she'd escaped from one cuff, and "you can see the outcome." She tilted her head in the direction of Wayne's car. "The man is a person of interest in an ongoing investigation." She knew the officer would ask what kind. "We need to call Richard Patterson. He's SAIC, special agent in charge. I'm sure he's wondering what happened to me."

Her certainty was confirmed when she heard the call come over the officer's radio:

"Attention all units, BOLO silver Chrysler minivan. License plate three-five-eight, one-seven-one. Driver may be armed and dangerous, known as OSI agent Wayne Howell. Suspected abduction of OSI agent, Melanie Drake. Last seen entering three-sixty-five southbound. May be headed to Prince William Forest area."

"I guess we beat everyone to it," the officer said wryly. "Speaking of beating. I can't imagine he was like that when he got to you."

Melanie grunted. "No. No, he was not." The officer walked her over to the ambulance. They swabbed the blood from her hands and then administered first aid. She touched the side of her face where she'd hit the steering wheel, right on top of her scar.

The EMT lifted her chin to check the bruise. "You know, you're lucky."

As if in a dream, she repeated the words that had been spoken to her as a child. "I know. It could have been worse." She smiled to herself.

"Very true," the EMT replied.

Melanie appreciated the swift work of Gilmour and law

enforcement to send an alert. She *was* lucky. She could have been dead before they got there. She insisted she was alright, but the EMT checked her vitals anyway. She watched the men extricate Howell from the car. By the looks of it, she'd probably broken one of his ribs, definitely his nose, given him a concussion, split his lip, and battered his manhood. Physically and mentally. They handcuffed him to a gurney and lifted him into the ambulance. Two police officers accompanied him.

Melanie looked up at the sound of an approaching helicopter. There was a small field on the other side of the interstate where it began to touch down. She spotted Gilmour and Patterson duck their way out and jog toward the underpass. Within a few minutes, they were on the scene.

"Mel! Are you alright?"

"Just a few scrapes and bruises." She held up her bandaged hands.

The attending officer introduced himself. "Sergeant Kincaid. As they say, you should see the other guy."

Gilmour and Patterson looked at him curiously.

"This one"—he jerked his thumb at Melanie—"I'd never want to get into a bar fight with her."

Melanie laughed for the first time that day.

"Do you want to go to the hospital?" Patterson asked.

"I'd rather not." The EMT handed her an icepack for her face. "Thanks." She smiled at the technician, then turned back to Patterson. "Too much red tape, and I'm okay. Shaken, but okay." She looked at Gilmour. "I might take you up on that Bulleit Bourbon offer." Over the past few years, Gilmour and Drake had developed a work friendship. Camaraderie. Gilmour joked that to be a true agent, she had to drink bourbon. Never Scotch. It was in the rules. "As much as I try to follow them, I am skeptical about this one."

They spent the next half hour giving Officer Kincaid all the necessary information for his report.

"Come on. Let's get you home." Patterson and Gilmour put an arm around the blanket-clad agent and walked her to the waiting helicopter.

"I retrieved your personal items from your car."

"All of them?" She wondered about her gun, phone, and tote.

"Yes. They're in a locker at the heliport," Gilmour answered. "The ginger ale cans included."

"That's a bit anticlimactic, wouldn't you say?" Melanie raised her bandaged hands and pointed at the locked box that contained the swabs from Howell's injuries.

A sense of relief swept across their faces as they lifted off.

It took the chopper fifteen minutes to travel the fifty miles back to Anacostia. Patterson brought the evidence to a locked facility, got his receipt, and then they reclaimed Melanie's things. Gilmour offered to drive her home. "Your car is impounded."

"Of course it is." Melanie shook her head.

"You did great work today," Patterson said.

Gilmour glanced in her direction. "Seriously. Both in the cafeteria and during your joyride."

"Actually, I did a crummy job in the cafeteria. He spotted me. Us, actually. We both did a crummy job. By the way, he said you need to take acting lessons."

Gilmour snorted.

Melanie continued. "Apparently, he has a nose for women. Whenever one enters the room, he notices. He's like a bloodhound, but that's an insult to bloodhounds."

Gilmour chuckled. "And you still have your sense of humor."

"Sense of humor? Me?" Melanie looked at him with a blank expression on her face.

He wasn't sure she was serious. "Yes. Droll, but you have one." They walked to where Gilmour's and Patterson's cars were parked. Gilmour helped her into the passenger seat.

"This should be a little more comfortable than your last ride."
He smiled.

Patterson leaned in. "You're grounded for tomorrow,
Drake."

"What about filing my report?"

"Are you sure you can write or type with those wads?" He
nodded toward her hands.

"Good point. I'll record it and then transcribe it."

"Excellent idea." He tapped the roof of the car. "Take it
easy."

Gilmour left the heliport and began to drive to Melanie's
place. He pulled into the parking lot of a liquor store. "Be
right back. Don't go anywhere."

Within minutes, he was in and out of the store.

"And what is in the brown bag?" She tried to get a peek.

"Bulleit, agent. Got a problem with that?"

"I do not." She leaned into the back of her seat and took
another look at her bandaged hands. They were beginning to
throb. "Why on earth would people want to do this volun-
tarily?" She raised one fist in the air.

"They usually wear boxing gloves," Gilmour replied.

"Duh. But like Officer Kincaid said, bar fights."

"It's called excessive consumption of alcohol. Makes people think they're tougher and stronger than they are. False
sense of bravado."

"Had many yourself?" Melanie liked Gilmour. She could
always count on him when the cases got gory. She much preferred stalking cyber criminals. At least she was now behind
a desk doing analytical work. Soon she would be back in college working on her ticket out of crazy town.

"Me? Bar fights?" He guffawed. "How do you think I
ended up here? It was going to be the military or the peniten-
tiary. I was a wild young man," Gilmour said.

"Really?" Melanie gave him a long, hard look. "How is it
that I didn't know this about you?"

"It's on the down-low. I was in my teens, associating with the wrong types of fellas. Got nicked for shoplifting, and it scared the pants off me. Back then, they weren't playing around. People got busted for anything and everything. It was a little-known fact that municipalities got kickbacks from the state for meeting a quota. X number of misdemeanors, x number of felonies, etcetera." He turned down the road that led to her apartment. "I got busted for stealing a protein bar."

"Get out!" She slapped him on the arm and then winced.

"I kid you not. Well, there were extenuating circumstances."

"Ah. Here's the loophole," Melanie joked, beginning to feel more like herself.

"Seriously. I was with a few of my buds. We were in one of those big box stores. I took a protein bar, but my friends tried to heist much bigger prizes like Xbox games, watches, and an assortment of tech accessories. I had about three dollars' worth of stolen goods, and they had thousands. Guilty by association."

"But you did steal a protein bar," Melanie said with a tight lip, trying to stifle a chuckle.

"To be honest? I wasn't really paying attention. I picked up a bar when I saw the security guards pulling my dudes aside. I absentmindedly put it in my pocket. It was an involuntary reaction. It wasn't premeditated," he protested.

"Obviously. If it was premeditated, and your target was a protein bar, then you don't deserve to go to jail. You need psychiatric help. You could have asked an unsuspecting stranger to buy one for you. Many people do, actually. People are nicer than we think."

"Says the woman who was abducted and almost killed."

"Putting recent experiences aside, the typical person is more inclined to be kind. I'm not talking about people with a personality disorder. Heaven knows we have plenty of them. But people. People like you and me. I bet you would buy someone a protein bar if they asked." She gave him a minute to digest what she was suggesting.

"Depending on the circumstances, probably yes. What I hate is when they ask you for money for food and you offer them a sandwich and they spit on you."

"That's not what I'm talking about." Melanie looked up at the ceiling. *Men really are different from women.*

"Look at all the people who tried to come to my aid today."

"Good point. I guess it's the agent in me that's blocking the idea of humanitarianism."

Melanie let out a big laugh. They pulled into the driveway in front of her townhouse. "Gilmour, would you think I'm a big baby if I asked you to go in first and check for goblins in the closets and monsters under the bed?"

Gilmour snorted. "Melanie Drake, I am going to resist the temptation to tease you because you had a rough day. I will gladly clear the apartment for you."

"Thanks." She sighed. It truly had been a rough day.

"No worries. And your secret is safe with me." He gave her a wink and lightly patted one of her bandaged hands.

She gathered her things and gingerly got out of the car. Gilmour lent her a hand. "I didn't realize how banged up I was."

"Listen, you took a beating, and you gave one back. And better. You knocked him out. Mel, that was very impressive work."

"It was the will to live," Melanie replied. She fished out her keys and unlocked the door. She motioned for Gilmour to go ahead of her. "It was also the will to get that miscreant for all the terrible things he's done, and to keep him from doing them again. It was a multilayer mission, although staying alive was at the top of the list."

Gilmour did what she'd asked and checked all the rooms, under the bed, and in the closets. "All clear."

Melanie threw her things on the sofa and headed to the kitchen. She pulled out two rocks glasses and handed them to Gilmour. "Two fingers, please." She smiled.

Chapter Ten

Tying Up Loose Ends

It had been several months since the harrowing incident with Howell. Melanie recounted her ordeal several times to various agents, lawyers, and prosecutors. Howell was charged with five counts of murder, five counts of sexual assault, five counts of kidnapping, and one count of assaulting and abducting a federal agent.

It was almost a full year before the case went to trial, but it was quick. He had a court-appointed attorney who did his job trying to defend his client, but he knew it was futile. Not even a *non compos mentis* defense was possible, although some would argue a serial killer is insane. The judge immediately ruled it out. There was no defense for Wayne Howell's actions, and the government had an ironclad case against him.

Melanie and members of the families of the victims sat through the excruciating details of the crimes. Weeks later, Howell was convicted of all charges. Yells and cheers filled the courtroom. The judge didn't bother to quiet them down. It was probably the only relief those in the courtroom were able to feel. Justice was served. The families cried and hugged

Melanie after the verdict. Their thanks were bittersweet. Ten days later, Howell was sentenced to life imprisonment without the possibility of parole, at ADX Florence, a maximum-security prison in Colorado, designed for criminals who were too dangerous to be in the general population of felons. He would never see the outside of the gray concrete walls again.

Not long after her ordeal with Howell, Melanie signed up for two psychology classes at Georgetown. Her plan was to continue working until after the trial and study for her master's at night. Once the trial was over, she put in her papers for an early retirement. The past fifteen years had kicked the tar out of her, with this last incident pushing her over the top. She was now convinced she had to start at the beginning. The years when children's moral compasses are formed. Giving children guidance was where she thought she belonged, and where she could really make a difference.

During her tenure at OSI, her parents had been supportive, but never thrilled. The work was dangerous and draining. They believed Melanie had other talents she could employ doing other meaningful work. They were overjoyed when she told them about her plans for the next chapter of her life.

Patterson, Gilmour, and several others took Melanie for a farewell dinner at Le Diplomate, a French brasserie with shiny red booths and a bustling atmosphere. She was going to miss her compadres, and as with every parting, all promised to keep in touch. Everyone knows that doesn't really happen. Maybe one or two would stay in contact, but for the most part, when you leave your job, you close the door. But her relationship with Patterson and Gilmour would persist, and they'd meet once a month for drinks or a quick lunch. They were truly the only friends she had. In the OSI, it was difficult trying to establish relationships, including romantic ones. Most of the time you couldn't talk about your work, or you were away at work. Melanie knew she'd cut herself off socially for most of her adult life. Things would be different moving forward.

Melanie was feeling optimistic about her future, but first she had to get that degree. Then get the job. Then the house. Then a dog. She was very focused on the dog part and knew before that could happen, she had to check the first three things off her list.

PART THREE

The Next Chapter

Chapter Eleven

Settling In

After Melanie left OSI, she enrolled full time at Georgetown. The sooner she could get through school, the sooner she could start the next phase. Even though her tuition was covered, thanks to the deal she'd made with Patterson, she would still have overhead such as rent, food, car, gas. Her folks suggested Melanie should move back home until she finished her studies; otherwise, she would have to take a part-time job to pay rent. That wasn't going to cut it. She had to focus on her studies. By living at home, she'd be able to save some money, finish her degree, find a job, and buy a house. This was her third round of moving back with her parents. *Déjà vu all over again.* She insisted on pitching in so she wouldn't feel like a slacker and took care of the grocery bills, even paid for maid service for the house, despite her parents' protests.

The two years blew by, and she received her degree with honors. Naturally. Melanie wouldn't have it any other way. Now she not only had book smarts, but she had also gained a lot of street smarts. She wished she could have skipped some of those lessons. She chose to stash them as far back in her mind as possible, hoping never to find herself in similar situations again.

A few months before she finished her classes, she began to check school systems for guidance counselor positions. She didn't want to move too far away from her family.

Her brother Justin had been stationed at Langley for the past several years. He'd met a lovely woman named Shannon who worked as a VIP concierge for foreign dignitaries. She arranged transportation, hospitality, dinners, lunch, whatever their spoiled little hearts desired. Melanie once joked that if Shannon could deal with those people, Justin would be a piece of cake. They'd married and planned to have a family in a couple of years. Melanie wanted to be around to influence her nieces and nephews. Teach them magic tricks. Read them stories.

Family was important to her. She still had no significant other, but she wasn't averse to it, either. She figured when she met the right guy, he would be the right guy. So far, none of them was the right guy.

Melanie was grateful to Patterson for assisting her with the paperwork for her tuition, and to Gilmour, who'd taught her how to separate reality from rumor. Too often, misinformation would spread, and agents had to decipher what was real, and what was a distraction. That particular talent helped her on and off the job. She phoned her former colleagues and invited them for a dinner celebration. Gilmour was single. Divorced. The job could do that to a relationship if you had time to develop one. She invited Patterson's wife. His second or third. She wasn't sure. The job could do that to a marriage, or two, *or was it three?*

Melanie made a reservation at Le Diplomate. She thought

it would be fitting to return to the last place where they'd shared a celebratory meal.

They greeted each other with warm hugs. Melanie realized how much she enjoyed their companionship. Things were going to change. From now on, she was going to put some balance in her life.

There was a job opening near Falls Church, at Jesse Moorer Elementary School. While she was filling out the application, she was stunned by one question in particular: Do you know how to use a firearm? As she continued to read through the guidelines, she discovered there was a monthly "Active Shooter" drill. It was disheartening to realize little kids had to go through such horrendous preparation. Children were no longer allowed to wear shoes with flashing lights. Melanie sighed. *How did we get to this point?* In her mind, the only upside was that she knew how to react. Anyone in her custody might have a fighting chance. She understood a Code Yellow meant there was a threat outside of the school building. Classes could remain ongoing, but no one was allowed to enter or leave the building. Code Red meant imminent danger. Classrooms were to be locked from the inside, lights turned off, and the children were to huddle together as far away from the door as possible. She prayed she would never be in either situation.

After she filed her paperwork and went through the numerous interviews with the principal, the board of education, and an advisory panel, she was given the job. With the start of the new school year, Melanie Drake, former OSI agent, would now be Melanie Drake, Jesse Moorer Elementary School Guidance Counselor.

Three weeks before school opened, she met with the faculty and was shown her office. It was near the main entrance, two doors down from the principal. The proximity made her wonder how many kids would go from one office to the next, hers being the "next." She was aware she would be vetting behavioral issues such as bullying and fighting, as well as poor academic performance. Gone were the days of simply telling a student they "weren't living up to their potential." Nowadays, mining for that potential was the first step. Too many children were anxious, sometimes picking up their parents' concerns. Yes, anxiety was a major epidemic, and for a lot of good reasons. Melanie's job was to help assuage those tensions and help give the children a sense of their own identity. It was a tough nut to crack, but she was up to the task.

During the few weeks before classes started, Melanie read through the files that were designated as a priority. She knew that meant there was a problem. She divided the piles into personality issues, academic issues, and one for crazy parents. To avoid lawsuits, the files weren't marked that way, but the teachers and administrators had their own color-coding system.

At the beginning of the new school year, some of the children were happy to be back, and some, not so much. It was easy to spot them. One girl, around eight years old, came in with whiskers drawn on her face. When Melanie said, "Good morning," the child responded with a *meow.* Kids identifying with animals were called "Furries." She hoped there wasn't a litter of them. She also wondered if one of her parents had helped paint the child's face.

She thought back to when she was eight. She'd been holed up in a cast, reading books and working on puzzles. Again, she asked herself, *How did we get here?* Social media was certainly one way people were being influenced. She thought a "National Unplug Day" would be beneficial, but it would never happen. Social media was as addictive as drugs and alcohol. It was the new addiction. She shook away her concerns and put on a happy face. Kids were about to enter the school.

She stood outside her office door. "Good morning, everyone. Slow down, please. Mind your manners. Be polite."

The bell rang for classes to begin, and the halls went quiet. They were hardly into the new school year and already Melanie had to meet with one of the students' parents. His name was Jerome. Jerome was seven years old. For the past week, he had entered the boys' bathroom each morning and changed into a dress. He seemed perfectly comfortable and acted as if it were normal. Most of Jerome's classmates didn't care one way or another. But all it took was one nasty tormenter who thought it would be fun to give Jerome a wedgie and hit him in the face. The kid joked he was giving Jerome "eye shadow." That kid got suspended, and Jerome removed his "costume" before he went home.

The problem intensified when Jerome's parents stormed through the door and demanded to know how their son got a black eye. They were already talking about suing the school before they sat down in Melanie's office.

Melanie suspected Jerome's parents didn't know about his interest in female fashion. "He was being teased by one of the other students, who gave him the black eye." She intentionally avoided the cause of the incident, hoping they would surmise why it had happened. But deep inside, she didn't think they had a clue.

"Being teased about what?" Mr. Walker's voice was gaining volume.

It was now Melanie's turn to inform them of the circumstances. Slowly. "He changed his clothes before and after class."

The father was outraged. "What are you talking about? Changing into what clothes? I see him leave in the morning. He's dressed just fine. I don't understand any of this." The man was rattled. Melanie could tell he was flummoxed, and imagined a number of thoughts were now running through his head.

The mother had a sheepish look on her face, indicating she might have an inkling of her son's masquerade. The father turned to his wife. "Do you know what this is all about?" His voice was reverberating off the walls.

"Mr. Walker, please keep your voice down." Melanie spoke in a composed manner. *Just weeks into the job and already a crisis. Yippee.*

"Where is he?" Mr. Walker bellowed.

"He's in class."

"Get him in here right now!" He shouted. "I want to know what in blazes is going on around here!"

Melanie knew this was going to be tricky. Was she supposed to warn Jerome to change his clothes? It was a turning point—she had to choose sides. School policy was that teachers, counselors, and anyone associated with school administration were not allowed to discuss the subject of gender with parents. Policy on discussing "furry" identities was still up in the air. The students' schooltime secrets were to be kept inside the hallowed halls of the educational system. The only thing the staff was allowed to discuss was disruptive, rule-breaking behavior, or grades.

The developmental process was no longer a homogenous undertaking. Life had become compartmentalized. There was a lack of shared communication. Hidden agendas abounded. *No wonder the world is such a mess.* Melanie forced herself to turn the channel in her head. *Look for the opportunities in the situation.* It dawned on her that school wasn't very different from her previous career. Everything was a careful balancing act to achieve the best outcome.

"Let me call his teacher." Melanie picked up the interoffice phone and asked to be connected to Jerome's teacher.

"Hi. It's Melanie Drake. Jerome Walker's parents are in

my office. They want to see him." She listened. "Yes." She was listening to the teacher tell her Jerome was wearing a dress.

"Should I tell him to change his clothes?" the teacher asked.

Melanie tried to couch her response diplomatically. "No. Just tell him they're here." She would let Jerome decide. Wow. That was a lot to put on a kid, but it was going to be an issue at some point. Might as well rip the bandage off now.

Mr. Walker stood and paced. "What's taking so long?"

Melanie checked her watch. It hadn't been ten minutes. She didn't answer him. She heard footsteps coming toward her door and held her breath. A gentle knock. "Come in."

And there he was. Jerome was dressed in a lovely pink ensemble. She had to give him credit. He was perfectly accessorized. The kid might have a future in the fashion industry.

Mr. Walker roared. "What do you think you're doing?"

Mrs. Walker stood and got between them.

"Answer me!" he shouted.

Jerome stood silently.

Melanie thought Mr. Walker was going to pop a vein.

"Go take that off!" Walker commanded.

"Okay, but someday you won't be able to pick what I wear."

A very astute comment coming from a seven-year-old.

Walker turned to his wife. "You knew he was doing this, didn't you?"

Mrs. Walker covered her face with her hands. "It only happened a couple of times when I was putting the donation box together. I thought he was going through a phase."

Melanie tried to cool the situation. "Please, everyone, sit down. Let's talk this through."

"I'm done talking. I'm taking my son out of this school. Clearly, he's been spending too much time hanging around with perverts."

"Perverts?" Melanie was troubled by that word.

"Who else is putting these ideas in his head?"

Melanie thought to herself, *Look around, you fool. Influence is everywhere.*

"Mr. Walker, I can assure you, we are not aware of any perverts working at or attending this school. I believe your accusations are uncalled for," Melanie said assuredly.

"Yeah. You're not aware. That's obvious, wouldn't you say?"

Melanie decided it was time to bring in some backup. She lifted the phone and pressed the button for the principal's office. "Hello, Mrs. Alexander? I have Jerome Walker's parents here." She listened for a moment. "That is correct. Thank you."

Mr. Walker didn't hear Mrs. Alexander's comment. "It's about the dress, isn't it?"

In less than five minutes, Audrey Alexander rapped on the door and entered. "Good morning."

"Good morning, my big fat hiney!" Walker boomed. "What in the hell are you running here? A drag show?"

Audrey resisted the temptation to laugh. "I'm sorry. A drag show?"

"Look at him!" He shoved his finger in Jerome's face.

No one said a word. "What do you have to say about this?" he fumed.

"Mr. Walker. It is school policy."

"What? Encouraging deviant behavior?"

Melanie had a lot of thoughts concerning deviant behavior. Dressing in girl's clothes was far from the kind of deviation she'd dealt with.

"Perhaps if we discuss this?" She faced Jerome and gave him a look of assurance. No one was going to hurt him in her room. Her concern was what was going to happen to him when he got home.

"There's no discussion!" Mr. Walker turned to Jerome. "Go take that disgusting thing off."

Disgusting? Hardly. Unexpected? Yes.

Jerome obediently walked to the boys' bathroom and discarded his ensemble. He fell into a sobbing pile on the floor.

After what seemed like an eternity, Melanie began to worry. "Excuse me." She dashed to the lavatory and found Jerome curled up in a ball. At first, she couldn't tell if he was bleeding. She quickly moved toward him. "Jerome? Jerome?" She lifted his head as he continued to sob. She cradled him in her arms and spoke softly to him. "It's going to be alright. We'll sit down and have a talk. We'll work this out. I promise."

He was trying to speak between hiccups and sobs. "You don't know my dad. He has a terrible temper."

That news did not come as a surprise. "Does he get angry with your mom?"

He bobbed his head. "All . . . all the time. When he comes home from work. He's always mad."

Melanie reached overhead, pulled down a few paper towels from the dispenser, and handed them to Jerome. "Come on. Let's get you cleaned up."

"Please, Ms. Drake, don't make me go home with him." He began to sob again.

"Has he ever hit you?" she asked as she stroked his hair.

Jerome buried his face in his hands. "He slapped me real hard."

"Have you ever seen him strike your mother?"

More nods. "He shoved her after he slapped me."

Melanie surmised the father was a bully. Displaced aggression, perhaps. For now, Melanie had to mitigate any physical threats against Jerome or his mother.

"You wait here. I'm going to get your mom, okay?"

Jerome nodded and wiped the snot running from his nose.

Melanie asked one of the hall monitors to stand outside the boys' bathroom. "Don't let anyone in or out. If someone tries to get past you, start yelling."

She marched back to her office. *So, Ms. Melanie Drake,*

you wanted to be a diplomat. Here's your opportunity to use diplomacy and negotiate.

"Well?" Walker exploded again.

Melanie ignored him. By now, a security guard was standing a few yards from her office door. Audrey Alexander had anticipated there could be a problem. Walker wasn't known for being affable or reasonable. He'd had a run-in with the softball coach the year before. He kept complaining Jerome wasn't getting enough time on the field. The problem was that Jerome didn't want to be on the field. He didn't want to play at all. The coach tried to reason with the man, but Walker growled in the coach's face and was banned from attending a game again. Not that he cared. His son wasn't destined for Major League Baseball.

Melanie looked at Mrs. Walker. "Could you please come with me?"

Mr. Walker started to move. Audrey stopped him. "No, sir. Just Mrs. Walker."

"I don't know what you people think you're up to!" Another gasket blown. Seemed like he had an inordinate amount of them.

That's when Mr. Lynch, the security guard, came into view. He said nothing. He just stood there, all six feet four inches, two hundred thirty pounds of him. Walker sagged. Little did he know Melanie Drake was as big a threat to his physical well-being as Mr. Lynch, and neither would have to use a weapon. Melanie kept her Glock in a lockbox, which was locked in her desk drawer. There were only two keys, one for each lock, and they were clipped to her new lanyard, which read:

MELANIE DRAKE
JESSE MOORER ELEMENTARY SCHOOL
FALLS CHURCH, VIRGINIA
GUIDANCE COUNSELOR

She fidgeted with her ID. This was a different kind of altercation. There was a child involved, in a school, with a very angry parent. *Diplomacy.*

Melanie escorted Mrs. Walker to the corner of the tiled room, where her son sat in a heap. Mrs. Walker sat on the floor, wrapped her arms around his shoulders, and began to rock him gently. Melanie could see his body shaking.

"I'll be right back." Melanie bolted back to her office. She stopped in the doorway. She was almost out of breath but held her composure. "Audrey, may I speak with you?"

The security guard moved closer to Melanie's door. Walker had better not have thoughts of going anywhere.

Audrey and Melanie moved out of earshot. Melanie began to repeat what Jerome had told her.

"The man has a temper." Melanie wasn't simply offering her opinion. She was quite masterful in sizing someone up quickly. "Jerome told me his father slapped him." Melanie knew kids embellished. But not in this case. "He also told me his dad shoved his mother."

"Oh boy." Audrey looked up. "Okay. Let's do it."

The two women walked toward the bathroom. Melanie reminded the hall monitor, "No one in or out unless I say so."

Hall monitors were teacher's aides. They would rotate during the day, keeping an eye on the corridors, checking student passes.

Mrs. Walker was still cradling her son, who had stopped crying. Audrey addressed her. "Mrs. Walker, do you have someone you can stay with for a few days?"

Mrs. Walker looked puzzled. "Why?"

"Considering the circumstances and your husband's mood, it might be wise to give him a few days to cool off," Melanie added.

"But he will be so angry." There was fear in her eyes. "Every night when he comes home, I think he's going to explode. This is going to put him right over the edge."

Melanie crouched down. "Jerome, can I tell your mom what you told me?" He nodded.

"Jerome said that your husband slapped him and shoved you."

Mrs. Walker was shredding the tissue in her hand. "Yes, but it was only that one time."

Melanie knew there could be a second, third, and many more times. It all started with the first one. "Mrs. Walker, I strongly suggest you give him time to cool down. We can work things out, but for now, distance, time, and considering the options would be good steps. We'll work with you to help come to a viable resolution."

Jerome looked up at his mother. "Can we go to see Aunt Colleen?"

"She lives over an hour away, sweetheart. You have school, and I have work." Mrs. Walker knew it was the right thing to do, but the thought terrified her.

"We can give Jerome schoolwork."

"But what about my job? I'm a nurse. I can't just leave."

"I realize it's difficult. But I can call your supervisor and explain that Jerome had to take a leave of absence from our school, and you have to accompany him. We'll tell her it's an academic program thing. I'm sure you're allowed personal time."

"Yes, but we're short-staffed. I wouldn't want to burden my coworkers."

Melanie took the reins. "Mrs. Walker. This situation is not going away. You need to take care of your son and yourself, first and foremost. Put your own oxygen mask on first." She referred to the instructions given to passengers during a flight emergency.

By now, tears were streaming down Mrs. Walker's face. Her hands were shaking. "What do I tell my husband?"

"Tell him you need a little break. We'll send him a text after you leave," Melanie said. "Do not tell him where you are going. Tell him it will be for a couple of days. You'll be in touch."

"I don't think he'll take that very well."

Jerome looked into his mother's eyes and pleaded, "Please."

"Okay." She sighed. "Tell me what I have to do."

Melanie helped her from the floor. "You are going to get in your car, drive home, and pack a bag for yourself and Jerome. Someone will meet you there. You will swap cars with them and drive that car to your sister's."

"But what about my husband? He'll follow me."

"He is going to be detained by Mr. Lynch. He can complain and protest all he wants, but he's not leaving the building until we get an all-clear."

"Can you do that?" Mrs. Walker asked with surprise.

Melanie wasn't sure what the correct answer was, but assumed it was technically *no*. She'd deal with that later. She didn't answer the question. Melanie's plan was to call one of her former colleagues to help out. If Gilmour wasn't available, he'd find someone who was. The important thing was to keep Walker at the school until Mrs. Walker and Jerome were miles away.

"What about my purse?" Mrs. Walker asked.

"I'll get it for you. Did you come in one or two cars?"

"Just one, but we both carry a set of keys to both. It's easier than trying to find where the other person left them."

"Good thinking." *And lucky for us.* "You sit tight and try to regroup. I'll be right back." Melanie left the bathroom while Audrey stayed behind.

Melanie tapped Mr. Lynch's shoulder. "Can you please hand me Mrs. Walker's purse?" She pointed to the bag sitting on one of the chairs.

"Someone tell me what is going on!" Walker demanded.

Melanie ignored him. He didn't deserve an answer, not even a lie. Lynch reached over and handed it to Melanie.

Walker must have gotten the message that no one was

going to give up any information. At least not in the short term. He took a seat and tried to control his urge to shove everything off Melanie's desk. *Wouldn't look good.*

Melanie dashed into the principal's office area. "I need an outside line, please. Private?" She gave a tight smile. "And Jerome Walker's address." She didn't have to explain. Walker's outrage could be heard several doors down.

The secretary nodded toward Audrey's office, made several clicks on her keyboard, and wrote the address down on a piece of paper. "Star, nine, one, and then the number."

"Thanks!" Melanie grabbed the paper and shut the door behind her. She dialed Greg Gilmour's cell.

"Greg! It's Mel. I have a situation at the school."

"Already?" He was half-teasing. "What, have you been there, like, ten minutes?"

"I'm serious."

"Okay. Go." Gilmour was at attention.

Melanie gave him the Walkers' address. "I need someone to go to the house and help a mother and son pack. They'll have to swap cars. Maybe you can rent one? We don't want her driving her own car."

"I'll loan her my SUV. It has GPS, so we can keep track of her if necessary. I have the old Jeep I can use."

"You are the best." Melanie knew she could count on Gregory. "We'll drive her car back to the school, and I'll drive you home later."

"You will explain all of this, correct?" It was more of a statement than a question.

"Yes, of course." Melanie was relieved. She wasn't sure how far over the legal line she was straying. Her first priority was to get mother and son to safety. She'd figure out the rest when they let Walker go.

One could argue he was being detained against his will. But he'd have to prove it and explain the circumstances. Melanie surmised Walker wasn't about to expose his temper to the board of education, or local officials. It could possibly open a major can of worms. Did he have "anger issues" on his work record? Melanie wondered. It appeared his relationship to his son and wife was stressed. She didn't want to diagnose him after one abrupt interaction, but she noted her training at OSI was coming in handy. She'd learned how to read potential volatile situations and how to diffuse them. It might not be that easy today, but she had to give it a shot.

She hung up the phone and returned to the bathroom. Jerome was now standing next to his mother. His face was cleaned up, and the dress was folded neatly. Mrs. Walker had her arm around her son's shoulders.

Melanie stooped slightly so she could be closer to Jerome's eye level. "Here's what's going to happen. We are going to get in your car and drive to your house. I'm going to help your mom pack a few things, and you'll pack some stuff, too. Go as quick as you can." She saw the concentration and determination in Jerome's eyes. He nodded. Melanie handed Mrs. Walker her purse. "A special agent is going to meet us at your house and give you a burner phone. You will take his car to your sister's. The agent and I will drive your car back here." She paused, letting the instructions sink in. "Call your sister from your car, then delete your call history. You'll leave your phone in your car so he can't track you."

Melanie knew this must be overwhelming. "Come on. We'll talk more in the car." Melanie checked the hallway. They went out the back door and around the building so Walker couldn't see them. Mrs. Walker's hands were shaking.

"What if he catches us?" She could barely spit out the words.

"He's not getting past Lynch, I can assure you."

Maynard Lynch was a former Navy Seal. His physical attributes were imposing, leaving one to guess what he'd done before he donned a security uniform. Whatever it was, it must have required tremendous physical prowess. When asked why he'd joined the Seals, Lynch's answer was, "Kids were always making fun of my name. 'May-nerd.' I wanted to bulk up. Be strong. The Navy seemed like a good place to start." He was forty-five when he retired from the Navy, and he wanted to keep working. Schools needed security, and he was well-trained. Everyone felt safe when he was around. Well, maybe not Mr. Walker at that particular moment.

"Call your sister." Melanie pulled out a small flip phone she kept in a pouch around her waist. It was a burner. She only used it when absolutely necessary, then discarded it, and replaced it with a new one. She always had one on her.

Mrs. Walker tapped in her sister's number.

"Hello?" Colleen didn't recognize the number.

"Colleen, it's me. We have an issue," she said grimly.

"What's wrong?" Melanie could hear her mood sink.

"Listen, I don't have a lot of time. I'm on my way home to pack a bag for me and Jerome. We're going to drive to your house." Patricia wasn't asking for permission.

"Of course. What's going on?"

"I'm on speakerphone with the school guidance counselor. It's her phone. Jerome is in the back seat." She wanted her sister to know they had an audience.

Today I am a former OSI special agent, Melanie thought to herself, but she wasn't necessarily going to share that information. Only if it became absolutely necessary.

"Hey, Jerome!" Colleen called through the phone.

"Hey, Aunt Colleen." Jerome's voice sounded weak but resolute. "I'm glad we're going to visit."

"So am I." Colleen sounded happy to see them, but not so sure about the circumstances. "Tell me, what's going on?" She tried to sound casual.

"There was an incident at the school. Robert lost his temper."

"Well, he's been wound rather tight lately," Colleen said.

Melanie decided to interrupt. "Hi, this is Melanie Drake. I'm the guidance counselor at Jesse Moorer. We need to give Mr. Walker some time to cool off."

"I totally understand. What do you have in mind?"

"An agent is going to swap cars at the house. We're going to drive Pat's car back to the school. He's also going to give Pat a burner phone with a couple of pre-programmed numbers."

"Oh?" Colleen started to sound alarmed.

"It's out of an abundance of caution. We don't want Mr. Walker to be able to track her phone."

"He'll know she came up here."

Melanie thought for a moment. "We'll put a GPS device on the car. As soon as he starts to move, we'll be alerted."

"Whew. Wow." Colleen was trying to process this new turn of events.

"I am going to try to have a conversation with Mr. Walker. Depending on his reaction, we may have to send a social worker to your sister's house to talk to you, but before we get the authorities involved, I'd like to have the opportunity to discuss this with him." Melanie looked over at Patricia and gave her a reassuring glance. "We'll work this out."

Pat gripped the wheel. "I can't take walking on eggshells every day. Jerome is terrified. We can't live like this day after day, wondering when he'll finally blow up." Tears began streaming down her face.

Melanie handed her a tissue. She turned to check on Jerome. He had a soft smile on his face. He was ready, even if his mother wasn't.

They pulled into the driveway. Jerome was the first to unhitch his seat belt and bolt toward the door. He had been making his list in his head and knew exactly what he wanted to bring with him. Pat Walker wasn't as organized.

The three went up the front porch steps. Again, Patricia's hands were shaking. Melanie took the keys, unhitched the

one for the car, and unlocked the front door. She followed
Patricia into the house. If Patricia Walker was like most
women, she would start with toiletries, then underwear, then
a few outfits and another pair of shoes. Patricia pulled out a
large suitcase from the closet. Melanie had learned how to
pack years before and used her skill to assist Patricia. She
began rolling up the clothes and placing them neatly inside.
In less than ten minutes, they were ready to go.

Melanie heard a car pull up. It was Gregory Gilmour. She
bounded down the stairs and flung open the door. "Thank
you so much." She gave him a hug.

"Anything for you, MelDrake." He turned to see a young
boy wrestling with something on the stairs. It was Jerome,
dragging a duffel bag behind him. "I'm Agent Gilmour."
Greg smiled at the boy. "You must be Jerome. Let me give
you a hand." He reached for the duffel, which Jerome gladly
released from his grip.

"You're an agent?" Jerome asked with wide eyes.

"Yes, I am." Gilmour showed him the badge clipped to his
belt.

"Cool. What kind of agent? Are you like a spy or something?"

"OSI. Office of Special Investigations."

"What kinda stuff do you investigate?" Jerome asked as
Gilmour showed him to his car.

"All kinds. Cyber stuff mostly." Gilmour figured that
would be the only thing he'd understand.

"Like catching bad guys on the internet?"

Gilmour was impressed that the kid had a vague idea of
what cyber stuff was. Then again, it was a whole new generation of kids and technology. "Yep. Chasing the bad guys on
the internet."

"Cool," Jerome replied.

"I'll go help Patricia. You get him settled," Melanie said.

Gilmour put his hand gently on Jerome's shoulder. "I'm

going to strap you in the back," Gilmour announced. He handed Jerome a small flip phone. "There is only one number that works on this, so don't try to call anyone. It's only in case of an emergency. Understand?"

"Yes, sir!" Jerome gave him a salute.

Melanie and Patricia came out of the house, pulling a large suitcase that was bouncing behind.

Gilmour grabbed the bag and introduced himself. "Gregory Gilmour." Then he put it in the back of his vehicle. He went around to the driver's side and gave Patricia the key and a phone. "Number for Melanie, me, and the police are programmed. If you do make a call, try to use a landline. Jerome has a small flip phone with just the emergency number. He knows only to use it . . ."

"In case of an emergency." Jerome finished Gilmour's sentence.

Gilmour smiled and continued. "Someone will be in touch. Hang tight. You're going to be alright."

Patricia looked very confused. "Someone?"

Melanie chimed in. "Once I get back to the office, I'll suggest some counseling, but that will be up to you and Mr. Walker. Meanwhile, breathe."

"What about my husband?" Patricia was still flummoxed. "What's going to happen to him?"

"Nothing at the moment. But if I need backup, Agent Gilmour will be right there."

"Don't forget to show him your badge!" Jerome exclaimed.

Patricia still had no idea who this man was or where he'd come from, except he was a friend of Melanie's. "Thank you. Thank you for doing this."

Gilmour opened the door for her. "Good luck. Remember, help is a button away."

Patricia started the engine, adjusted the mirrors, and backed out of the driveway. Jerome was waving vigorously from the back seat.

Melanie and Gregory got into Patricia's vehicle and headed back to the school.

"So, now will you tell me what is going on and how I got snookered into pulling a not-quite-legal something?"

Melanie began to relate the story of Jerome's latest fashion trend . . . how someone gave Jerome a black eye, but the father didn't know why until he barged into the school threatening to sue.

"Uh boy."

"Yep. His father freaked out when Jerome appeared in my office wearing a dress."

Gilmour rolled his eyes. "So this guy is a real banana?"

"Major. At our school, we're not allowed to discuss anything that hints at cross-dressing with parents unless they are already aware."

"What do you mean?"

"Say a kid named Jerome wants to be called Jennifer at school. We cannot tell the parents."

"Why not?"

"Privacy issues. There are court cases on the state and federal level. Many argue the Fourteenth Amendment broadly gives the parent the right to direct their child's upbringing," Melanie replied.

"Does that apply to everything or just gender?" Gilmour was surprised by the need for secrecy.

"For now, it's identity. The problem stretches further, because we don't know what the rules are yet, so everyone acts with trepidation. If you do one thing, you enrage the parents. If you do something else, you enrage someone else."

Gilmour scratched his head. "Wow. Politics in elementary school."

Melanie continued. "Parents have no idea what their kid is doing in school unless they break something or beat someone up. Oh, the rules are so shaded in gray."

"That must drive you bonkers!" Gilmour grinned.

"Ha ha."

"What do you think is going to happen?" Gregory asked.

"That kid is going to be the deciding factor," she replied.

"Yeah. I didn't get a warm and fuzzy, father-and-son relationship vibe from the kid. Looked like he couldn't get out of there fast enough."

"They left of their own accord," she pointed out.

"How about aiding and abetting?" Gregory asked.

"Abetting what? There's been no crime committed." Melanie huffed.

He chuckled. "Not yet."

"Let the judge be the judge of that. Mr. Walker would have to file a missing person's report. He's not going to do that. Why? Because he's about to receive a text message right now." Melanie reached for the phone Patricia had left behind and typed a message.

Jerome and I are taking a little break for a few days. I'll be in touch.

"Now he can't claim she is missing," Melanie said proudly and proceeded to erase all other text messages except that one and delete Patricia's contact list and call log. She wasn't going to make it easy for Walker. The less info at his fingertips, the better. She tried to reserve judgment, but wanted to err on the side of caution.

They pulled into the visitor parking area of the school. "So do I get to meet this guy?"

"I thought you'd never ask." She waved him toward the door.

The halls were unusually quiet. Melanie checked the big clock. The peacefulness wouldn't last much longer. The bell would ring for lunch, and Mr. Walker was going to be given some very disturbing news.

Lynch spotted them walking down the hall. He gave them

a thumbs-up, an "all good" nod and a wink, and greeted Gilmour. "Nice to see you, man." Lynch held out his baseball-mitt-sized hand.

"Good to see you, Lynch."

No other words were spoken. Only eye contact. Melanie got the impression Mr. Walker had cooled his heels.

Agent Gilmour and Melanie entered her office. "Mr. Walker, this is Special Agent Gilmour."

"Special Agent? What's this all about?" His voice sounded more concerned than angry.

"Everyone is fine. But I am here to inform you that your wife and son will be spending a few days out of town."

He held up his cellphone. "I just got a text." He slumped down in the chair. Now it was his turn to rock back and forth.

Melanie took the brave step of approaching Walker. "Mr. Walker, would you like to speak in private?"

He jerked his head. "With who?"

"With me. Or Agent Gilmour?" She looked pleadingly at Gregory. He gave her an *I just might strangle you* look.

She mouthed the word *Please?*

Walker surprised her with, "I suppose you're okay."

"Do you want to do it now?"

"Maybe tomorrow."

Melanie thought if she gave him too much time, he might back out.

"How about this? We take a walk to the coffee shop and have a cup." She knew it wasn't protocol to meet with a parent off school grounds, but it was an opportunity that might not present itself again. She looked at Gilmour. He gave her a signal he'd be on her tail.

"Uh, okay." Walker sounded compliant.

"Do you want to freshen up in the bathroom?" Melanie motioned for Gilmour to escort him.

"Yeah. Yeah."

As they were walking away, Melanie asked Lloyd what had transpired. They hadn't been gone very long.

"I had a quick chat with him."

"You did?" Melanie wanted to know his tactics. He seemed to have effected a complete turnaround in record time.

"All I said was, 'Hey, man, don't blow it. You have a lovely wife and a good kid. I know Jerome. He's kind. He helps his schoolmates with work. He's the first one to grab a Band-Aid if someone scrapes their knee. The world needs a lot more people like him. Doesn't matter what people look like on the outside. It's what's inside that counts. If your family breaks up, everyone loses.'"

Melanie was in awe. "What did he say to that?"

"He hung his head. I think he was embarrassed. You know something, MelDrake? People need to learn how to communicate better. I'm not meaning you or anything. I mean friends. Family. Man, people need to get their heads out of their phones and start talking to each other."

"You won't get an argument from me. I'm all for an Unplug Day!"

Audrey Alexander overheard the conversation. "I think that's a splendid idea. October is the month of respect. Every Friday, we'll have everyone unplug their computers. We'll have interactions by playing face-to-face games instead of online. Pictionary, stuff like that."

"Audrey, that's a wonderful idea," Melanie said.

"Speaking of playing games. We need a new soccer coach." Audrey dropped the ball into Melanie's lap, no pun intended.

"Are you looking at me?" Melanie checked over her shoulder. "You mean Lynch, right?" She gave a nervous smile.

"No, I mean you. I know you played a little soccer, and we need a coach. Listen, the rules are different for kids this age. Practice is twice a week."

"After school?" Melanie closed one eye, as if someone had squirted a lemon into it.

"It's only an hour. Until we can find a replacement."

Melanie made a sputtering sound. Her day was getting more complicated by the minute. "Audrey, I'm in the midst of finding a house."

"Your parents are in real estate, aren't they?"

That blew Melanie's excuse. "Yes, but they don't normally work in this area."

"I have a friend who might be able to help. Give me the details later, and I'll have her get on the case."

Melanie knew she wasn't going to be able to wriggle her way out of this. "Alright. I'll give you my wish list this afternoon."

"First day of soccer practice is in two days."

"Yippee." Melanie sneered.

Mr. Walker was heading back from the bathroom.

"Ready?" Melanie asked.

"I guess so." He shrugged.

Audrey gave her a curious look.

"We have to discuss a few things."

"Outside of school?" Audrey was concerned Melanie was overstepping.

"Won't be long." Melanie was very good at answering questions without actually answering them.

She unlocked her desk drawer, removed her purse, and re-locked it. Gilmour was still standing in the hall. He gave her an inconspicuous nod. He wouldn't be far behind.

Walker and Melanie left the building in silence. She knew she was taking a big risk. Not physical harm, but her job. She would deal with the repercussions later. Right now, she had to try to save a family.

It was a five-minute walk. Before they reached the coffee shop, he stopped. "I'm really sorry about this morning." Then silence again.

Melanie didn't respond. She didn't want to lie and say,

"Oh, it's okay," because it wasn't. She would consider accepting his apology after their chat. Too many people throw out expressions of regret like throwing confetti on New Year's Eve.

They stood in line to order their coffees. Mocha latte for Melanie and decaf for Mr. Walker. *Good move.* After they got their java, they found a quiet corner to sit.

Melanie began. "Mr. Walker, you should know that our school policy is not to discuss gender issues outside of the classroom."

He looked confused. "Gender issues? Why not?" His voice was calm.

"There are a number of legal battles around the country citing the Fourteenth Amendment, which in some interpretations grants parents the right to determine what their children are taught in school."

"Has that changed?" He furrowed his brow.

"Not exactly. As of now, school districts can make their own decisions."

"Was anyone going to tell the parents they don't have a right to know what's going on in school?" He rubbed his forehead.

She didn't want to get into politics, so she moved on. "It's tough raising a kid today. But I have to tell you, Jerome is a very bright, considerate, and compassionate boy. Those qualities have to come from somewhere." She paused, giving him an opportunity to think about what she and Lynch had said to him about his son.

"Yeah. He studies hard." Walker looked down at the table. "I know I got a little rough with him once."

Only once? Melanie thought. "Do you want to tell me the circumstances?" She was being very, very careful.

"He was messing with his mother's makeup, and I slapped it out of his hands."

"What happened after that?"

"His mother came running into the room, and I shoved her." He held his head in his hands. "I am not proud of it."

"Mr. Walker, I must ask you—and please be honest—was that the only incident?"

He looked up abruptly. "Why? What did she say to you?" His voice had gotten louder.

"Nothing. I'm simply trying to see the whole picture." She took a moment. "I hate to see families in strife, especially if there's a remedy." Melanie wanted to get as much insight as possible. "Tell me more about you. What kind of work do you do?"

"I work as a supervisor at the local bottling plant."

"Do you like your work?"

"It's alright, I guess."

"Are you friendly with your coworkers?"

"Yeah. We take fishing trips once in a while. Bowl a few, but nothing regular."

"I'm getting the feeling there is something about your job you don't particularly like."

He grunted. "Yeah, my boss."

Melanie chuckled. "I think bosses are the reason most people don't like their jobs."

"Believe it or not, I went to business school, and now I spend my day on a loading dock." He sounded demoralized. "I thought I'd start on the ground floor and work my way up, but I never got very far."

Melanie understood. "Can I tell you something?" She didn't wait for permission. "I went to school to work in foreign affairs. I thought I could change the world."

Walker snickered. She could tell he was starting to feel comfortable with her. "Then I found out I needed a master's degree, and I didn't want to be bogged down with debt."

"How did you end up here?" He finally took a sip of his tepid coffee.

"I applied for a job with the government, and after fifteen years, I went back to school."

"Fifteen years?" He looked genuinely surprised.

"Yes. It was a long and winding road getting here."

"So did you give up on saving the world?" He smirked.

"Nope. I figured maybe I could do it one kid at a time."

He actually chuckled. "And you're starting with mine."

"Mr. Walker, may I ask you another question?"

"Go for it."

"Do you feel angry a lot of the time? Like the world has something against you personally?"

"Well, yes and no. I guess I get irritated more than I should." He sat back. "Almost everything aggravates me. The light is taking too long to change; the mailman is late; I can't find the remote. That kind of stuff."

"And when you get home, all your frustrations are about to burst through the seams. Am I right?"

He let out a huff. "That pretty much sums it up."

"Do you drink?" She knew she was crossing a line into dangerous territory, but in for a penny, in for a pound.

"One beer a day." He put his hand on his heart. "Swear. I'm not going down that road. I've seen too many people destroy their lives inside a bottle."

"Have you considered changing jobs?"

"Where would I go?" He looked at her.

"You said you have a business degree."

"Yeah. That was almost a dozen years ago. A lot has changed."

"What about taking some online courses? Brush up on a few things."

"I thought about it, but, you know, life keeps getting in the way."

"Life surely has a lot of detours. It's a series of adjustments. I'm a huge advocate of making the best out of what you're handed. The idea is never to give up. You never know what opportunities lie ahead." Melanie hoped some of her wisdom would reach him. "I'd be happy to help you find some classes you could fit into your schedule." Melanie had a plethora of recommendations in her office. "But first we need to figure out how to keep your family together."

Walker looked at her again. "How? What about my son? He must hate me."

"I don't think he hates you."

"Then why is he doing this to me?"

"Mr. Walker, Jerome isn't doing this to hurt you." Melanie wasn't entirely sure about that, but she had to mollify this man if she wanted to succeed. "Perhaps it's just a phase. Kids go through them all the time."

"Have you seen it often?"

"I have to be honest. This is my first guidance counselor gig, so I can't give you any empirical data. Perhaps talking to him about his clothing choices might give you some clarity?" she suggested.

"How is that going to happen if his mother has taken him away?"

"We can work on that. What if we set up a counseling session with the three of you?"

"Would you be the counselor?"

"No. I'm not well-versed on family affairs, but I would certainly support any recommendations and follow up at school."

"Can you arrange for it?" His willingness seemed genuine.

Melanie sensed he was remorseful and ready to give counseling a try.

"Yes. But you need to be able to accept any choices Jerome makes."

He was silent. Then said, "My kid. *Mrs. Doubtfire.*"

Melanie burst out laughing. "Now there's the spirit."

His expression changed. "Come to think of it, that movie

was on a few weeks ago. Okay. You have my total attention. I will do whatever you recommend, a counselor recommends, or what RuPaul recommends."

"Mr. Walker, you do have a sense of humor. You should lean on it more often. Instead of getting angry at things that annoy you, try to make a joke of them. For example, when the light isn't changing fast enough for you, look up at the traffic light and say, 'I know you're doing this on purpose.'"

That made him laugh. "Yeah, I guess it's pretty stupid to get angry over something like that." He paused. "I don't know why I let that stuff get to me."

"Like I said, that's something you can work on. Lights are going to do what they do; people are going to be jerks when they want to. It's all about how you react to those stressors."

Melanie checked her watch. Gilmour was sitting outside the café just in case things got dicey. She caught his eye and gave him another secret sign that things were going well.

"I'd better get back to my office." Melanie stood. "Mr. Walker, why don't you come with me, and I'll put you in touch with a counselor. I suggest you make a few appointments just for yourself. Get a handle on your temper. After a few weeks, we can bring Mrs. Walker and Jerome into it."

He was nodding thoughtfully. "Where will Pat and Jerome be in the meantime?"

"They'll be staying where they are for the time being, but we can put a schedule together. And I'll give you a list of schools where you can take some online courses."

"Okay. Sounds good." He held the door open for her. "Ms. Drake, you just might save the world."

Melanie let out a guffaw. "One kid at a time."

They walked back to the school, with Gilmour following them. Again, Walker held the door open for her, and they made their way to her office.

Lynch and Audrey had been waiting anxiously for them to return. "All good?" Audrey Alexander called out.

"All good," Melanie responded, with a sense of satisfaction.

"Please take a seat." She motioned toward a chair and shut the door. She could hear Lynch's footsteps moving closer to her office. He'd be right outside if she needed him. She picked up her phone and buzzed Audrey's office. "Could you please tell Agent Gilmour I'll be a few minutes?" She listened. "Thanks."

"Agent Gilmour?" Walker asked.

"An old colleague." Melanie pulled up her file of family counselors. She wrote down two names. "These are very good. I'd suggest you make an appointment with each of them, explain the plan, and see which one you feel the most comfortable with. Not the one who you think will go easy on you. But feeling safe is very important. Physically and emotionally." She turned to her monitor. "Now, let's find a few online courses. What area are you particularly interested?"

Walker told her he wanted to work in administration. As an office manager. Something along those lines. Again, Melanie checked her roster and wrote down a few institutions for him. "The first two offer job placement, but obviously it will be up to you."

He took the paper from her. His hands were shaking. "I cannot thank you enough. I feel as if a weight has been lifted off my shoulders."

"I am very happy we found a way to improve things for you."

"What about Pat and Jerome?"

"After you choose your therapist and have had three sessions, you'll arrange for a group session. You'll phone me and give me the information, and I will pass it along to your wife and son."

"Will you be at the session with all of us?"

"No, I'm afraid that's out of my jurisdiction. To be perfectly honest, all of this is out of my jurisdiction."

"Well, it should be in your jurisdiction. You're good at it."

"That's the nicest compliment I've had all day." She stood, signaling the meeting was over, and opened the door to the eavesdroppers.

Walker followed. He held out his hand. "Thanks very much. I will be in touch with details."

"You're very welcome. Good luck. I am looking forward to seeing all of you at the open house in November."

Walker nodded at the two men standing in the corridor and left the building.

Gilmour was the first to speak. "What did you do? Pull a few magic tricks?"

Lynch did a double take. "Magic tricks?"

"Oh, you don't know about the "Magnificent Mel-Drake?"

"MelDrake?" Lynch was further confused.

"We haven't had Show and Tell yet." Melanie made a frowny face.

"So, you do know magic tricks, or is he busting your chops here?" Lynch asked.

"Both," Melanie and Gilmour said in unison.

"Oh, I can't wait for Show and Tell now!" Lynch laughed.

"Seriously, Mel, how did it go? He seemed repentant."

"We spoke about what a good kid Jerome is. I discovered Mr. Walker is not unlike many people. He's terribly unhappy with his job. Feels like he's at a dead end. Been shortchanged."

"So he's angry with the world," Lynch added.

"Pretty much."

Audrey Alexander jetted out of her office. "Melanie, what was that all about?" She was half curious and half perturbed.

"Sorry. I thought I could get to the bottom of this in a neutral atmosphere."

"That is against school policy." Audrey's voice was stern.

"If it's any consolation, he's going to go to a therapist to figure out his anger issues, and then start family counseling, provided Mrs. Walker is so inclined. He's also going to investigate continuing education classes."

"You did all that over a cup of coffee?" Audrey seemed skeptical.

"I was using my skills to the best of my ability." Again, not directly answering the question. "Rooting out the cause of the problem is the only way you can find a cure. You can't fix something unless you know where the problem lies. I got the impression that no one has ever asked Mr. Walker about his feelings."

Gilmour grunted and added, "Men and their feelings. They don't know how to make that connection or express them. That's why most of them act out." He added, "Drake is a top-notch investigator, you know."

Audrey let out some air. "Don't let it happen again. Please." She returned to her office.

Melanie whispered, "You're welcome," causing Lynch and Gilmour to chuckle. Audrey waved a hand at them without turning around.

"She's just doing her job," Lynch said.

"And I was doing mine."

"By breaking some of the rules?" Gilmour teased.

"You just shut it if you want to get a ride home." Melanie turned and went back to her desk. She phoned Patricia's burner phone and explained what had transpired. Patricia sounded hopeful and was willing to give family counseling a try as long as Jerome was okay with it. Melanie wasn't ready to say "Mission Accomplished," but her gut told her she had made some progress that day.

She walked down to Audrey's office to clear the air before she left with Gilmour. She gently knocked on the door frame. "Got a minute?"

Audrey gestured toward a chair.

"I apologize for breaking the rules today. I'm usually a stickler about following them. But to be honest, I didn't think about rules this morning. All I could think about was that poor kid and his mother and what their future could be if the family breaks up. I thought if I could speak to Mr. Walker in a safe space, he would open up, which he did. He suffers as many people do. He hates his job because it's not what he ever wanted to do. I know that feeling. I just never acted out. Well, that's a story for another day. My point is, I am hopeful. I'm not sorry, but I am taking responsibility."

Audrey knew there was a big difference between an apology and accountability. "Consider coaching soccer your penance." She shuffled a few papers. "Now go home and take that agent with you."

Melanie got up and turned to leave.

"Mel?" Audrey called her. "Great job."

Melanie resisted the temptation to gloat when she walked over to Gilmour.

"Get your hand slapped?" he asked playfully.

"Not exactly. But I didn't get a gold star, either." She unlocked the drawer, removed her locked gun, and put it in her tote. She scribbled a list of what she was looking for in a house.

Lynch grunted. "It's a sorry day when teachers and counselors have to carry guns."

"Very true. But I've had this for several years. Believe me, possessing it was not my choice. Part of the job."

"And now it's part of this job," he lamented.

"Let's hope, pray, chant, meditate that the world will be right-sided again soon. There really are more good people than bad." She patted Lynch on his big, burly shoulder. "Have a good night."

Gilmour shook the security officer's hand. "Good to see

you. Keep an eye on that one." He jerked his head in Melanie's direction.

Lynch made a fork with his two fingers, pointed them at her, and then at his eyes.

Melanie knew he was joking about watching her, but she was glad he was around. She took one more pass at the principal's office. "Here's my wish list. Happy house-hunting." Just as she was leaving the office, Audrey called out her name. Melanie turned in time to catch the whistle Audrey tossed in her direction. "Thanks a pant-load."

Melanie and Gilmour drove the twenty-five minutes to his house. "Greg, you were a lifesaver today. Not just for me. I told his father that I think Jerome is going through a phase."

"Could be. It may have nothing to do with his gender identity. He could be the next Benny Hill." Gilmour was referring to the famous British comedian whose show aired in the U.S. from 1969-1989. It was sketch comedy, with Hill often dressing like a frumpy woman. "Do you know at one time, over twenty-one million people watched that show? And then there was Barry Humphries' Dame Edna from Australia." He clicked his tongue. "We need to get our sense of humor back."

Melanie pulled into Gilmour's driveway. "Stop in for a nip?" he asked.

"Sure. Why not." Melanie unhooked her seat belt and followed him inside.

He made his way over to a credenza and poured two fingers' worth of bourbon into tumblers. He handed one to Melanie. "You earned this."

"Thanks. So did you." She raised her glass.

"So what's the plan for house hunting?"

"My folks are looking into a few places between the

school and their house. Audrey is also on the lookout, because I am going to be the substitute soccer coach."

"Well, that shouldn't be too difficult. At least there are rules to the game." He chuckled.

"Yes." Melanie went down the list: "Do not touch the ball. Only the goalkeeper can pick up the ball. Play must happen inside the rectangle box."

"And there are penalty kicks when a player breaks the rules," Gilmour added.

"Precisely." Melanie felt the tension release from her shoulders. She hadn't realized how tight she was until her muscles began to relax. "You know something? This job isn't any easier than working cases." She snickered.

"Look on the bright side. You're not profiling criminals."

"No. Just irate parents."

"You did great today, Mel."

"Sometimes people just need to talk to someone. I don't think Mr. Walker is a bad guy, but he let all his frustrations build up and was a walking time bomb. I also think giving him some professional advice made him feel less defeated. He's what, thirty-five maybe? He has time to change his career path. Look at me, for example."

Gilmour let out a hoot. "Melanie Drake. There are few people like you. You have grit and determination. Most people give up too easily."

"That's because they don't have mentors, or confidants. Come on, Greg, who do you share your feelings with?"

"What do you mean?" He knew exactly what she meant, and she was right. "I have friends."

"I know you have friends, but I am willing to bet you never discuss your feelings with them."

"Maybe I don't have any," he joked.

"You could be right." She winked and set her glass on the

coffee table. "I gotta go. Big day tomorrow. Gotta get ready for soccer."

"Thanks for the exciting day." Gilmour walked her to the door. He gave her a long, big bear hug.

Melanie had to admit, even if it was only to herself, it felt good. That's another thing the world could use a little more of: good hugs.

Chapter Twelve

Present Day
A New Routine

As promised, Principal Alexander had several listings for Melanie to look at after soccer practice. They were all within an easy commute from school, but the prices varied greatly. There were three on the list that she was going to check out during the week.

When the bell rang for dismissal, Melanie took her spot in the corridor, reminding kids, "Slow down, please. Mind your manners. Be polite."

She begrudgingly lugged her duffel bag to the girls' locker room. Squeals and laughs bounced off the tiled walls. She smiled, knowing there were happy kids around. Then she wondered how happy they would be once Melanie started enforcing the rules. She didn't want to embarrass the girls by changing in front of them, so she went into a stall and slipped into a pair of jogging pants, a T-shirt, socks, and sneakers. She debated about her OSI cap and decided it gave her some authority, especially if there were going to be helicopter parents around.

She put the whistle that hung from a cord over her head. It touched the front of her school lanyard. She put the whistle to her lips and gave it a practice run. Two quick, short toots! "Everybody! Out on the field!" she said with a surprising note of excitement in her voice. Maybe she would enjoy this after all.

She counted fifteen excited eight- and nine-year-olds. All were in their gym clothes. Once they made the team, they would be fitted for their uniforms. Of course, everyone was going to make the team. Melanie would find something for the most awkward kid to do.

Melanie had them line up in single file. Each girl would get her chance to see how far she could kick the ball. Melanie took notes. There were a half dozen who might have some promise. She only needed seven to make up a team if they played other schools. Then she paired the girls up and had each duo stand several feet apart. "I want you to try to kick the ball to your partner." Balls were flying everywhere. "Easy does it. You're not trying to kick a forty-yard field goal."

She took a seat in the second row of the bleachers and watched the girls valiantly aim the ball. *It's going to be a long season.* After a half hour, she blew the whistle again. "I'm dividing you into two teams. One will wear orange socks; the other will wear blue. You'll get them with your uniforms next week. Okay, everyone. Time to change." The after-school bus would be pulling in soon, and she had to change into something more appropriate to meet the real estate agent. There was more giggling wafting above the lockers. She wondered if they were laughing at her the same way she and her friends had laughed at their gym teacher. *Nah. I'm much cooler than she was.*

With everyone accounted for, they marched to the side of the building, where the bus would take them home. Melanie watched until the vehicle left the parking lot. She typed the address of the first house into her GPS. It said it would take seventeen minutes. When she arrived, the agent was already there, in her pink pantsuit, big hair—as in way too big—and too-white teeth. *This woman watches too much television.* She smirked to herself. *Whatever, as long as she can find me a place to call home.*

They went through the usual greetings and introductions. "I think this is going to be perfect for you!" the agent exclaimed.

If you say so. Melanie smiled and followed the giant piece of bubblegum into the house. It had a large eat-in kitchen that could use some renovating, a half bath on the first floor, three small bedrooms, and a full bath upstairs. She was already calculating how much she would have to put into it before the house was what she really wanted. She took the tour, front and back. It was okay.

"So what do you think?" The agent smiled. Melanie swore a beam of light bounced off one of her teeth.

"It's lovely, but I'm not feeling it." Melanie had no time to waste, nor did she want to waste the agent's. "It needs work and it's already hitting the top of my price range."

"Oh, of course!" the agent gushed. "Let's move on to the next one. It's a bit of a fixer-upper, but it might fit into your budget."

Melanie was game and followed the agent to the next house, which was about five minutes farther away. When they pulled up, Melanie could already see the fixer-upper part. It was in dire need of a paint job and landscaping. She speculated what the place would be like inside. The agent opened the front door with a bit of a shove. "That can be easily fixed." She smiled.

It looked like someone had attempted the "fixing up" and stopped in the middle of the job.

"Yes, you can see there's been some work already started."

"And?" Melanie wanted to know the reason it stopped.

"And the owner was transferred to somewhere in South America. Nairobi, I think."

Melanie didn't know whether she should laugh or cry. "Nairobi is in Africa."

"Oh, I know it begins with an *N.*" Her expression was as dumb as she was.

"Nicaragua?" Melanie prompted her.

"Yeah. That's it. Spanish, right?"

Melanie now understood why people wanted to slap other people. In the agent's case, maybe it would rattle some of those brain cells. *Did she not learn geography?* As far as she knew, they were still teaching it in school. Another case of someone not paying attention.

Melanie reached into her bag, grabbed her pad and pen, and started taking notes. "How long has it been on the market?" she asked, wanting to end this suffering ASAP.

"Just this week. You're lucky to be the first one to see it."

In spite of its ramshackle condition, the space itself had promise. The previous owners had already broken down the wall between the dining room and living room and installed a new support beam. That was a huge plus. She wanted as much of an open floor plan as possible. The house needed Sheetrock, a new floor, and molding. She'd convince her brother to paint.

As she walked to the back, she saw that two existing windows had been replaced by French doors. One set led outside from the living room; the other was near the spot where a dining table could go. More pluses. The agent continued to blab while Melanie was envisioning how the place could look. *Eventually.* She wandered over to the kitchen area. It was all but gutted. That could definitely be a plus, but it would require immediate attention if she wanted to move in anytime soon. The agent broke into Melanie's musings. "I have a great kitchen cabinet guy and a plumber. We could get you in here in a couple of weeks. Of course, it would all depend on what kind of cabinets you wanted."

Melanie was thoughtful as she opened the door under the stairs. "Basement?"

"Yes. It's a full basement." She switched on the light and gestured down the steps. Then she turned and pointed to a washer and dryer hookup in an alcove off the kitchen. "The owners were planning to install them in the kitchen area next to the side door, but never got around to it. It just needs some bi-fold doors, and *voilà*! You have a laundry area on the main floor."

Melanie nodded as she scribbled more notes. "Let's take a look at the second floor."

The agent led the way. The master bedroom was average. She'd be able to fit a queen-size bed and some furniture. There was a full-size bath, albeit in need of renovation, but it was functional. Melanie tested the plumbing out by flushing the toilet and running the water. There was a door from the main bath that led to the master bedroom. Convenient. The other two rooms were on the small side and needed new windows and floors. That would be a project for another day. The house could be livable in a month. There was something about it that made her want to pursue it further.

She went back to the main floor and strolled outside through the French doors in the living room. A small, raised deck ran along the back of the house from one set of French doors to the other. Tall evergreens lined the perimeter of the property, concealing the stockade fence that divided it from the neighbors' house. It was peaceful. Private. She imagined what she and her mother could do to the landscaping. She sat on the wooden steps that led from the deck to the yard. She did some rough math. It would cost her a lot of money to make it move-in ready, but the owners wanted to get the house off their hands before they left the country. Otherwise, it would be sitting there uninhabitable for who knew how long. She wrote down a number on a piece of paper and handed it to the agent. "Offer this."

The agent didn't balk. She knew Melanie's parents were in the same business, so she wasn't dealing with an amateur. Plus, Melanie had a very nice down payment from the money she'd saved over the past three years. It would take her another few years to finish the place the way she wanted, but once the first floor was done, she could move in and take her time with the rest.

The agent rushed out to her car and phoned the owners. Melanie could see the woman's head bobbing. She was smiling. *Always a good sign.* The woman finished her call and sprinted up the also-in-need-of-repair sidewalk. She was grinning from ear to ear. "This is an all-time record for me. I've never closed a deal so fast in my ten-year career!"

Melanie wondered if her offer was too high. It was the asking price less fifteen percent for the renovations. It appeared everyone had done their homework. "I'll have the contracts drawn up immediately. Do you have a bank for your mortgage?"

"Yes. Unless you have someone you'd recommend. As soon as you send me the contracts, I'll get the paperwork moving."

"Excellent! I'll be in touch!"

Melanie watched the pink bubble bounce into her car. She waved and drove away. Melanie sat on the front stoop. She pulled out her phone and dialed Gilmour.

He answered on the first ring. "Don't tell me you got suspended from school or kicked off the soccer team."

"Neither. I just bought a house." She gave him the address.

"See you in a few," he replied.

She called her mom to give her the news. It dawned on her that she'd called Gilmour first. *Huh.*

"Mom! I did it. I just agreed to buy a house. It needs some

work, but it's in a nice neighborhood. Lots of trees, and a yard where you and I can go crazy!"

"Sweetheart! That's wonderful. It didn't take you very long."

"I know. But when something feels right, you've got to go with it." Melanie was truly overjoyed. She felt her life was finally shifting into a rhythm she could move with comfortably. A slow, easy samba. "I'm going to have to get the kitchen done and some other things like a floor, Sheetrock. You know, the essentials." Melanie chuckled.

"I thought you said *some* work."

"Some work here. Some work there. But it's all manageable."

"How long do you think all of this is going to take?" her mother asked. "I have plans for your room," she ribbed.

"Ha ha. You're a regular Carol Burnett," Melanie tossed back to her. "It will depend on how long the bank takes, and then the cabinets will be about four weeks. Probably six, maybe eight weeks before I can move in."

"Oh, honey, I am very happy for you."

"Thanks, Mom." She heard a car coming down the street. She waved at Gilmour. "I gotta go. We'll talk later." She didn't want to tell her mother she'd called him first.

He pulled into the driveway and parked behind Melanie's car.

"So this is it, eh?" He gave her a big smile.

"Yep. It's a fixer-upper, but I can do it in stages. Most of the work will be in the kitchen, but I'm not ordering custom cabinets. There are so many standard designs to choose from—I'm not going to pay stupid money for them."

Gilmour laughed. "I don't ever recall seeing you so excited about something. Not even your kumbaya with that Mr. Walker dude."

"Come." She dragged him to the deck outside the French

doors. "Imagine what trouble my mom and I can get into with this space?"

Gilmour looked around. "Stockade fence?"

"Yes, and it's in good condition."

"Excellent. It'll make a great yard for Cosmo and Kramer."

"Who?" Melanie was puzzled.

"The two K-nines from the Air Force."

"The dogs that were on the mission in Belgium?"

"Yes. Them."

"What do they have to do with my backyard?"

"They need a home. This is perfect for them."

"Whoa. Wait. You want me to adopt two German shepherds?"

"Yes." He stared at her.

"You're really serious, aren't you?" Melanie placed her hands on her hips.

"They both got injured in an explosion."

"Oh no!" Melanie's hands flew up to her face. "What happened?"

"Obviously a bomb went off. Cosmo was blinded in one eye, and Kramer is deaf in one ear."

Melanie sputtered. "Oh, geez. So now I am going to adopt two disabled dogs."

"I knew you'd say yes."

"Wait! I didn't say yes."

"Yes, you did. You just said, 'So now I am going to adopt two disabled dogs.'"

"That was sarcasm, Mr. Smarty Pants."

"Mel, please?"

She could see the urging in his eyes. "There's no place for them to go," he added in earnest.

"What about you?"

"I signed up for two puppies that were abandoned on the base."

"You did? When?" Her eyes widened.

"The same day I put your name in for Cosmo and Kramer."

"What?"

"Since the Air Force is the executive agent for the DOD's military working dog program, they put up notifications of dogs being retired."

"Why don't their handlers take them?"

"They're on to training new dogs."

"So, let me see if I've got this straight. You put my name on a list for Cosmo and Kramer, and you adopted two puppies."

"Correct." He pretended to flinch so she wouldn't punch him.

"What about the puppies, again?"

"Someone left them outside the base. In a crate."

"People!"

"At least they left them someplace where they had a good chance of getting a home."

Melanie huffed. "New job. New house. New roommates."

"See how easy that was?"

This time, she slapped the back of his arm with the back of her hand. "Ouch!" Again, he was pretending. "I think this deserves a celebration. Do you have any plans for dinner?"

"I do now." She smiled. "You're paying."

"See you soon," she said to the house as she patted the front door and then scampered to her car.

Gilmour pulled out, and she followed. There was a family-owned Greek restaurant a few blocks away. They were greeted by an older woman who spoke with an accent. Melanie introduced herself. "I just put a bid on a house about a half mile away."

She described the house to the woman, who was familiar with the neighborhood.

"You will like it here. Come sit." The woman showed them to a table and handed them menus. "What can I get you to drink?"

"What do you have in the way of wine?" Gilmour asked.

"We have nice Greek wine. Not sweet," she said. She motioned that she would be right back. In just a few minutes, she returned with two glasses and a bottle of Volcanic Slopes from Santorini. "You taste. You like. You no like, we try something else."

Gilmour and Melanie swirled the honey-colored potion, sniffed, and tasted. "I like. You like?" he asked Melanie.

"Yes." She studied the bottle. It was made from the Assyrtiko variety of grapes.

"*Kalós,*" the woman responded, meaning "good" in Greek. "We have delicious fish tonight." She recited the menu, which was filled with delectable entrees.

They ordered a platter of dips with hummus, taramasalata, and tzatziki, with spanakopita, and grilled octopus on the side.

Melanie was animated as she discussed her plans for the house. Gilmour saw Melanie Drake in a completely different light. For once, she was thinking about herself. He chuckled.

She stopped short. "What's so funny?"

"You. Your excitement is charming."

"Charming? Me?" Melanie peered over her forkful of octopus.

"Yes, you." Gilmour felt as if he were encountering a side of Melanie he hadn't met before. "You're always business. Facts. News. Real news. You do your homework. What I find fascinating is you are quite meticulous and methodical, but you decided to buy a house within, what, fifteen minutes?"

Melanie placed her fork on the table. "You know how sometimes you just know something? We do it all the time with our job. Sometimes knowledge and experience mesh to help us interpret certain situations."

"There you go. I rest my case." He continued to savor his dinner.

"But you're right. It was a quick decision, but I made it based on what I wanted, what I could afford, and how it felt."

"Intuition?" he asked.

"Gut feeling," she answered, knowing those two words always settled better with men.

He smiled, knowing she was patronizing him. "I'm really happy for you, Mel. You have a new job and soon a new house."

"With two German shepherds." She raised her eyebrows. "You are going to have to help me figure out a bathroom area for them."

"As a matter of fact, I did my research. They make artificial grass for outdoor dog potty use."

"Dog potty use?" Melanie snorted. She lowered her voice as the waitress brought their entrees.

Gilmour reached into his blazer pocket and pulled out a piece of paper. "It was on the same posting with the dogs. I guess they want to make it easier for people to say yes. I went to the website and downloaded the PDF. They use it to train dogs, and it can be used outdoors."

"You *have* done your homework."

"I had to. I'm getting two puppies, remember?"

Melanie studied the ad for the fake grass. "I can partition it off with landscaping. They'll have a private potty." She had a big grin on her face. "I'm not going to be in the house for at least six weeks. Where will Cosmo and Kramer live until then?"

"Believe it or not, they are going through debriefing, and of course medical exams. If you're not ready when they're released, I'll keep them until you are. You'll can come by every night."

Melanie shook her head. "Let's not forget soccer practice."

"Can you bring the dogs to school?"

"Huh. Good question."

"I suggest you ask first before you get your hand slapped again."

"Well, duh. So tell me about your puppies."

"They're some kind of mixed breed. I think they have some lab in them." He tapped his phone and showed her a photo. "About four months old."

"They're adorable." Melanie bubbled. "Do they have names yet?"

"I was thinking maybe Ben and Jerry."

"You're going to name your dogs after ice cream?" Melanie squeezed more lemon on her fish.

"What's wrong with ice cream? If I recall, you happen to like it."

"Have you spent any time with them?"

"Uh, no." He tightened his lips. "I took one look at them in that wooden crate and said, 'I'll take them.' "

"A side of you I've never seen before."

"So we're even."

"Where are they now?"

"At the vet, getting checked, vaccinated, chipped, and fixed." Gilmour rattled off the doggie to-do list.

"When do you get them?"

"If their tests are good, and their surgery goes well, it'll just be a couple of days."

"Well, a lot has happened today." Melanie sopped up the olive oil and lemon sauce with a slice of pita bread. "Including finding a really good restaurant in my new neighborhood."

Gilmour smiled. His relationship with Melanie was moving from work buddies to a fine friendship.

Chapter Thirteen

Moving In and Moving On

Melanie knew she would qualify for a mortgage. It was a matter of how long the paperwork would take for her approval. Tammy, the real estate agent, had a business relationship with one of the local banks and helped push the loan through within two weeks.

While she was waiting, Melanie had the kitchen measured for cabinets and a countertop. It was a railroad design, with cabinets along the walls. The space led to a dining area that faced the backyard and opened to the living room on the left. She chose a simple design with white doors and brushed nickel hardware. The countertop was a simulated gray slate. It was a neutral palette that would allow her to add color on the walls, or furniture, which was also something she had to consider. But before she could purchase a sofa, she had to install a finished floor. She decided she would run the same light gray oak throughout the main level. It would give the space a sense of continuity. An electrician installed recessed lights in the kitchen and checked all the outlets. She was willing to pay for whatever needed to be done to pass the bank and the building department inspections. True, she was taking a gamble by putting out her own money, but it simply felt right. If all went according to her plan, she would be in her new house before the holidays.

Within two weeks, the bank called, informing her she was approved for the loan. They set the closing for three weeks from that day. Melanie scrambled to be sure everything else was moving as scheduled. She felt as if she were part of a juggling act, managing work, coaching, renovating, and preparing to be responsible for two new creatures.

With the help of her mother, she found an estate sale where the entire contents of a house was up for grabs. For now, all she wanted was a dining room table and a sofa. She didn't want to buy anything new until she and the dogs assimilated to each other and the new environment. It was going to be a lot of newness and renewal in the next few months.

Time was moving quickly. The next six weeks passed in a whirlwind. She closed on the house, had the Sheetrock and floors installed, and the walls painted very pale gray. Next came the kitchen. She'd picked cabinets that were in stock, as well as countertop material, and the installation went smoothly, though it was a hustle to get everything done by her move-in date.

Cosmo and Kramer were about to be relieved of their military duty. She appreciated Gilmour's very generous offer to look after them while he was trying to train his own puppies. It was a lot to expect, even though he'd made the offer, probably out of guilt. After all, he'd signed her up for something before consulting her. Any normal person would have gone ballistic, but as with almost everything else, she took it in stride. Besides, one of the main reasons she wanted to buy a house was so she could have a dog. Instead, she'd have two. What was one more in the grand scheme of things? Plus, they'd keep each other company while she was at work and coaching.

Melanie had worked with Cosmo and Kramer a couple of years before. She was profiling a serial bomber in Belgium and looking for a way to track him. The dogs provided the perfect solution. When they located the building, the dogs detected the bomb, and it was defused. There was no sign of the bomber until they heard a small explosion a half block away. He was arrested after he blew his foot off.

Two years later, Kramer and Cosmo were called to duty again for a bomb threat but had been injured in the process. Cosmo had lost the sight in one eye. He could still see out of the other, but that wasn't good enough for the military. Kramer became deaf in one ear, but he behaved as if he had no idea his hearing was impaired. If you asked him, and if he answered, he would tell you he was just fine. Then your name would be Dr. Dolittle.

Even though they could still sniff out bombs, they couldn't pass the overall physical test, so it was time for them to retire. She was required to attend an indoctrination seminar to become acquainted with their special needs as well as commands, so there wouldn't be any miscommunication between woman and doggies. They were only five years old, so they had plenty of spunk in them. Secretly, Melanie was overjoyed she was taking command of the pups. She'd missed them after their mission was complete.

Finally, the first week of November, her house was habitable, and she moved her possessions in. Over the years, she hadn't accumulated much. She was always on the move and either lived at home or in furnished or semi-furnished rentals.

Melanie had a few favorite things. There was the turquoise Fiestaware she'd bought at a pottery outlet, and the Tramontina stainless cookware she'd bought on a whim. She rationalized that if she had good cookware, she might actually cook. Not a chance. Not until now.

Her brother and a couple of his buddies retrieved the dining table and chairs, and the sofa from their parents' garage. The sofa was about ten years old. Deep blue with traditional rolled arms. She'd spruce it up with some colorful throw pillows. The dining table was a light ash with white vinyl seats that she reupholstered in a smoky tweed. All it took was few yards of fabric and a staple gun. Another talent she could add to her personal toolbox.

Thanksgiving was only a week away, and the students were engrossed in Thanksgiving decorating, stories, and the school play. There was only one more soccer practice left. During the fall, her school didn't play against other teams. It was a time to learn the rules and the basic techniques. Real games against other schools would start in the spring; and the girls would start practicing again indoors after the Christmas holiday break. Melanie conceded that coaching wasn't as grueling or boring as she'd feared. A few of the girls quit after the first couple of weeks, leaving her with eleven. Thankfully, it was the better players that stayed, which made her job easier. The others had gotten discouraged or just didn't want to get dirty.

It was during the last soccer practice that Melanie spotted a man several hundred yards away. He had a familiar gait. The closer he got, the more she thought it might be her old boss, Rich Patterson. Then he waved, confirming her guess.

"Hey! What are you doing here?" She waved back and gave him a big grin.

He smiled, but it wasn't as robust as her greeting. Something was up. "Is everything alright? Family? Work? What?"

"Everything is fine." He gave her a quick hug. "Got a minute?"

"I will as soon as practice is done. Five minutes. Tops.

Take a seat." She pointed to the bench on the side of the field. She blew her whistle. "Throw-in!" A player from one team kicked the ball outside the sideline, giving the other team the opportunity to throw it back in. Preferably to a teammate.

Melanie's stopwatch beeped, signaling it was game over. She blew her whistle again. "Okay, everybody! Get cleaned up." The girls hustled past her, all of them speaking or giggling at the same time. She turned to Patterson. "Don't go away. I have to make sure they don't pull each other's hair out. I'll be right back."

Rich got up and wandered toward the bleachers. He was leaning against the side when Melanie came back outside.

"So what brings you to my little corner of the world?"

"We need you back," he said without batting an eye.

"You what?" Melanie was shocked and just this side of horrified. "I can't do that. I have a job. Responsibility. I just bought a house, and tomorrow I'm picking up my new fur family."

"I know. Gilmour told me."

"Gilmour? He knows about this?" Melanie furrowed her brow. "Why didn't he tell me?"

Patterson gave her a look that said, *Do I really need to explain it to you?*

"Come on, boss, I can't go back to that life. It almost killed me."

"This is something completely different."

"How so?"

"For one thing, it doesn't require your full-time employment. It would only be one or two assignments a month. At night, after work."

Melanie exhaled the words, "Okay. Clarify please."

Patterson looked around to be sure no one was within earshot. "Let's sit down."

Melanie had an uneasy feeling about this conversation. It was dredging up a lot of bad memories.

"Now before you get all PTSD on me—"

She interrupted him. "Wait a second. I was never diagnosed with PTSD."

"True, but you cannot think that situation with Howell didn't affect you in some way."

"Oh, him and a dozen other horrible missions I was on."

"Understood. But hear me out." He placed his hand on her arm. "Mel, you were an exceptional agent. You excelled at everything you took on and anything that was handed to you. What I am about to describe is light years from your previous line of duty."

"So what do you need me for?" Now she was curious.

"I need you to be an escort for international billionaires."

Melanie blurted out, "You want me to do what? And with whom?"

"It's not what you think," he replied.

"The escort part or the billionaire part? Or is it the international part?"

"Listen. There are international billionaires from some, shall we say . . . *iffy* areas of the world. They come to Washington, New York, and Miami to conduct business. When they have dinner parties, or cocktail parties, or other social gatherings, they want to be in the company of attractive, intelligent women who can carry on a conversation. They don't want bimbo bubbleheads just sitting there looking good. They're too easy to find. Then after dinner or whatever the occasion, you get to leave, and their dessert arrives." He used a euphemism.

Melanie was listening intently. "Dessert." She chuckled. "Explain how this is going to work."

Patterson told her there were two sting operations planned. One was an art exhibit at a diplomat's residence, and the second was a dinner party scheduled at a different diplomat's private club. There would be approximately ten men seated at the table.

"Who are the other women?" Melanie asked.

"They're usually from an agency. A very exclusive international agency."

"So how do I fit in? And why?" Melanie was truly intrigued. "Won't they know I'm from a different agency? No pun intended." She snickered.

"We need you to work counterintelligence."

"But how?"

"NSA, CIA, FBI. The entire alphabet of government intelligence agencies gets tips on everything from drug smuggling, diamond smuggling, human trafficking, guns, ammo. You name it. In each case, there is an elite billionaire involved in organizing the gathering. It takes money to pull off these jobs."

"Right." Melanie knew what he was referring to. "But what exactly would I be doing? Sitting? Talking? Obviously, listening."

Patterson smiled. "All of the above, but you might find this surprising—we're really interested in your sleight of hand talent."

"My what?" she exclaimed, her eyes the size of saucers.

"Yes, those little tricks from Uncle Leo." Patterson saw she wasn't quite buying it.

"You're joking, right?"

"Mel, I am dead serious. We need you to plant a bug on these men. The devices are smaller than a pencil eraser. Drop one in a pocket. It can transmit up to a thousand feet. There might be an occasion for you to drop a GPS device. All you have to do is get close enough. I know you can do this, Mel." He hesitated. "I need you to do this. There's no one else I know who's both capable and completely trustworthy."

Melanie knew he was serious. There had been too many high-risk security breaches occurring of late. It was a sad state of affairs when the people who were supposed to be protecting the nation's most sensitive information carelessly tossed it out to the world and enemy hands. She understood his caution. "You know I can't say no, so where and when do we start?"

"The first job I want you on is an art exhibit," Patterson said.

"Okay."

"There's a new artist who is putting on an exclusive show in Georgetown." He used finger quotes for the word *artist*. "No one has ever heard of him, and from what I understand, his work is garbage."

"Beauty is in the eye of the beholder." Melanie smirked.

"Yeah, well, we suspect these pieces of art are a cover for something else. We just can't figure out what. There's a guy from the Middle East who is spending beaucoup bucks on something that the art experts say is junk. So he's either gone totally crackers, or there is something in this transaction that very few know about."

"And I'm supposed to find out what it is?"

"We suspect drugs, but we have no evidence, cannot get a warrant. We're dealing with diplomatic immunity."

"Now there's a real Get Out of Jail Free card." Melanie bit her lip.

"The exhibit is a week from tomorrow."

"Huh? Say what?" Melanie blinked several times. "A week from tomorrow?" She pursed her lips after she stopped biting them. "How am I supposed to get ready for something like that in eight days?"

He handed her an envelope. It contained a thousand dollars cash, and an American Express credit card. "You'll go shopping. Get a few outfits, wigs, shoes. Very upscale."

"Now you're talking!" Melanie's tone became more dynamic as she peered into the packet of goodies.

"We're going to establish a few different identities for you, so as soon as you get the wigs, we'll need photos. Create at least four personas."

"Roger that." Melanie took a very deep breath and let it out slowly.

"I know you can do this, Mel. Compared to some of the work you've done, this is a walk in the park." He wrote down a date, time, and address and handed it to her. "A town car will pick you up and bring you to the exhibit. It will be waiting outside the exhibit venue in case you need to make a quick exit."

"Will I be wired?"

"Yes. Bluetooth. No real wires, per se. You'll have a pencil eraser-sized mic and an earpiece you can clip on to an earring. I'll hook you up just before you leave your house."

"Okay, boss." She snickered. "Thought I'd never say that to you again."

"You can take the girl out of OSI, but . . ."

"Yeah. Yeah." Another deep huff. "Can I go home now?" She placed her hands in a prayer-like pleading position. "I have to pick up my pooches tomorrow morning, and then it's the school Season of Giving Festival Play."

Patterson smiled. "You look good, Mel. You've put a little meat on your scraggly bones, and you don't have that permanent frown on your forehead."

She leaned in and whispered, "A little Botox can work wonders."

"Well, it's good to see you smile."

"I trust your escapades won't wipe the smile off my face."

"Think of this mission as a role in a spy movie."

"As long as I don't get caught, and James Bond's got my back."

"Will Gilmour do?"

"Gilmour?" she asked quizzically.

"Yes, he'll be somewhere in your orbit. Never far away. When you spot him, ignore him."

"Understood." She heard the final bell ring, signaling the building was closing. Out of an abundance of caution, the school locked its doors at four thirty unless there was a planned activity. No one was allowed to be alone in the building. "Okay. I've gotta run." She gave him a peck on the cheek. "You'd better make sure I don't regret this." She walked quickly to the administration parking lot and headed home, stopping at a pet center on the way. Melanie still had a few things to pick up to welcome her new doggies.

When she pulled into the parking lot, she phoned Gilmour.

He picked up right away. "Patterson talked to you." It was a statement, not a question.

"How long have you known about this?" she asked suspiciously, trying to figure out the timeline.

"Just a couple of weeks."

"You signed me up for the dogs before or after?"

"Before, Mel. I wouldn't dump so much on you all at once," he said sincerely. "Just think, you'll be able to come home to them twice a day. Imagine how happy they'll be."

"Boy, you know how to put a spin on things, don't you?"

"I do my best."

"So what do you think? Or should I ask, how much do you know?"

"Where are you now?"

"Outside of Pet-a-Palooza. I have to pick up a few things I ordered. Why?"

"I'll meet you at your place. Say, half hour?"

"Sure. Why don't you pick up some takeout from Mykonos?"

"Great idea. See you in a bit."

Melanie's head was spinning. So much to filter. First and foremost were Cosmo and Kramer. She went into the store and gave her name. A smiley-faced employee greeted her. "Yes, Ms. Drake. Your order is in the back. I'll have someone get it for you."

"Thanks." She pulled out her debit card and paid for the two matching large gray dog beds, twenty-five pounds of kibble, two cases of canned food, and a variety of dog chews. A pooper scooper, bags, and a container. She did a double take when the store associate came around with a hand truck. She admitted it looked as if she'd spent over 500 dollars. Which she had. She gave the young man a tip for helping load everything into her car. Gilmour would do the unloading when she got to her place.

Melanie backed her car into the driveway, unlatched the hatchback, and left it open for Gilmour when he arrived. She opened the back gate and surveyed the yard. It wasn't in the best shape, but it would have to do for now. There was a five-by-five area sectioned off with fencing that matched the stockade. It was Cosmo's and Kramer's private toilet, where the fake grass was installed. The privacy fencing blended well with its surroundings, and the potty area couldn't be seen from the house or the patio. There was plenty of room for the dogs to run around and be safe inside the confines of the yard.

Melanie heard a car pull up. It was Gilmour. He got out of his vehicle with two large shopping bags. "Delivery!"

Melanie stuck her head into one of the bags. "Smells divine!"

He handed her the bags. "Let's get this stuff out of your car first." He let out a low whistle. "How many dogs are you expecting?"

"Very funny. By the way, how are Ben and Jerry?"

"I think they've doubled in size in the past couple of weeks."

"Do you know what kind of mix they are?"

"Is Mastodon a dog breed?" He laughed. "Vet thinks they're Labskies. A cross between a Labrador and a husky."

"Yikes. They're gonna be huge."

"You should see their paws. They're the size of ping-pong paddles."

Melanie laughed out loud. "Looks like we got ourselves a big hunk of canine love." She carried the food into the kitchen while Gilmour unloaded the car.

"Hey, whatever happened to that Walker guy and his family?"

"Funny you should ask. I got a phone call today from Mrs. Walker. She, Jerome, and her husband started Zoom sessions with a family therapist, and now they are doing it in person. She and her son moved back home two weeks ago. Jerome is back in school and is going to be a tree in the school play."

"That sounds promising. And neutral."

"Mrs. Walker agreed to let Mr. Walker go up to her sister's house and visit on the weekends. She told me they had many heart-to-heart discussions. They even watched *Mrs. Doubtfire* together. Apparently, Jerome had seen some of the film before school started. He explained to his father that he wanted to try out dressing like a girl. He thought it was funny. Obviously, no one else did."

"So all good in MelDrake land?"

"I hope so, because you have some 'splaining to do." She set the table and put the food on platters. "But, yes, all good. I really helped a kid. And his family. Wonders shall never cease."

Gilmour poured each of them a glass of wine and took a seat across from Melanie. He began to explain the situation. "Too many foreign diplomats with dirty money are slipping past the authorities."

"But they can't be arrested."

"For the most part, no. But that doesn't mean we can't foil their plans. If things go wrong for them, they'll have a higher power to answer to."

"The money god?" Melanie dipped some bread into one of the dips.

"Whichever one is funding whatever their operation entails."

"Pretty clever." She licked her lips. "On both sides. Think about it, getting stuff smuggled via diplomats. It's kind of brilliant."

"But we are brillianter," Gilmour replied with a made-up word.

"Indubitably." She pointed a piece of pita at him. "And that's a real word."

During dinner, Gilmour confessed he knew very little about the operation they were about to undertake. "According to Patterson, the diplomats gather sporadically. How often? We don't know."

"He said maybe once or twice a month."

"Probably. We don't want to draw attention by foiling too many of their plans. I suppose the higher-ups will prioritize the cases."

"Yeah, whose priority?" Melanie rolled her eyes.

He moved on. "Apparently this first job has something to do with the art world, right?"

"Yes, but I don't think it has to do with someone curating a collection of junk."

"Smuggling something." He shrugged.

"I guess we're going to find out."

"We're certainly going to try."

"The best part is that I'm getting a new wardrobe. And a new identity. Or four." She touched the side of her face. "I'm going to have to apply some heavy makeup on this."

Gilmour took a closer look. "It's barely noticeable, but you're right. You have to look different and can't have a telltale sign."

"Slide that over to me, please." She pointed to a pad and

pen at the other end of the table. She began to make a list of things she needed to buy: "Clothes, shoes, wigs, makeup. Heavy-duty makeup."

"What time will they drop off your pooches?" he asked as she was writing names of designers on the page.

"Around three. Then I have to leave at six for the school play."

"What are your plans for Thanksgiving?" he asked.

"Shannon, my sister-in-law, is having us over. She plans so many parties, she could do Thanksgiving dinner for twenty in her sleep."

"I'll be going to my folks in Alexandria. A quiet dinner for thirty or forty."

"You have a huge family." Melanie knew Gilmour was one of five, and his siblings were married with kids.

"Yeah. It's loud, but it's fun. I especially like watching the nieces and nephews play together."

They cleared the table and chatted a bit longer, speculating on the illegal activities they would be attempting to discover.

Chapter Fourteen

Thanksgiving

The day before the four-day Thanksgiving weekend, Melanie left school at two thirty. Her new fur family was about to arrive.

She checked and rechecked the doors, the gate, the potty area, the scooper, bags, and container. She was excited and nervous. It was a big responsibility, but the dogs were already trained. All she had to do was teach them to be house pets and her cuddly pals. There was a small area at the end of the kitchen where she'd set up their food and water station. Instead of regular dog bowls, she'd bought them matching Fiestaware. *Why not?* Theirs were navy blue so she would not confuse them with the turquoise, human plates.

She heard a vehicle pull into the driveway. It was a K-9 kennel transport. She went to the front door and waited on the porch with the necessary identification. A young officer greeted her with an electronic tablet. "Ms. Melanie Drake?"

"Yes, that would be me." She showed him her driver's license.

"Ready to meet your new kids?" He smiled.

"We're old friends. Worked a mission together." She followed him to the back of the vehicle and opened the matte black doors and unhooked the dogs' leads.

Cosmo jumped out first, then Kramer. Melanie squatted down and wrapped her arms around both their necks. "Hello, my darlings!" Cosmo began to nuzzle her. "You remember me?" Kramer followed suit. "Oh, you guys! I am so happy to see you!" Her eyes welled up, and so did her heart. She felt a loving warmth engulf her. Then she began to babble in doggie-speak. "Oh, my bubbies . . ." She kissed each on the head. "Look at mommy's new babies. Aw, that's my good boys." At least that's what it sounded like.

She stood to address the officer, who was smiling at the reunion. "What happens next?"

He handed her their leads and asked her to sign the tablet with a stylus. He shook Melanie's hand, thanked her for giving the dogs a home, saluted them, and went on his way.

Melanie bent down again. "I am so happy to see you." And she really and truly was. She would thank Gilmour later. *Let him sweat it out just a bit longer.* She chuckled to herself.

"Come on, fellas. Let's check out your new digs." The dogs followed with their tails wagging. They seemed to know this was going to be their new home.

Melanie spoke to them as if they were people this time. "Come with me." She went into the kitchen and showed them where their kibble and water bowls were. The dogs immediately sat at attention. "This is your dining area." They looked up at her and then down at the empty bowls. "Are you guys hungry?"

Cosmo made a soft yap.

"Okay. First, I shall show you your posh bathroom facility." She opened the side door and led them to the enclosed area to the right. The dogs walked on the fake turf, sniffed around, and marked it with a little piddle.

"You guys are really smart. And territorial." She patted

them on the head. "Good boys." She turned and went back into the house, the dogs following on her heels. She scooped a bit of dry dog food into their bowls. "Have a snack." The dogs obediently went to the dishes and chowed down. After a few minutes, she called for them to follow her.

"Now this is the living room. Each of you has your own bed. Take your pick." The dogs looked up at her. "Okay, I'll pick." She went to one of the beds and sat down. "Cosmo. Here." She patted the soft fabric, and he obeyed. "Sit. Lie down." And just like that, he was in comfort land. "You're next, Kramer." Melanie shifted to the other dog bed and repeated the action. Similarly, Kramer sat, and was in comfort land, too. "Okay, guys. I have to get changed and go to a school play. I won't be gone long." She opened a wooden box on the mantel and pulled out two very large dog chews. "Here you go. No eating the furniture."

Melanie climbed the stairs two at a time. She was feeling rather buoyant. She had an instant family, and she was going to see one of the children she'd helped play a tree.

While she was sifting through her closet, she tried to imagine what styles she should buy for her new gig. She was five feet seven inches and 150 pounds. Yes, she had put on a few pounds, but they were in the right places. Her three-day-a-week Pilates classes made sure of it, and most of her clothes still fit her well. Her new job would require her to wear completely different outfits. One each for her four personalities. She'd do some research later. It occurred to her she would have to do her shopping either on Black Friday or Stupid Saturday. Maybe the high-end shops wouldn't be as crazy as the big box stores. She had never heard of a stampede at Gucci or Dior and decided she would take her chances at Tyson's Galleria. She got goosebumps thinking about her shopping spree. Melanie wondered what the credit limit was on the card. She figured if she went over it, she would find out! This was going to be fun!

Meanwhile, for the school play, she decided on a deep burgundy pantsuit, with wide slacks and a long, tailored jacket. A citron brooch against the burgundy gave her a festive, seasonal look. She made her way down the steps. Two German shepherd heads snapped to attention. "It's only me. How do I look?" She made a face. "I guess they didn't teach you that in doggie school." She blew them a kiss and headed out to see the play.

The auditorium was filled with almost three hundred people. Parents, grandparents, siblings, staff, and friends. The air was electric. For many, this was a first, including Melanie. Her first elementary school play as a guidance counselor. Her own first performance had been at the school talent show, where she'd performed her favorite card tricks. Who would have guessed she would be using those talents again? This time it would be in a very different way, for a very different reason.

Audrey Alexander entered the stage. "Good evening, everyone! Welcome to the Jesse Moorer Elementary School Season of Giving Festival!" A huge round of applause, hoots, and shouts filled the room. "I'd like to point out that all the decorations along the walls are by our students. As you can see, we have some very talented pupils." More hoots and applause. "This evening's play is about the importance of sharing. Each class will make a contribution to the feast of Thanksgiving, not only onstage, but also in the form of generous donations for the Food Pantry." More thunderous applause. "So, without further ado, I'd like to present Ms. Tilbury's first grade." Another round of applause as twenty six-year-old children entered the stage wearing costumes representing farm animals. They began to sing and dance to "Old MacDonald Had a Farm." Melanie tried valiantly not to laugh too hard as the cows bumped into the chickens. It was adorable. And hilarious. After they took a bow, two children wheeled out red wagons filled with canned corn and

canned beans. Next up was the second grade. Their song was
"Baby Shark," with Jerome dressed like a palm tree. She
spotted his parents in the second row. They were smiling and
bobbing their heads to the music. When the song was over,
Jerome and another child pulled their red wagons across the
stage. This time, they were filled with canned tuna and canned
salmon. Each class had a theme that coincided with the pantry
products the students were donating. Melanie was clapping
her hands when she caught Lynch's eye. He was positioned at
the foot of the stairs at stage right. She motioned toward the
Walkers. He gave her a thumbs-up.

The play went on for another hour and a half, with parents shooting videos and photos, trying to capture their children's performances. At the end of each routine, the children
presented Audrey with wagons of food. By the end of the festival, the school had collected hundreds of canned goods,
and boxes of rice and pasta. The event was an enormous success. As the audience ambled out to the hallway, Mr. and
Mrs. Walker approached Melanie.

"Ms. Drake, I want to thank you for everything you've
done for our family. We very much appreciate your going the
extra mile for us. Especially me." Mr. Walker was very con-
genial.

"I'm so happy things are working out," Melanie replied.

"Yes, thank you, Ms. Drake." Mrs. Walker took Melanie's
hand and gave it a squeeze. "From the bottom of my heart."

"I took your advice and enrolled in two online classes,"
Mr. Walker continued. "There's a position open at my company that will take me off the loading dock and into the office as soon as I complete the courses. I told my boss I wanted
to apply for it and was going to school. He suddenly had a
different opinion of me and offered to help. Fancy that."

"I am very happy to hear it." Melanie was thrilled. "Communication can be a wonderful thing."

Jerome wiggled his way through the crowd, palm leaves

slapping everyone along the way. "Thank you for everything. Have a happy Thanksgiving."

"Same to you. Remember, my door is always open." She smiled at the reunited family. "For all of you."

After several minutes of small talk, Melanie had to make a quick exit. She had two new family members waiting for her. She was relieved Shannon hadn't asked her to make anything for their Thanksgiving dinner. "Just bring wine," was the request Melanie had hoped for.

When Melanie returned home, Cosmo and Kramer were sitting at attention near the front door. "Hello, my furry friends." She bent over to give them pats and hugs. "You guys settling in okay?" She went into the kitchen and let them out. "You know where your bathroom is, right?" They scampered right over to it. "Apparently so," she said out loud and waited. She wanted to observe their pattern. Would they wander around the yard or come straight back inside? Within minutes, they were back at the door. She thought they might need a little coaching, but that could wait until morning.

She looked down to see if they'd eaten any of their kibble. The bowls were empty. "Aw, you guys want something else?" They looked up at her, trying to understand this new language. She opened a can of food and put it in two separate navy-blue bowls and placed them on the mat. The dogs didn't move. Melanie remembered they were trained to respond to a command. "Okay. Go for it." She wasn't sure if that was the proper way to say it, but they seemed to get the gist and went for the food. Her own stomach grumbled on cue. She hadn't eaten anything since lunch.

She peered into the refrigerator. There were some leftovers from the Greek takeout. She fixed a plate and poured a glass of wine. She scooted past the two big dogs, went into the living room, and turned on the TV. One of the channels was

broadcasting the Macy's Thanksgiving Day Parade preparation, showing the balloons being inflated. She had to admit,
she liked this part better than the actual parade. The dogs returned to their beds and settled in. Within an hour, she was
ready to hit the sheets. It was going to be a big day tomorrow. It was the first holiday dinner hosted by her sister-in-
law, and then she would be on a shopping spree for the next
two days. She made a note to buy colored contact lenses and
fake nails. She normally wore her nails short with a French
manicure, but she would change it up according to her disguise. As soon as she stood, the dogs lifted their heads. "Do
you want to come upstairs with me?" She brought her dishes
into the kitchen and put them in the dishwasher while the
dogs waited for their next command. "Okay, guys, come!"
Both sprang to attention and met her at the bottom of the
stairs. "Why can't men be as accommodating?" Kramer
cocked his head. "I said, why can't men be as accommodating?" He just stared. "And there it is. The blank stare." She
chortled. "Come on." She climbed the steps, and the two
dogs followed.

When they reached the bedroom, the dogs sat at attention.
Melanie wondered if they would climb into bed with her. It
could be rather tight. She was glad she'd opted for the king-
size bed. It took up a few more inches, so she'd put her
dresser in one of the other bedrooms. Then she wondered if
she should go downstairs and get their dog beds. She looked
at the dogs. "I guess I didn't think this part through." There
were two small area rugs on each side of the bed that could
serve the purpose until they decided on sleeping arrange-
ments. Or she could buy two more dog beds for her room.
Another thought for another day. For the next few, she
would be concentrating on creating the various faces of
Melanie Drake.

The next morning, she woke up and swung her legs off the

bed, hitting Cosmo in the head. She'd forgotten about her new roommates for a moment. He let out a soft noise. Not a whimper, but more of a *Huh? Why did you do that?*

"Sorry, pal. We're going to have to get used to the new situation. Remember, life is a series of adjustments. More on that later." She stepped into the ballet flats she used for slippers and donned a robe. The dogs sat and waited for the next command. "Come." And they did.

She let the dogs out and fixed a cup of coffee for herself. Once again, they returned immediately to the door. She decided to take her coffee outside and let them have some more fresh air. She sat on the steps of the deck. They sat at attention next to her. "Go play." She waved her arms. Maybe they needed something to fetch. She reached over and picked up a twig lying on the ground and flung it as far as she could. "Go!" The dogs bolted immediately toward the piece of wood. She noticed Kramer got there first. Melanie thought Cosmo probably needed more time to adjust to his new surroundings because of his impaired sight. He galloped behind Kramer as the other dog brought the stick back to Melanie. "Good job!" She patted both of them. She threw the stick again, but this time, not as far. Kramer still beat Cosmo to it, but he let Cosmo pick it up and bring it back. Melanie watched in awe. "Talk about being a team player."

Again she praised them. She finished off her java and stood. The dogs sat waiting for her command. "Come on." She made her way to the side door and let them in. She decided this would become part of her morning routine. Coffee with the dogs and a stick. Maybe a ball, too.

She went into the living room, and they followed her. "You guys can sit and watch the parade. I have to change." They understood the word *sit*. It was *parade* and *change* that probably confused them.

Melanie went into the small bedroom that was now serving as her dressing room. She didn't have a lot of clothes at the moment, but that was going to change shortly. She wondered where else she would be able to wear her new wardrobe once this mission was over. She would try to keep that in mind when she went shopping.

She picked out a pair of black trousers and a rust-colored turtleneck sweater. Her blunt, collarbone-length hair was pulled back with a matching headband. One black lacquer bracelet sat on her wrist outside the cuff. Presentable, casual, and holiday-ready.

As she was about to leave, she let the dogs out one more time. Melanie was thankful she didn't have to go through potty training with them. She walked them to the living room. "You guys stay. I'll be back in a few hours." She used the hand signal to tell them they could lie down. Another thing she was thankful for. She hardly had to teach them anything. She'd work on the playtime thing with them. And the snuggling thing, too.

She grabbed the insulated wine bag and placed two bottles of sauvignon blanc in it, then headed toward the door. "Be good. See you soon!" she called out to her guys. She laughed at the realization she had someone to talk to. "At least they're not judgmental." She wondered, "Or are they?" Again, she laughed.

Melanie drove the forty minutes to her brother's house. Her parents were already there, waiting for Shannon's mom and dad to arrive. Justin greeted her with open arms. "This is great! Our first Thanksgiving here, and with you!"

Melanie took a step back. "Okay. What have you done with my brother? He's never this happy to see me."

Justin burst out laughing. "Dad paid me to say it."

"That's more like it." She smiled and handed him the wine. He set it down on the small side table in the foyer.

Shannon came from the kitchen, looking as if she had just stepped out of *Vogue*. "Fifteen minutes," she called to the two women who were preparing the meal. A man stood behind her, carrying a tray of champagne glasses. Why on earth had Melanie thought Shannon would be cooking? Or serving? *She plans parties for a living. Duh.* Justin took Melanie's coat and hung it in the closet. The bell rang, and Shannon's parents entered the foyer. Justin took their coats as the man with the tray passed around the glasses. She held up her flute. "Cheers!" A variety of salutations were expressed by everyone else.

Shannon ushered her guests into the living room, where a fire crackled inside a large white marble fireplace with a black slate hearth. When Justin was stationed overseas, he'd shipped a Persian rug home, and it was now the centerpiece of the living room. Overstuffed chairs, a love seat, and sofa sat on the perimeter of the rug, facing the warmth and the glow.

Everyone took a seat except Shannon. She stood in the doorway, whispering instructions to the man who'd served the champagne. He quickly disappeared and then reappeared minutes later with a tray of hors d'oeuvres. After everyone took a few pieces, he placed the tray on the glass cocktail table.

"Dinner will be served in about fifteen minutes. Until then, I think we could use a refill." Before she had time to ask, the gentleman in the white jacket brought another bottle of champagne into the room.

Melanie had never seen her sister-in-law in action before. She was slick. No wonder she was able to cater to the elite. After several more minutes of chitchat, a dinner bell rang in the dining room. "Dinner is now being served," she announced, and slowly swept her arm in the direction of the dining room.

The table was beautifully set with a centerpiece of seasonal flowers, branches, and tea lights. Burgundy napkins were folded in the shape of a rose with a place card and centered on plates from the Wedgwood Cornucopia china collection. Schott Zwiesel wineglasses and Mepra Vintage flatware finished the place settings. Melanie was totally impressed. Shannon had gone to a lot of trouble. On second thought, her staff had gone to a lot of trouble. She didn't want to throw shade on her sister-in-law's fabulous table setting, but it was nice to have people to do all the work.

Melanie liked Shannon. At first, she'd thought Shannon and her brother might be mismatched. Shannon came from money and influence, but she never appeared to be spoiled. She didn't act in the way other rich girls would behave. Shannon had a successful business, and she worked hard at keeping a lot of people happy. It couldn't be an easy job. Melanie rethought her first reaction. Shannon had really gone to a lot of trouble to make this dinner beautiful, and delicious. Melanie also considered how smart it was for Shannon to have a staff prepare and serve. It allowed Shannon to enjoy her family and the dinner. Together. No one had to get up and help clear the table or do the dishes. Yes, Shannon was one smart cookie.

When it came time for dessert, Shannon suggested everyone return to the living room. Moans of delight echoed around the table as people pushed themselves away. Melanie was the first to enter the living room and began to browse the bookshelves. Lots of biographies about international heads of state, religious leaders, and scientists. She couldn't tell which books belonged to her brother and which to Shannon. Perhaps that was their common ground.

The others came shuffling in, commenting on how full they were and that they'd never be able to eat again. "Until leftovers," Justin joked. "Honey, I hope you told them to save some stuffing for me."

"They made a special batch just for you." Shannon smiled. Melanie appreciated how considerate Shannon was of her brother. Maybe she and her sister-in-law could become good friends now that Melanie was settled in her new job, with a house and dogs.

"We should have dinner or brunch one day," Melanie suggested while the miniature apple tarts and pumpkin soufflé ramekins were being passed around.

Shannon almost looked surprised. She and Melanie hadn't spent much time together and never went out alone. Shannon thought Melanie was a bit of an introvert. What she didn't know was that Melanie had gotten used to not being able to open up to people outside her agent sphere.

"I'd like that." Shannon placed her hand on Melanie's shoulder. "Let's put something on the calendar when I get back to my office on Monday."

"Perfect," Melanie replied.

Justin sidled over to where the women were talking. "What are the two of you up to?"

"Nothing." Melanie looked up in the air, as if she were trying to hide something.

"Come on. Spill," Justin insisted.

Melanie reached over to touch the side of his head. "What do we have here?" She produced a playing card.

Shannon laughed out loud. "I had no idea you could do that!"

"Yeah. When we say Melanie is up to her old tricks, we have to clarify which one it is."

At that point, Shannon's dad wanted to see a few more.

"I'm going to need a full deck, because as my brother would attest, I'm not playing with one." Everyone chuckled. Ever since she'd started her new job, she always carried at least one playing card with her for good luck, and for any kid who might be crying on the playground.

Shannon went over to the antique desk in the corner and brought over a fresh deck. She handed it to Melanie. "Let's see what you have up your sleeve," she teased.

Melanie shuffled the cards and did one of the simplest tricks her Uncle Leo had taught her. She was asked several times how she did it but repeated what she always told people: "We magicians are not allowed to reveal our secrets. It's our code."

The magic show brought the late afternoon to an end. Justin retrieved his guests' coats, and Shannon handed everyone a goodie bag filled with cardboard containers of turkey, ham, stuffing, sweet potatoes, broccolini, and biscuits. "I won't have to cook for a week!" Melanie exclaimed. "Thank you so much, Shannon. It's been a fantastic day. Food, beverages, décor. All of it." Melanie kissed her on the cheek. "We will plan that brunch."

Shannon smiled. "Yes, we shall."

The guests exited at the same time, bidding each other a fine evening. The Drakes walked Melanie to her car. Her mother was the first to speak. "I'm so glad you and Shannon are going to get together."

"Me too, Mom." Melanie gave both of her parents a peck on the cheek. "Christmas Eve at my house!" she called out to everyone. "I'll hire Shannon," she whispered to her mother.

Chapter Fifteen

Gucci, Armani, Dior, Oh My

Melanie set her alarm for an early start on Friday. She wanted to do a little online browsing before she began her shopping expedition. Otherwise, she could be overwhelmed, confused, and get nothing accomplished. Her first look was at Dior. She saw a beautiful gold lamé midi dress with a plunging neckline. Price tag, $6,900. She gasped. "Patterson would kill me." She continued to look through other websites and discovered most of the clothes cost several mortgage payments. An Armani washed silk jumpsuit was the least expensive at $3,595. She picked up her phone. Patterson answered on the first ring.

"What's up, MelDrake?"

"Do you know how much some of these outfits cost?" She'd known designer clothes were expensive, but seeing the price tags took her breath away.

"They want four high-end personas. That means high-end clothing."

Melanie hesitated. "Do I get to keep any of it?"

Patterson snorted. "Is that all you're concerned about?"

"No! But you do realize I have to get shoes and handbags, too? This could run into tens of thousands of dollars!"

"Then make sure you get something you will wear again."

"Does that mean I get to keep the clothes?"

"Let's just say, if the operation goes well, you could very well uncover millions of dollars of illegal transactions."

"Kinda my commission?" Melanie said lightly.

"Perhaps. Just don't go too crazy like spending seven thousand dollars on a Valentino evening bag."

"Roger that. I think I've got it covered," Melanie said.

"Good luck!" Patterson said as he ended the call.

Melanie put the credit card in her wallet along with a few ten- and twenty-dollar bills, just in case she had to tip anyone. Shopping at exclusive boutiques was not part of her routine.

She checked on the dogs, who had been outside for almost an hour. Cosmo and Kramer were sunning themselves on the deck. Melanie smiled. It wasn't going to take them too long to adjust to their new digs.

It was supposed to be a crisp sunny day, and she decided to leave the doggie door unlatched so Cosmo and Kramer could come and go as they pleased. She checked the back gate to be sure it was locked. She doubted anyone would attempt to enter a property where two large German shepherds lived, and good luck if they did.

Melanie drove to Tyson's Galleria and used the valet parking service. She had her list and began at Neiman Marcus in the Dolce & Gabbana shop, where she walked to the sales associate and asked for the banded stretch lace cocktail dress in black. "Size eight, please."

"Of course, signorina," the woman said with an Italian accent. "One moment." A few minutes later, the woman reappeared with the knee-length, sleeveless dress. She showed Melanie to a private dressing room, where she quickly pulled

off her slacks and sweater and wiggled into the beautiful con-
fection. She gave a spin before the mirror. "Perfect." She
hung the dress up and handed it back to the sales associate.
"I'll take it."

"Would signorina care to try others?"

"No, thank you." She slipped back into her clothes, and
out came the credit card. When they were at the register,
Melanie asked, "Could I leave the bag with you? I have a lot
of shopping to do."

"Yes, of course. We have a valet service that will bring
your purchases to your car when you are finished shopping."

*Of course you do. Heaven forbid someone should have to
lug around shopping bags filled with thousands of dollars'
worth of goodies.* Melanie played along. "Oh, yes. It's been a
while since I shopped here." The woman gave Melanie her
receipt and a call tag.

"The valet is on the main floor near the south entrance."

"Thank you. You've been very helpful." Melanie decided
to wait until she'd purchased all the clothing before she
bought shoes and handbags. She checked her list. Next was
Dior.

Again, she approached a sales associate and told her exactly what she wanted. "The Cady gold lamé midi, please.
Size eight." Just as before, the salesperson retrieved the dress
and showed Melanie to a dressing room. Off came her slacks
and sweater and on went the fluid, lamé dress, cascading
down her body. "Wow!" Melanie almost didn't recognize
herself. The gown was stunning. She gently removed the
dress and handed it to the salesperson. Another, "I'll take it!"

During the transaction, she showed the woman her call
tag, and she replied, "Certainly. We'll send it down for you."

Next stop, Armani. "The washed silk jumpsuit in gray.
Size eight, please." It was the same routine.

Lastly, Chanel. This time, it was a short cream-colored
bouclé jacket, with a cream-colored silk blouse and matching

silk Bermuda-length shorts. She'd wear sheer white stockings with it.

Now it was on to shoes. First stop was Gucci. Black moire fabric, slingback heels. As she walked past the stores, her attention went to a spectacular pair of Louboutin yellow patent leather pumps. She could wear them with the Chanel outfit. That might be the only time, but they were on sale! Originally $800, but today, they were merely $500. She couldn't resist. She'd never had a pair of stilettos and went into the store to try them on. They certainly made her much taller, but they also accented her long, well-toned legs. "Why not?" She gave herself permission. She also spotted another pair of Christian Louboutin shoes. These were a neutral block heel sandal that would go with anything.

One more pair and she would move on to handbags. She stopped at the Bottega Veneta shop and bought a pair of black ankle boots with a mid-heel. She'd be able to wear those again, too.

She browsed the handbag boutiques on the main floor of Saks. First was a Mach & Mach iridescent top handle bag, then an Alexander Wang faded neon, and a black silk Oscar de le Renta purse. She also stopped at a few perfume counters. She couldn't risk smelling the same, either. She bought the smallest versions of Baccarat Rouge 540, Chanel Coco Mademoiselle, and Tom Ford's Black Orchid. As much as she liked Carolina Herrera's Good Girl, she didn't understand why the bottle was in the shape of a stiletto. What were you supposed to do with it when you were finished with the perfume? She adored Creed's Wind Flowers, but it was too expensive for her to justify the $425 bottle, so she settled on Hermès Eau des Merveilles Bleue. It was much more reasonable at $150. She snickered at the word "settled."

Melanie made her way to the main level and approached the valet station. She showed him her call tag. "Does madam also have a car with us?"

Melanie dug the ticket out of her purse, which was looking very shabby after all the gorgeous and glimmering things she'd seen during her quest. She handed the ticket to the young man. "We'll have your car and purchases for you momentarily."

Melanie sighed. *So this is how the one-percent lives.* She remembered when the saying used to be "the other half."

It was almost four o'clock by the time she pulled into her driveway. She was bushed. Who knew spending tens of thousands of dollars on clothes could be so exhausting? She could hear a bark coming from the other side of the fence. At least one of her boys was enjoying the fresh air. She would have to learn the difference in their barks.

She clicked the hatch open and grabbed half the shopping bags. They even smelled expensive. She brought her purchases into her newly appointed dressing room and hung them on the rolling clothes rack she'd bought. She decided it would be much more convenient if she could keep all of her clothes in one place instead of swapping them in and out of storage boxes when the seasons changed.

Melanie paired the shoes and purses with the dresses. She gazed at her new wardrobe. It was rather spectacular. Tomorrow would be wigs, nails, and contact lenses. She made an appointment at a specialty shop and told them what she was looking for: one short cropped blond wedge; one wavy auburn shoulder-length; one black chin-length bob, and one white blunt cut to her collarbone, with bangs. The salon told her they could accommodate her, and she should come in the morning for a fitting.

She needed a nap. She flopped on her bed and went out like a light. The next thing she heard was the sound of dogs barking in the yard. She woke with a start. First off, she wasn't used to hearing dogs bark, and second, she had no idea what time it was. But it was dark. She checked her watch. It was after seven o'clock. She heard a car door shut and looked out the window. It was Gilmour. She'd forgotten he was stopping by to go over some details.

She slapped some cold water on her face, dragged a brush through her hair, and ran a tube of lipstick across her mouth. She stared at the lipstick for a second. She'd never cared about how she looked in front of Gilmour before. Why now? Maybe it was all the heady perfume she inhaled while shopping. Every boutique was filled with the delicious scent of something.

Gilmour used the door knocker he had given her as a housewarming gift. It was a bronze Irish horseshoe and this-tle with HERE'S LUCK inscribed on it.

"Coming!" Melanie raced down the stairs.

"Did I wake you?"

"Actually, you did."

"Long day at the boutiques?"

"Actually, yes. Who knew?" Melanie stepped aside to let him in. "Let me see what my dogs are up to." She could hear them barking in the yard.

A few minutes later, Melanie returned with Cosmo and Kramer. "Sit." And they obeyed. "Imagine how easy life would be if people behaved like they do?"

"Settling in okay?"

"Yes. I thought it was going to be a big adjustment, but they are so well-trained."

"They have no idea how good they have it now." Gilmour patted each of them on the head.

"Oh, I don't know about that. Yesterday they got to lie around and watch the Macy's parade."

Gilmour chuckled. "Mel, I have to say, you've blossomed in your new life. You look happy."

"Amazing, isn't it?" She gestured for him to take a seat. He maneuvered around the German shepherd obstacle course and eased into the sofa. "Did you bring food?"

Gilmour laughed. "Was I supposed to do that? I thought you were going to cook."

"Hardly. I had way too much to do today. Shopping and all." She went into the kitchen and opened the fridge. "Leftovers?"

"Oh, no. I don't think I can stuff more stuffing in my face. How about we order some ribs? There's a new place a few miles away. It's called Memphis Pig Out. They might deliver." He pulled out his phone, looked it up, and called. Much to his delight, he learned two "meat and threes" specials could be delivered in a half hour. He called out to Melanie, "What sides do you want?"

She figured the usual collard greens, corn, mashed potatoes, and sweet potato fries were available. "How about one of everything?"

"It's called "meat and threes" because you get three sides."

"Okay. You pick one type of potato, and I'll get the other one."

Gilmour placed the order and walked into the kitchen.

"Did you see Patterson?" she asked.

"I did. The exhibit is next Thursday. He told me to remind you he needs photos for your IDs."

"I'll be ready for them on Monday, I hope. It's not easy creating a new persona on such short notice."

"Come on, Cracker Jack. You can do it," Gilmour encouraged her.

"Well, I have all my outfits. I can't believe I spent over twenty-five thousand dollars today. That's almost a year's worth of mortgage payments!"

"And there are people who live like that all the time."

"Do you think it makes them happy?" Melanie asked thoughtfully.

"What, the money?" he asked.

"Spending it."

"Apparently so. People spend money on the dumbest things."

"Conspicuous consumption. It was an eighties thing."

"And it's back."

Melanie pulled out one of the dining room chairs and slid her yellow pad over so it was in front of her. "What's the plan?"

Gilmour explained she would be a guest at a private exhibit at a diplomat's house. "One of the grand brownstones in Georgetown."

"And why am I being invited?" Melanie asked, wanting to know her cover story.

"You are a curator for a Greek tycoon. He heard about this new artist, and you asked if you could see some of his work. The artist informed your assistant that none of the pieces on display were for sale, but if the gentleman wanted to commission something, it could be arranged. I suppose the artist wanted to sound legit."

"And you think he's not?"

"I think *he* thinks he might be, but Mahdi Alkali may have other ideas." He took out his notes and continued. "Here is a floor plan of the townhouse. The main living area is on the second floor." He pointed to one of the rooms. "This is where the paintings will be on display. You'll chat up a few people, and then you'll slip this into Alkali's pocket." He handed her a very small object, the size of a pencil eraser, just as she had been told.

"What about me?"

Gilmour handed her a velvet pouch. It contained a silver and black Edwardian brooch. "Can you wear this with any of your new threads?"

"Yes. I can wear it with the black dress, front and center. Does it have matching earrings?" Melanie was quite serious. She needed an earpiece.

"Yes, my lady." He produced another pouch.

"These aren't real, are they?" Melanie had to ask. Everything was a secret sideshow.

"No, but the jeweler we use promised no one will be able to tell unless they have an eyepiece."

"Where will you be during all this?"

"I'll be your humble servant. They got me a gig passing hors d'oeuvres."

"So when I arrive, what's my first move?"

He handed her the engraved invitation. "Show this to the gorilla at the door. As soon as possible, introduce yourself to the host. Then a little later, you plant the device on him."

"Is it GPS or audio?"

"Audio. We want to hear what he's saying to people. The agency's van will be in the alley, marked like the rest of the catering vehicles."

The dogs stood at attention when a car pulled into the driveway. Gilmour got up to see who it was, the dogs following. "Delivery!" he called out.

"I'll get the dishes." Melanie quickly pulled out the tableware as Gilmour paid the man.

Gilmour came into the kitchen with his head partly hidden by the bag. "This smells delicious! I don't remember the last time I had ribs."

Melanie grabbed a roll of paper towels. "I think we're going to need these."

The only sounds after that were groans of delight, finger licking, and lip smacking. "I'm really liking my neighborhood," Melanie exclaimed.

As they were finishing up, Gilmour asked, "So will I be able to recognize you?"

"That would be the true litmus test, now, wouldn't it?"

She scraped the dishes and put them in the dishwasher. "What about the other escorts? How many people will be attending?"

"Guest list says fifty. Some of the men will be with their wives, but there will be a smattering of other sophisticated women such as yourself."

"This should be very interesting."

"Yeah. Ready to take a walk on the wild side?"

"According to Patterson, it's supposed to be a walk in the park." She let the dogs out one more time. "Your turn." She pointed to the door. "I've got to get my beauty sleep."

The next day was another shopping jaunt. This time to the wig boutique. The wig fitting was a hoot, and she was lucky enough to get exactly what she wanted. Each outfit required a certain look if she wanted to appear authentic. You didn't wear Chanel with a Mohawk. She stopped at a national eyewear chain and picked up four pairs of contacts: violet, turquoise blue, green, and gray. She stopped at a drugstore and purchased several pairs of press-on nails in French, red, and gray. She wondered who'd come up with the idea of painting fingernails. Of course, Melanie had to find out and discovered it was believed the practice began over 3,000 years ago in China, where the color of one's nails represented one's social status. She speculated what the color gray represented. When she finished, she went to a secret location to have photos taken with the variety of wigs and different makeup looks. Good enough for fake passport and driver's license photos.

Chapter Sixteen

Back to Business

The Monday after Thanksgiving weekend was a slog. Everyone was overstuffed, over tired, over football, parades, complaining, arguing about politics, and hearing the same stories year after year. Melanie hoped there wouldn't be any crying or fighting. She was tired from running all over the county, pulling together the many sides of Melanie. She reviewed everything in her head. She couldn't think of anything else and hoped there would be no surprises. This assignment was as big a surprise as she could stand.

Melanie knew she had to get home early and get some rest. She had to be on her toes for Thursday's soiree at Mahdi Al-kali's. Lots of foreign diplomat license plates filled the city streets, as well as the suburbs. It was curious that most people didn't know what these diplomats did. It seemed as if they hung around embassies and ordered each other around. It was as if they existed under an impenetrable cloud. She wondered how Shannon got into the business of catering to these mysterious people. She decided she'd ask her over brunch.

She checked her desk planner. Luckily, it was a light week.

There were no parent-teacher conferences, no soccer practice, no school plays. The biggest challenge was all the paperwork. She was inundated with surveys, questionnaires, and reports about sharing information with parents. She was submitting the same information over and over to different groups. Why wasn't there a template so she didn't have to repeat her responses? *Ah, bureaucracy.* Everything seemed to be a political football. She thought she had gotten away from most of it when she left the agency, but no. Bureaucracy was everywhere. Melanie sighed. She remembered her new slogan: change the world one kid at a time. Maybe when they were grown-ups, people would be kinder and more tolerant. She prayed.

The week started with a new schedule for Melanie, Cosmo, and Kramer. *Up at six o'clock. Dogs go out. Melanie makes coffee and toast. Dogs come in. Dogs get fed. Dogs go out again. Melanie takes a shower and gets dressed. Dogs come in. Melanie goes to work. After work, Melanie goes home. Dogs go out. Dogs come in. Melanie fixes dinner for herself and the dogs. They watch TV. Dogs go out. Melanie goes to bed.* She found the routine reassuring. *At least until Thursday.*

Then the day came. The morning routine was normal, although she had a bit of the jitters. Decaf. It had been several years since she was in action. The past two years, she'd been in graduate school, and before that, she was doing desk duty. She took a few meditative breaths and continued on the day's path.

The morning at school was the usual. Good morning, behave, etc. She kept checking her watch, the hall clock, and the timepiece on her desk. The minutes were moving at a snail's pace. She couldn't phone Patterson or Gilmour with any questions. Going forward, everything except her surveillance device was on paper.

When the final bell rang, she jumped from her seat. Partly from nerves, and partly to get this mission moving. She arrived home by four. The dogs were now greeting her at the door, always sitting at attention. "Smart fellas. Didn't take you long to figure out I was your new mommy, eh?" Their tales pounded a rhumba rhythm on the floor. "Come on." She entered the kitchen and let the dogs out.

She showered and dried her hair, and wrapped it in a skullcap. Next came the makeup. She started with a heavy concealer for her scar. A porcelain foundation to contrast with the black dress. Her eyeshadow was dramatic, with black eyeliner circling the deep blue contact lenses, finished off with dark eyebrows. She enhanced her cheekbones with contrasting blush. Ruby red lipstick, and a black wig. She took a long look and smiled. She barely recognized herself. She pinned the brooch in front of her sternum, the best placement for picking up her conversations. She slipped on the slingback shoes, grabbed the silk purse, and gave herself a spritz of Coco Mademoiselle. She went to the back door to let the dogs in. They stopped, sniffed, and tilted their heads. "No, Mommy doesn't smell the same or look the same. But I can assure you it's me." She held the door open, and they obediently went inside. They knew their dinner was waiting, regardless of who this strange woman was.

At five thirty, a black town car pulled into her driveway. She looked at the dogs. "Okay, my canine pals, it's showtime!"

Melanie had read somewhere that rich people rarely wore coats because they were chauffeured everywhere, never having to stand in the cold.

The driver greeted her at the front door. "Good evening, Ms. Carlyle. My name is James Collier." He was carrying a gorgeous silk and cashmere wrap. "In case you get a chill."

"Thank you." She couldn't help noticing the tag on the shawl: Brunello Cucinelli. *There goes another 1800 dollars.*

This one I'm keeping. She checked her handbag for the fifth time to be sure she had everything.

It took about forty minutes to reach the diplomat's residence. There were well over a dozen black town cars, limousines, and SUVs double-parked, most with diplomat plates. All had dark tinted windows. Melanie could tell which vehicles were police by the configuration of the headlights.

James came around and opened her door. "You may leave your wrap with me if you so choose." He had a slight accent. UK? New Zealand? She didn't and couldn't ask. No small talk.

"Thank you, James." Melanie snickered to herself, wondering if that were his real name.

"According to the schedule, I am to pick you up in two hours, unless you need me here sooner." He handed her a small device, the size of a flash drive. "Just press this button and I'll be outside."

"Thank you." Melanie, now known as Sylvia Carlyle, showed the security staff her invitation and her identification.

"Good evening, Ms. Carlyle. Enjoy the exhibit." The man had a Mediterranean accent. Possibly Albanian.

Melanie Drake, aka Sylvia Carlyle, gracefully and confidently climbed the marble steps as if she was supposed to be there. Another gentleman in a black suit, black turtleneck, and an obvious earpiece opened the door for her. She showed him the invitation, as well. "Enjoy the evening." Definitely Albanian. Melanie was well aware the Albanian mafia was active all over the world, including the Middle East. It came as no surprise the agency had their eye on Mr. Mahdi Alkali.

Melanie entered the main living room and was handed a cocktail. Something exotic, she assumed. All heads turned as she passed through the crowd. She had an air of assurance, and beauty to match. She sidled up to Mr. Alkali and extended her hand.

"And who is this wonderful work of art?" he said as he kissed the back of her hand.

Smarmy. "Good evening. I'm Sylvia Carlyle. I appreciate your allowing me to view Mr. Bayard's work."

He gave her a curious look. Melanie knew she had to explain her presence. "I'm the curator for Mr. Poulos, the Greek shipping magnate. He is interested in Pierre's work. I know none of the work here is for sale, but Mr. Poulos asked if I could review it for him, so he could, perhaps, have something commissioned. I trust I am not intruding." She focused her steely blue eyes on his.

"No, not at all. You bring more beauty to this affair. Please, follow me. I'll give you a personal tour." They crossed through the foyer, and a guard unhooked the red velvet rope.

Melanie couldn't believe how easily she was accepted as Alkali showed her to the large room that held the exhibit. She surmised dressing well, smelling good, and flirting could take a girl a long way.

"How long have you worked for Mr. Poulos?" he asked.

"Just a few months. I was studying abroad when I met him. He wanted someone to cover up-and-coming artists in the States."

"Tell me more about Mr. Bayard. How did you discover him?" She peered at one of the paintings. The plaque said MORNING'S BRIGHTNESS, but it was a very bad imitation of Jackson Pollock, who had absolutely no brightness in his work or his life. Bayard's piece was orange and red splatter. Melanie thought some of the kids in her school could do a better job finger painting. She murmured, "Interesting," a polite way of saying "I don't get it."

"Yes. I think all of his work is interesting." He emphasized the word as if he knew she was mocking it.

Trying to regroup, Melanie moved to another piece that showed more promise. This one was called MIDNIGHT'S DARKNESS, an apt description of the dark streaks of blue, gray, and black. "Now this one speaks to me." She stepped back to get a different perspective.

"Ah. That is one of my favorites." Alkali seemed pleased.

"How many pieces do you own?" Melanie asked.

"Fourteen. All are on display here." He scanned the room. At that point, another man speaking in Arabic came over to Alkali. "If you'll please excuse me? The artist is about to arrive, and we must close the room for a short time."

Melanie linked her arm through his as he escorted her to the large hand-carved double doors that led to the foyer. He showed no sign of awareness when Melanie slipped the eraser-size device into his pocket. "Please enjoy the food service. We shall have the official opening in just a few minutes."

He retreated into the room with the paintings. A man with a tray of exotic cocktails came up to her. "Would madame care for a Bekka Highball?" It was Gilmour, serving up a mixture of Calvados, Lillet Blanc, white grape juice, champagne, and tonic. "It's rather refreshing."

Melanie took a glass from the tray. As she sipped, she muttered, "Made the drop."

The crew in the van parked in the alley could hear her loud and clear. Now it was time to listen to what was going on behind closed doors.

"These are not my frames!" Bayard shouted. "I frame my own work. It's part of the artistic experience."

"Please, Pierre. I prefer the more ornate look," Alkali said calmly.

"This will not do. I will take all my work back!" Bayard was practically screaming.

"Pierre, please calm down. I will pay you double."

Bayard was apoplectic. "Do you think I will compromise my work for money?"

"The fact that you have already sold your paintings to me

indicates you will, and you did. A small adjustment is all I ask." Alkali finished with, "They technically belong to me now unless you want to unwind our deal." He paused. "It is a generous offer."

Bayard knew he was not going to pay back the $200,000 Alkali had given him. He'd already spent most of it on a car, clothes, and a deposit on a rental in the Hamptons for the summer. Another two hundred grand would get him a villa in Ibiza.

"Fine. But I want that money deposited in my account before the night is over."

"Of course," Alkali said quite calmly. "I'll arrange for it right now." Alkali reached into his pocket to retrieve his phone. He found something that looked like a ball of lint and flicked it onto the floor. He exited the room and spoke with one of his associates, who quickly disappeared.

The agent who was listening popped out his earpiece. Gilmour heard the clatter, as well. "Houston," he muttered to Melanie. That was code for *We have a problem.* Both knew she couldn't get down on her hands and knees to look for the piece. She would have to proceed without the listening device.

She took the first opportunity to get the attention of the artist, introducing herself as a curator in search of new talent. She asked simple questions such as where his studio was, what time of day he preferred to work, what medium was his favorite. After he finished answering her inquiries, the next question was easy. "Do you frame your own work, or do you have a woodworking artist do it for you?"

Bayard's nostrils flared a bit. "I always frame my own work. It's part of the process. But those are not mine." He nodded toward the room with the velvet stanchion. "He made the swap after I sold the paintings. I really had no idea he was going to do that." Pierre tried to hide his annoyance, but was not doing a very good job of it.

"That's a shame. People do not understand the blood, sweat, tears, and joy that go into creative work."

"You got that right." The artist seemed less peeved now that he'd let off some steam to someone who clearly appreciated the artistic process. "Follow me." He led Melanie to the velvet stanchion. The guard let them pass through.

"I saw some of the pieces earlier. I particularly liked MIDNIGHT'S DARKNESS."

"Come. I'll show you." The two walked over to the painting. He showed her the area where his frame should have been. "Mine are much thinner. Not as deep."

Melanie took a closer look at the depth of the frame. "Yes, it does seem a bit cumbersome."

"Finally! Someone who understands!" Pierre announced.

A bell rang from the front room. Alkali made an announcement. "Ladies and gentlemen, I am pleased to present my personal collection of Pierre Bayard's work." People clapped politely and made their way into the big room. They milled around, making comments in a foreign language. Melanie could only imagine what they were saying. She set her untouched Bekka on a side table and meandered around the room until she was near Gilmour, who was standing with a fresh tray of cocktails.

Melanie plucked a new one from the tray and checked to be sure no one was in earshot. "There's something behind the paintings. I am sure of it."

The agents could hear Melanie through her encrusted brooch. "Not deep enough for a substantial amount of drugs. Must be papers of some kind." She took a sip of her drink, pretending to peruse the room while Gilmour stood at attention, pretending not to notice her.

Melanie cozied up to Alkali again. "I shall have to leave

shortly, but I wanted to thank you again for a lovely evening. I was wondering if I could impose and come back for another look?"

"Ah, alas, my lovely, the paintings are being shipped tomorrow morning."

"What service do you use?" A totally plausible question.

"I use Navis to do the packing. They will transport the paintings to my private jet."

"Navis is probably the best." She didn't want to push it and ask where he kept his jet. Most likely the agency already had that information. "Thank you again, Mr. Alkali."

"Please call me Mahdi. It would be most enjoyable to be in your company again." He handed her a business card with just his name and phone number, engraved in gold.

"Thank you, Mahdi." Melanie's fight-or-flight instinct was kicking in, but she knew she had to make as graceful an exit as her entrance.

When she reached the sidewalk, she spotted James several yards away. He walked toward her, carrying the cashmere wrap.

He opened the door and drove around the corner to the entrance of the alley. Gilmour was waiting and jumped in.

"You could get fired for abandoning your post, sir," Melanie chided him.

"Good work, Sylvia."

The driver looked in the rearview mirror. "Good to see you, boss."

Melanie turned to Gilmour. "Boss?"

"He's one of ours, Mel."

"I figured as much, but one of yours?"

"We gotta keep a tight ship. James, put the pedal to the metal, please, and take Ms. Carlyle to her humble abode."

When they arrived at Melanie's, she invited Gilmour in for a nightcap. "I think we earned it."

"James, do you mind waiting for a bit?"

"Not at all, sir." The driver got out and opened the door for Melanie. She pulled the wrap tightly around her. This one wasn't getting away.

When she unlocked the door, the dogs were waiting and cocked their heads again. "It's me!" She pulled off the wig and skullcap and ditched her shoes.

"By the way, you looked stunning tonight."

"Who wouldn't, wearing ten thousand dollars' worth of clothes?" She chuckled and led the gang into the living room.

She poured a cognac for each of them as the dogs settled into their beds. She curled up on the sofa, with Gilmour only a few inches away. They clinked glasses.

"What's the next step?" she asked.

"Since Navis is not covered under diplomatic immunity, their truck will be pulled over for a traffic violation tomorrow. The police officers will find a small amount of cocaine in the driver's seat." He used air quotes for *find*. "That will require the van to be confiscated and investigated."

"How long will it take before we find out what Alkali was trying to smuggle?"

"You and I will know by the end of the day. I don't know whether or not the State Department will make the finding public."

Another clink of the glasses. "Here's to Pierre Bayard, whose hissy fit will lead to a discovery."

The following evening, Melanie got the phone call she was hoping for. "Mel. You hit the nail on the head. It was paper. Very important paper. Highly classified paper."

"Whoa. For real?"

"For real, MelDrake. Congrats."

"I know this is a rhetorical question, but how does this kind of thing happen when we are supposedly so security conscious?"

"People get sloppy. Look at how many classified documents have been found in people's libraries, golf courses, home offices? And then there are young cyber people within the army intelligence community who are not qualified to handle such sensitive information."

"Like the national guardsman who posted documents on that gaming site."

"Yep. And look how long it was exposed before anyone noticed?"

"You're right. Sloppy."

"Well, at least we stopped one potentially dangerous situation."

"Do you know what's next on our magical mystery tour?"

"I think it's diamonds."

Melanie's eyes got wide. "Really? Do tell!"

"I can't. Not because it's classified, but because Patterson hasn't brought me up to speed yet."

"I can't wait to showcase my next outfit."

Chapter Seventeen

Diamonds Are a Girl's Best Friend . . .
Unless They're Blood Diamonds

It was finally the weekend after a very busy week. Melanie spent Saturday catching up on chores. Boredom was a welcome change from all the activity of the week. She was still mentally unpacking the events of the art exhibit. A lot had happened in a short amount of time. She wondered, and hoped, the other operations would go as smoothly.

She heard a vehicle pull into her driveway. It was the Pooper Scooper Brigade, a service that came by twice a week to dispose of the bagged doggie doings. They'd installed a pull-out bin that was accessible from both sides of the fence. It was big enough for an eight-gallon bucket, and small enough that neither a toddler nor the dogs could fit inside. It was brilliant.

By the end of the day, the laundry had been sorted, dishwasher emptied, bird feeder filled, and the front porch swept. She planned on a quiet dinner with her two companions and early to bed. Brunch with Shannon was on the next day's agenda. They were going to Café 44 at 44 Canal Center

Plaza on the Potomac. After brunch, they planned a visit to the sculpture garden.

Melanie was looking forward to forging a friendship with her sister-in-law and having a girls' afternoon together. *So this is what normal feels like?*

Around six o'clock, her phone rang. It was Gilmour. "Got a minute?"

"I was just about to make some pasta and a salad."

"I'll bring a bottle of wine."

Melanie pulled the phone away from her ear and gave it an *I don't recall inviting you* look.

As if he were reading her mind, Gilmour promptly followed with, "If you don't mind me barging in."

"Get a nice pinot noir." And she hung up. She was beginning to enjoy this new aspect of their relationship. Before she'd left the agency, they'd sometimes shared work-related meals, but recently, they were spending more time together.

"Okay, guys. Another dinner guest," she said as she placed their bowls on the floor. They never went to the food until she said, "Okay." She looked at the two magnificent animals. "We are so lucky to have each other, aren't we?" They looked up at her. She believed they were finally beginning to understand Melanie-speak.

About an hour later, Gilmour arrived with two bottles of Sonoma Coast Sojourn. He handed them to her.

"Did you know pinot noir is considered the healthiest wine to drink?" She continued, "It's because of the high levels of resveratrol. The grapes have thin skin, fewer calories, low alcohol content, and low sugar."

"When did you become a sommelier?" he teased.

"I do my homework, remember?" Melanie went to a drawer, grabbed a corkscrew, and handed one of the bottles back. "Get busy."

"Aye aye, mate!"

Melanie checked the lemon zest and parsley sauce she was making for the pasta.

"Smells delicious." He leaned in over her shoulder.

Melanie could feel the warmth of his face so close to her cheek. It was odd. Odd in that it felt quite normal. "Get away," she teased, "and pour us a glass of that lovely vintage."

"I was letting it breathe."

"It can hyperventilate in the glass," she joked, and placed the fettuccini in the boiling water.

"Is there anything I can do?"

"Set the table?"

By now, Gilmour had eaten enough meals at Melanie's that he knew where the tableware was kept. She watched him out of the corner of her eye. He seemed very comfortable. Relaxed. Come to think of it, so was she.

Melanie fixed a green salad with fresh herbs, and removed the bread that was warming in the oven. Everything was on the table, ready to enjoy. "Mangia!" she called. The dogs' ears perked up. "Do you speak Italian?"

"I think every living being reacts to the word!" Gilmour chuckled.

They talked about stuff. News. Politics. Movies. Music.

"I'm having brunch with Shannon tomorrow."

"A sister-in-law outing?"

"Kinda. I can't remember the last time I hung out with a woman my age. For fun." Melanie described their plans.

"Good for you."

"Yes. I need to get in her good graces before they start popping out kids. I want to be their favorite aunt."

"Won't you be their only aunt?"

"Only if Shannon's brother decides to remain unmarried."

"Is that on the horizon?"

"Doubtful. He just broke up with his girlfriend. Besides,

he lives in Minneapolis. He has a huge job with a banking firm. I doubt he'll be heading east any time soon."

"Well, if I know you, you are sure to be their favorite aunt."

When they finished dinner, they shared the cleanup and reconned at the dining room table.

Melanie was the first to speak. "What's the deal? I thought the next gig wasn't coming up for a while."

"They had to move it up, unless you'd like me to request a delay?"

"Funny." She rested her elbows on the table, chin in hands.

He pulled out his pad and pen and braced himself for her reaction. "It's Thursday."

"Oh, come on!" Melanie groaned. "I've barely recovered from this last escapade."

"There is a dinner at an exclusive club which is being hosted by a special envoy from France. Chatter is that diamonds from Zimbabwe were smuggled in, and they are going to be handed off to an insurgent group."

"Insurgents? Here?" Melanie had thought domestic unrest was winding down.

"No. El Salvador, and probably Haiti. The theme of the dinner is supposedly a cigar tasting. Cuban cigars."

"So someone from France is hosting a dinner in order for someone to hand off diamonds from Zimbabwe to fund an insurgency in Latin America?"

"You wanted to get into international affairs? Here you have it."

"So which country is behind this deal?"

"Unfortunately, we are dealing with international mercenaries. While some still sign up for serious battle, many have discovered it's easier to smuggle. Less physical risk, and they can avoid aligning themselves with any political party. The jobs are quicker, and the payoff is huge."

"Even mercenaries get to change their career paths," Melanie mused. "Do we know who will be carrying the diamonds and how?"

"We're not sure if Monsieur Escoffier is in on it. His history here in the States is squeaky clean. He may be a pawn. Sometimes these dignitaries are asked to host events as front men." He continued, "The only caveat for the dinner is that the men wear the club blazers during the meal."

"People still do that?" Melanie made a sour face.

"Oh, my dear MelDrake. Do you really think much has changed in the sphere of worldly men?"

She grimaced. "How far we've come and yet not so much."

Gilmour began giving her the rundown. Again, she would be picked up by James and taken to the club. There would be six men and six women at the event, including Melanie.

"Do you know who I will be seated next to?"

"I have no idea, so you're going to have to keep your eyes and ears peeled."

He pulled out another pouch. This time, the camera was hidden in a David Yurman necklace: the Streamline pavé tag in sterling silver; one side was encrusted with diamonds.

"Wow. This is stunning." She held it up to the light.

"We thought a diamond necklace might intrigue the interested party. Oh, and this is the real thing. Boss didn't want you to wear paste, especially if real diamonds are involved in the deal."

"Wow," she repeated. "I'll wear it with the Armani silk jumpsuit, the Mach & Mach bag, and the ankle boots."

"Getting a little kinky?"

"Don't be a doofus. It's *edgy*."

"And what color hair?"

"Everything I'm wearing is geometric, sculptural. Probably the white chin-length bob and gray contacts."

"Now *that* sounds kinky."

She slapped him with a kitchen towel. "Get your mind out of the gutter."

"I can tell when I'm not wanted," he joked.

"And where will you be in this?"

"I'll be doing janitorial duty."

"What do you mean?"

"I'll be the valet in the men's room. Handing out towels and cologne."

"Do you get tipped for that?"

Gilmour burst out laughing. "If only." He gathered his things, put the paperwork in a bag, and handed it to Melanie. She knew what to do with it. As she walked him to the door, she tossed the bag into the fireplace.

Melanie checked the clock on the mantel. It was past nine. The dogs were waiting at the back door for their final nightly run around the yard.

Melanie met Shannon at 44 Café at noon. It was a beautiful fall day with clear blue skies reflected in the Potomac.

They ordered mimosas while they perused the menu. "I'm so glad you suggested this." Shannon smiled across the table. "I don't think we've ever done anything like this before, have we?"

"Not that I can recall."

"It's really bad if we can't even remember whether we were ever alone together, isn't it?" Shannon said with surprise.

"I know. Shame on us." Melanie lifted her champagne glass.

"Indeed. Shame on us," Shannon replied facetiously.

The conversation was pleasant. Delightful, actually. They realized they had a lot of interests in common: art, literature, music, and space exploration. Melanie told Shannon she'd recently purchased a telescope so she could watch the night sky. "You should come over when we have the next meteor shower."

"I'll bring the champagne!" Shannon offered.

"Good deal."

When the check came, they immediately agreed to split it down the middle. "We're both working women." They almost said it at the same time.

From there, they strolled to the sculpture garden. Shannon explained she had to arrange for a small group tour for the family of Taiwan's ambassador. That reminded Melanie to ask, "How did you get into this business?"

"When I was in college, I got a summer job as an au pair for a family from Germany. I lived with them, took care of the kids, and also helped with the planning of dinners and parties. The following summer, I was an au pair for a Brazilian family. Similar duties. By the time I graduated, I'd developed a good reputation and was hired by a catering company. I was getting paid a decent salary, but after two years I thought I could run a small operation on my own. It seemed as if I was doing all the work anyway. So, I took out a small business loan and applied for a grant for women in business. I have a regular staff of five and subcontract the rest of the work to small businesses such as myself. It's a nice network. Everyone is bonded and goes through background checks."

"That is very impressive." Melanie wasn't lying. She was impressed. What she'd heard validated Melanie's initial impression that Shannon was a smart cookie. "So what's your next gig?"

"Oh, you'll love this. I have to oversee a cigar-sampling dinner at a stodgy old men's club."

Melanie almost choked on her iced latte. She coughed to conceal her shock. "What kind of dinners do they serve at stodgy old men's clubs?" Melanie thought the universe was either intervening on her behalf or plotting against her.

"It's a five-course menu. First course is chilled lobster with beluga caviar and a dab of crème fraîche. Second course is scallops in a roasted pineapple chutney."

"Sounds delish." Melanie's brain was bouncing inside her head. This was going to be trickier than she'd thought.

"Then there will be a short break, with a dollop of sorbet and a small pony of a digestif.

"That will be followed by grilled baby lamb chops served on a bed of parsnip puree, with roasted corn." Shannon thought for a moment. "Let's see, I think they settled on the mini beef Wellington. It was that or short ribs served on polenta."

"And for dessert?" Melanie couldn't imagine eating anything else, but she was curious.

"A Viennese table. Pastries, cakes, a huge selection."

"So what do you have to do to prepare?"

"Get the menu together, order centerpieces, arrange staffing. Dinners are easier than events. Dinners have a schedule. Parties are all over the place. People arrive on time for dinner. They show up whenever they want when it comes to a party. It's easier to keep track of the liquor consumption at a dinner. Sitting down for a meal also helps the level of sobriety. People go nuts at parties. Drink more than they should. Eat more than they should and say more than they should."

"Because they drank more than they should." Melanie understood completely.

"I don't think I've worked an event where there wasn't some kind of argument."

"With all these dignitaries and politicians?"

"They're the worst. You are living in the Ego Capital of the World."

"And I thought it was Hollywood." Melanie chortled.

"It's just a different set of smoke and mirrors," Shannon said as they were leaving the sculpture exhibit. They walked to the parking lot and said their goodbyes. "This was such a good idea, Melanie. Let's not wait another two years before we do it again. I hope to see you sooner than later."

Melanie thought, *not if I see you first.*

As soon as she got in her car, she phoned Gilmour and used their code word, "Houston."

"I'll meet you at your house."

They both arrived at Melanie's at the same time. Gilmour jumped out of his vehicle. "What's up?"

"Shannon is the caterer for the dinner party this week."

"Oh boy." He followed Melanie into the house, where the dogs were sitting at attention in the foyer.

"Come on, fellas." She led the dogs to the back door, let them out, and unhitched their door so they could come back in when they were ready.

Gilmour and Melanie pulled chairs out from the dining table. "How do you want to handle this?"

"I'm just going to have to do a bang-up job on my disguise. I think the white wig and overexaggerated makeup should work. I'll make a fake birthmark on the other side of my face to distract from my scar. The wig should also cover most of it."

"Are you sure you want to do this?"

"I seriously doubt Shannon is in on the diamond exchange. If she recognizes me, I'll have to tell her I'm on an assignment."

"Do you think that's wise?"

"Got any other suggestions?"

"Can you trust her?" Gilmour asked.

"Geez, I hope so. She's married to my brother." Melanie hung her head. "Okay. We will proceed according to our loosely concocted plan. Are you sure the diamonds are going to be handed off at the dinner?"

"From what we've been able to gather. We don't know who or how, but we are certain the courier will be someone attending the dinner."

"I'll keep my eyes and ears open."

"And I'll always be close at hand, handing out towels to the uber rich."

* * *

Work at school was moving along at a steady pace. Soon the kids would be jacked up about the forthcoming holidays, and Melanie was enjoying the calm before the storm. Kid storm and diamond storm. She knew it was going to be complicated. At the dinner, she would have to put her powers of observation into high gear. *Who seems the most nervous? The most detached?* She put those thoughts on hold. It was time for the school announcements.

Principal Alexander's face appeared on the large screen above the blackboard in the front of the classrooms. "Good morning, everyone." She paused so all the kids could reply. The principal announced the lunch menu, a fire drill, the next food drive, bake sale, and sign-up for the holiday festival. All of this information would also be sent via email, text, and a printed flyer—covering all bases of communication. She finished up with, "Everyone have a good day. Please be kind."

Melanie thought that was a nice finish to the morning news. "Please be kind." The contrast between her two careers was remarkable, yet in one way, they were connected. Previously, she was working on ending a problem. Now, she was working on preventing people from turning into a problem. She was working on the same issue from opposite ends of the spectrum.

Melanie checked her desk diary. There was nothing scheduled. No meetings, no conferences. She phoned Audrey to ask if she could take a personal day on Friday. "I still need more time to unpack a few things. Get an electrician. All that kind of stuff." Perfectly plausible reason to take a day off. Especially the electrician part. You had to be on *their* schedule. Not that she had to explain herself, but she was used to having a cover story. Regardless of her explanation, she really did need a day off. A day off from everything. The past week and a half felt more like a year and a half.

* * *

With the exception of knowing Gilmour would be on scene, and James, who would be her driver, she was flying blind. By the time Thursday rolled around, she was mentally ready to take on the identity of Moira Rockwell. As soon as she got home, she began the transformation. She applied a very heavy concealer over her scar and waited for it to set. Then she applied a layer of heavy cover foundation. The steel-gray contacts would match her dress perfectly. She created a dramatic look by blending gray and violet eyeshadow and finished her exotic look with silver eyeliner. The white wig completed her contemporary Cleopatra appearance. Next, she created a fake birthmark on her cheekbone about an inch below the outer corner of her eye, then finished everything off with a spritz of Hermès and a pale lavender lipstick. She stepped into the silky jumpsuit and adorned her neck with the David Yurman necklace, then clipped on the matching earrings, which concealed an earpiece. The black ankle boots gave her just a bit of an edge. She stood in front of the mirror. "Hello. My name is Moira Rockwell. Pleased to meet you." A rush of adrenaline raced through her veins. Even though this was a much more challenging assignment than the first, she felt ready for it. She was aware the last one had been relatively easy, but it was a good rehearsal for what was to come.

James arrived at seven o'clock. Melanie paused in the doorway. The wrap. She thought it might bring her luck. Not that she was the superstitious type, but it couldn't hurt.

James did a double take. "You look marvelous, Ms. Rockwell."

"Thank you, James." Melanie had to agree. She was looking forward to seeing the expression on Gilmour's face.

She rode a little over a half hour before the car pulled up to a gated driveway. He pressed the button and announced the arrival of Moira Rockwell. The gates swung open slowly to a long brick drive that led to the multimillion-dollar historic Georgian mansion. A small brass placard at the base of one of the topiaries specified MEMBERS ONLY. James opened the rear passenger door, and Moira ascended the marble steps. Before she could knock, a man wearing a butler's uniform opened the stained-glass door. He looked exactly as if he'd stepped out of a scene from *Downton Abbey*. Or was it *House of Usher?* She stifled a giggle when he said, "Good evening." Definitely *House of Usher*. "You're the first guest to arrive. May I show you to the sitting room?"

"Yes, thank you."

"May I offer you a cocktail while you are waiting?"

"Yes. A negroni, please."

The man bowed and disappeared through another door.

Melanie made a sweep of the foyer. The sitting room was to the right of a massive staircase. Straight ahead, a hallway led to two large hand-carved doors, with another bronze plaque. This one said PRIVATE. On the opposite side of the sitting room were two more large wooden doors. That plaque read DINING ROOM. Just before the entrance was a single Dutch door labeled: VALET. Their fancy version of COAT ROOM. She was curious where the bathrooms were, but didn't dare ask. Not yet, anyway. She wanted to scope out the dinner guests as they arrived. Within minutes, "Jeeves"—Melanie's imaginary name for the butler—returned with the sparkling red potion. She'd never had a negroni but knew it was trendy and felt the cocktail went along with her persona. Trendy and edgy. She smiled to herself.

A few minutes later, two men arrived together. They both had dark complexions and black hair. They were speaking Spanish. *Maybe they're bringing the Cuban cigars?* A man appeared from behind the PRIVATE doors to greet them. He had a French accent. Melanie presumed it was Monsieur Escoffier. He snapped his fingers, and Jeeves appeared. "Henri, have zumone open zi valet, *s'il vous plait?*" *Okay, so his name isn't Jeeves. It was fun for a minute.*

Melanie stood off to the side, eavesdropping. She heard one of the agents in her ear. "Move in closer."

She cleared her throat. All heads turned in her direction. "Pardon my interruption. I am Moira Rockwell." She extended her hand. Escoffier kissed the back of it. "*Enchanté,* mademoiselle."

"*Le plaisir est à moi,*" Melanie answered. *The pleasure is mine.*

"Ah, you speak French?""

"*Un peu.* Very, very little." She smiled.

He turned to the two gentlemen and introduced them as Guillermo Gutierrez and Ricardo Torres. Melanie noticed Mr. Torres's hands were not as well manicured as Mr. Gutierrez's. His hands didn't match the expensive designer suit he was wearing. She glanced at his shoes. They, too, were at odds with the rest of his clothing. She would keep an eye on him.

A valet opened the coat room and began to exchange club blazers with the men's suit jackets, giving each of them a plastic tag. Melanie wondered how many jackets the club had and in what sizes.

Three women entered the vestibule. After they were introduced, she learned that Annika and Elsa were from Sweden, and Olivia from Finland. That made four, including Melanie/Moira. She made small talk with the women, making sure her microphone was facing the men so the agents could pick up on their conversation. Henri opened the door as four more men entered the vestibule at the same time. Escoffier introduced everyone. Munir Balgesh from Pakistan; Yassin Cumbe from Mozambique; Geoffrey Leeds from Australia. It was quite a mix of accents and styles, each gentleman turning over his hand-tailored suit jacket for a dull wool blazer with the club crest.

Two additional women walked through the main door, Maxine Rieux from France, and Isabella Fromentini from Sicily. Lots of chatter as clothing was swapped. Fortunately, there was no dress code for women. They were only allowed into the club when invited to an event.

Escoffier opened the double doors to the dining room. *"Voilà!"* It was a grand room that could accommodate more than a dinner for twelve. Buffets and sideboards lined the perimeter walls, where paintings that could possibly be original Gainsboroughs hung between the large casement windows. The scenes could have been torn from the pages of Voltaire's *Candide*. Melanie wondered why men had worn those ridiculous wigs. Another stupid idea.

Escoffier showed everyone to their assigned seat. Melanie made sure her David Yurman necklace caught the panorama of the room. She wondered if Shannon was on the premises. She hoped not.

Melanie was seated between Cumbe and Geoffrey Leeds. Annika was on the other side of Leeds. There were six on each side of the very wide table. Conversation would be a little challenging if she wanted to speak to someone sitting across from her.

Wine was served, along with the first course. Melanie was looking forward to the menu, a copy of which was on each place setting. Shannon was right. It was beef Wellington. Escoffier tapped his glass with his knife to get the group's attention.

"Bonsoir. Welcome." He made a short speech and introduced everyone. "Tonight, we will enjoy a wonderful meal, fine wine, and good companionship. Then later, we will be sampling some of the finest cigars in the world with demitasse and dessert. Bon appetit!"

Everyone lifted their glass and declared their own salutation. "Chin-chin!" "Salud!" "Skål!"

Melanie particularly appreciated Leeds's toast: "To those

who have seen us at our best and seen us at our worst and can't tell the difference!" She was relieved he had a sense of humor.

Leeds was very charming and a big fan of Bach. Melanie wasn't particularly fond of the composer's work but could speak about it in depth. "Personally, I prefer Vivaldi." She smiled. "*The Four Seasons* is masterful. And to think they wrote all that music by candlelight."

"Extraordinary," Leeds concurred.

The first course was exactly what Melanie had been salivating for. Lobster with a dollop of caviar. The wine was crisp and cut the saltiness of the fish roe. As the first course plates were being removed, one of the side doors opened. It was Shannon, checking to see if everything was in order. Melanie turned in the opposite direction, pretending to remove a crumb from Leeds's sleeve with her napkin. "Oh here I go again. I'm always feeding my clothes." He smiled. "Thanks."

From the corner of her eye, she saw Shannon leave. Even though she couldn't hear what her sister-in-law said to Escoffier, her microphone picked it up. An agent's voice spoke inside Melanie's ear. "She's gone for the evening."

Melanie let out a whoosh of air.

"Already full?" Leeds joked.

"It was delicious. A bit rich, but I would do it all over again. Just not right now." She chuckled.

As more wine was poured, the conversations became louder. Melanie was careful not to imbibe heavily. She had to be alert. *Be aware.* One thing was certain, Mr. Torres did not look comfortable. Did he not think his behavior was obvious? Then again, men could be oblivious to their own behavior and everyone and everything around them. *Poor dears. When are they going to realize women are superior?* She laughed to herself. She wasn't man-bashing. Simply observing.

During dessert, Torres got up from the table. She watched him shake Escoffier's hand. He was leaving. She excused herself to go "powder my nose." She was stunned when all the men stood up as she rose from her seat. *At least they're polite.* Torres opened the big door for her and walked over to the valet door to retrieve his suit jacket. He looked around for some assistance, but there was no one to assist him. Melanie lingered in the vestibule and watched Torres go inside the coat room. When he exited, she swore he was wearing a different jacket from the one he'd arrived in. It didn't match his pants. She had to think fast. Gilmour was already in the hallway. One of the agents had alerted him when Melanie left the dining hall. She motioned with her hand to get something to drink. She decided to take a risk and engage Torres in conversation as he was adjusting the ill-fitting jacket. She hoped Gilmour would appear with a glass of something quickly.

"Mr. Torres. You are leaving so soon?" She could see the perspiration collecting on his forehead. "Is everything alright?" She stood between him and the main door.

"*Sí.* Yes. Fine." He pulled out a handkerchief and patted his head.

"Oh, I think perhaps you should sit down and have a glass of water." She took his arm and tried to guide him to the sitting room.

He briskly pulled his arm away. "No! Please! I am fine."

Gilmour appeared with a glass of water and handed it to Melanie.

"Here, drink this." As she handed the glass to Torres, she purposely fumbled and spilled the water all over the front of his jacket. "Oh, I am so sorry!" She took his handkerchief and started to blot his jacket. That was when she felt it. Something that felt like pebbles sewn into the jacket lining.

He was huffing. "Please! I am fine!" His arms were flapping wildly.

Melanie watched Gilmour speak into the cuff of his sleeve. He motioned for Melanie to continue to try to detain Torres.

"Oh, I feel awful. I hope I didn't ruin your jacket."

Torres calmed down a bit. "Please, señora, I must leave now. I have emergencies."

Melanie glanced at Gilmour again. He gave her a nod.

"Oh, of course. Again, my apologies." She walked him to the main door and held it open as she watched him hurry to the black town car waiting at the foot of the steps. Torres didn't recognize the driver who got out and opened the rear passenger door.

"Good evening, sir. I'm Charles. Your driver wasn't feeling well and asked me to cover for him. I hope you do not mind. You are going to Dulles Airport?"

Torres looked him up and down. The driver was dressed in the same uniform as the first one had been wearing. "Yes, *por favor. Rápidamente.*"

Melanie recognized the voice of the driver. It was James. She shut the door and nodded to Gilmour. He spoke into his sleeve again, and Melanie returned to the dining room.

Leeds stood and pulled out her chair. "We were beginning to wonder what happened to you."

"Thank you. I was speaking with Mr. Torres. He had to leave early." She scanned the table. The only one who looked in her direction was Yassin Cumbe from Mozambique, neighbor to Zimbabwe, a place notorious for its blood diamonds.

The chatter around the table continued for another hour. Melanie was able to breathe normally as she listened to one of the agents tell Gilmour the plan was a go.

Cigar smoke filled the room, and fine brandy was served. Her eyes were stinging, although the aroma wasn't as unpleasant as she'd thought it would be.

Several miles away, a half dozen police cars were blocking an intersection. They appeared to be checking inside vehicles.

When the black town car approached the front of the line, a patrolman asked for identification. James showed him something that looked official. The patrolman asked if he would roll down the privacy glass that separated the front from the back seat. Torres didn't move. The officer leaned in. "May I see some identification, sir?"

"I have diplomatic immunity," Torres said.

"I still need to see some identification."

Torres checked his breast pocket. Then his pants pocket. He knew he'd collected his passport from his original jacket. Had he dropped it in the confusion with that woman? "I don't seem to have it on me."

"I am going to have to ask you to step out of the car, sir."

Torres was beginning to shake. "I promise you I have the correct documents. They are at the club." Torres began fishing for his phone. That, too, was missing.

"Sir, please step out of the car," the officer insisted.

James took the cue. He opened the driver's door and then the rear passenger door. Torres begrudgingly got out of the vehicle. What he didn't notice was the small razor in James's hand. Before anyone could take another step, diamonds began to rain down from Torres's jacket. Two agents wearing black suits appeared from behind one of the police cars to cuff Torres and take him away. Two other agents photographed the scene and removed the evidence. When they finished, they gave James the signal he was free to go.

James pulled back into the club driveway just as Melanie appeared on the steps. He got out and opened the door for her. "Did you have a pleasant evening, miss?"

"It was quite interesting." As they continued toward the road, another stretch limo passed them and continued to the front of the mansion.

"Dessert." James jerked his thumb at the car.

Melanie knew exactly what he meant. By the time they reached the main road, Gilmour was waiting on the corner.

He climbed into the rear seat. "And how did we do this evening?" Melanie quizzed him.

"I don't know how you did it, but lifting his passport *and* his phone?"

"It's called distraction." Melanie grinned. "And don't ask me how I did it."

"Magic Circle?" Gilmour asked.

Melanie made a zipper gesture across her lips.

"It turns out Torres's diplomatic passport was a fake. There was no record of it in the database. Good thing you nicked it. Made the officer's job a little easier."

"What would have happened if Torres was able to show his ID?"

"We knew one of the men was a fraud, so everyone was on the lookout for possible fake identities. They would have had to detain him and go through the motions, forcing him to miss his flight to El Salvador. Then the red tape would roll, keeping him here until they could sort things out. You saved them a lot of time."

"Does that mean I get a bonus?" Melanie joked.

"Isn't the wardrobe enough?" Gilmour grinned.

"I am going to have to find a place to wear it." She opened her purse and handed him Torres's fake ID and phone. "Should we call his family and tell them he won't be home for dinner?"

They burst out laughing, including James, formerly known as Charles.

Chapter Eighteen

Lights Out

Melanie patted herself on the back for her quick thinking and sleight of hand, then congratulated herself for taking the day off. She didn't have to get up to let the dogs out, since Kramer had taught himself how to unlatch the doggie door. She reminded herself that only an idiot would try to break into a house with two very large, very strong, and very loud German shepherds. She slept well most of the time, but last night, she was in the slowest wave of Delta. She stretched slowly and swung her legs around so she was sitting upright on the edge of the bed. The dogs must have sensed the lady of the manor was awake. She could hear them scramble into the house and up the stairs.

"Good morning, my sweet boys!" She kissed them both on the head. "Did you fix breakfast for me?" Kramer cocked his head. "No? Well, that's just fine." She pretended to be offended. "After my big night last night, one of you could have fixed coffee." The dogs looked toward the window. A car was pulling into the driveway. It was Gilmour. Cosmo and Kramer bolted down the steps. Melanie looked at herself in the mirror. "You are *so* not ready for the public." She tousled her hair and slipped on a pair of shoes. The lounging pajamas she was wearing were good enough to open the door.

"So now you show up unannounced?" She turned and walked toward the kitchen. "I hope you brought coffee."

"Good morning to you, Miss Sunshine. I tried to call, but your phone kept going to voice mail. When I hadn't heard from you, I was a little concerned so came by to do a wellness check."

"Yes, I am well, and good idea about the coffee." She grabbed two turquoise mugs from the cabinet and poured the coffee from the cardboard cups. "Don't even say it."

"What? Why dirty a cup when it's already in one?"

"I said, 'don't even say it.' Geez, even Kramer has better hearing than you." Kramer raised his head at the mention of his name.

"Aren't we in a fine mood today?" he mocked.

"You, maybe. Me? I'm not awake enough to make an accurate assessment." She grabbed the bag he was holding and plucked out a warm cranberry scone. "But maybe these will help."

"You're welcome." Gilmour bowed.

Melanie grinned. "Thank you. I was kidding. I feel great today. Well, not great. Not yet. But I will in a few minutes. Perhaps after my second scone." She looked over at her phone. It was sitting on the counter. Unplugged. "No wonder." She got up, licked the sticky sugar off her fingers, and charged the battery. "I must have forgotten when I got home."

"Mel, you did an amazing job last night." He sipped his coffee. "You're right. It tastes better in a real mug. No paper aftertaste."

"See? When will you realize that there is no sense in arguing with me? I am always right. Geesh." She flicked him on the back of his head.

"Ouch."

"Sissy." She took another bite of the scone. "So you were really worried about me?"

"After last night? You could have run off down under with Mr. Australia."

"Oh, stop. I was doing my job." Melanie thought she'd heard a tinge of jealousy. That could be a good thing. Maybe. "I have to admit, nicking Torres's passport was risky, but the phone was even trickier. I had to reach pretty close to his other jewels."

Gilmour almost spit out his coffee. "You're pretty funny in the morning."

"Any idea when our next big caper will be coming up?"

Gilmour cleared his throat.

"Oh, I don't like that sound."

"Maybe you shouldn't do such a good job," Gilmour said.

"This one is a little more complicated."

"How is that possible?"

"You have to go to New York. An overnighter."

"Why?" Melanie looked concerned. "And what about my real job?"

"An international tech tycoon is flying in for a summit with a bunch of other tech millionaires . . . billionaires. Hard to keep track."

"Probably billionaires. Millionaires was so last week," Melanie said as she peered over her mug.

"His name is Sven Reinhardt."

"Oh, you've got to be kidding. There is someone who has the name Sven?"

"Yeah, yeah." Gilmour continued. "He wants to have dinner with an elegant, sophisticated woman."

"Where do you find these people?" Melanie asked earnestly.

"Come on, Mel. Big Brother is watching and interfering. Anyway, you're supposed to meet him for dinner at Casa Cruz."

"Whoa. Isn't that the most expensive restaurant in New York?"

"Yes, but you will also be within meters of original works of art. Warhol. Haring."

"Not a fan of Warhol. So pretentious."

"Wear the gold lamé Dior." Gilmour winked.

"Wait a sec. Did I tell you I bought a gold lamé Dior?"

"I did your expense account." Gilmour raised his eyebrows.

"Okay, and then what?"

"A small gathering at his hotel suite for other tech giants."

"What's the scheme?"

"We think someone is selling a type of malware that can cut through most of the security walls protecting our major electric grids. If it gets into the wrong hands, someone can turn out all the lights. As in all of them. A total collapse."

"But I thought there was a failsafe roll-out."

"So did the NSA. Now there seems to be another tech genius who could hold the country hostage."

"How do I fit in?"

"The only info we have is that the malware is going to be delivered via flash drive by one of these billionaires."

"I don't get it. Why would a billionaire want to hold the country hostage? Doesn't he already have enough money?"

"Remember that line from *Scarface*? You get the money first; then comes the power."

"That's not how it goes." Melanie did her best impersonation of Al Pacino and repeated the line correctly.

Once again Gilmour almost spit out his coffee. "Mel, I don't know what's gotten into you."

"Finger paint, cutting construction paper into flowers. Sniffing glue." She laughed. "Maybe not sniffing glue, per se. But I do get to sit in on some of the art classes."

"Can we please get serious?"

Melanie sat straight. "Yes. Sorry. I have a caper hangover." She reached for her pad and pen.

"You weren't drunk last night." Gilmour knew she'd had fewer than two glasses of wine over a three-hour stretch.

"Hung over from the gig. Duh."

"Oh, I get it." He let out a huff. "After dinner, you will accompany Reinhardt to his suite at the Baccarat on Fifty-third. You'll love the opulence and ambiance."

"Wait a minute. I am not doing that." Melanie's nostrils flared.

"No. It's not what you think. There will also be a few of these tech dudes with their wives or mistresses. It's a techie soiree. He's booked the Baccarat suite. It's almost eighteen hundred square feet, and a dollar a square foot per night."

"Geez. That's much bigger than my house. And probably my yard, and my mortgage payment." *Funny how things are always being compared to a mortgage payment once you buy a house.*

"Right. There will be plenty of room for you to maneuver. Honestly, I don't think you'll be put in any kind of compromising position. We don't think he has an overactive libido. Never had a steady girlfriend, never married, rarely seen with the same woman more than once. He's very refined and enjoys female company. That's the best info I can give you."

"And where will I be staying?"

"At the Warwick. Around the corner. It's a very lovely hotel."

"Yes, I know it."

"You'll check in using your next identity. Leonora Stavolo. You're a high-end real estate agent. Nothing less than two-million-dollar showings."

"Where am I from?"

"Minneapolis. You're in New York to find a loft for a client."

"I can fake that."

"Good girl."

"So what's supposed to happen at this soiree?"

"We think it's where the negotiation will take place. We'll have the room rigged, but we need eyes on the scene."

"Got it." Melanie was writing down the details. "When is this supposed to happen?"

"Next weekend."

Melanie wasn't the least bit surprised these jobs were coming fast and furious. The agency had a quota to fill before the end of the year if they wanted to maintain their budget.

"And how am I getting there?"

"Amtrak. Private car will pick you up and bring you to the hotel."

"What about my clothes? I can't wear the gold lamé on the train."

"Go buy yourself a travel outfit."

"What am I going to wear on the way home?" She gave him a mischievous grin.

"Okay, two travel outfits."

"And shoes," she added.

"And shoes." He shook his head.

"Oh, come on, Greg. I earned it."

"You did."

"We're talking about next weekend, as in the one after this one?" She wanted to be sure.

"Yes. Next Saturday, you'll be on the eleven o'clock Acela, arriving at Penn Station at two thirty."

"Oh, good. I don't have to take another day off work for work."

"Correct." Gilmour got up.

"So this really wasn't a wellness check. This was a 'let's bring Mel some scones, get her hopped up on sugar, and then give her the next assignment' check."

"Guilty as charged." Gilmour tightened his lips. "Okay, spunky. I have work to do. Enjoy your day off."

"I have to go shopping." She gave him her MelDrake death stare.

Melanie took her time easing into the day. Scones, coffee, and a new assignment that required thinking and planning. She went online to search casual travel ensembles. There was a Brunello Cucinelli cashmere, toast-colored drawstring pant with a matching hoodie, and Armani drawstring pants and matching zipper warm-up jacket in deep burgundy. A pair of Prada Double Wheel sneakers finished off the casual, elite traveler.

Fortunately, the commotion at school that week was only a dull roar. She was beginning to understand the dynamics of how holidays, weekends, and school projects affected the children. Especially the children of divorced parents, of which there were many. Melanie often wondered if it was better for the children when the parents split amicably, or minimally tolerated each other to preserve the family unit. It could go either way for the child. Melanie was discovering that children have keen insight and are often underestimated. Their intuition is acute before the world suffocates them with platitudes, misinformation, and doubt. The saying "out of the mouth of babes" has merit. They are unfiltered. Honest. Why did adults think they were pulling something over on kids by pretending to be one big happy family, when their offspring could sense their anger and resentment? Such a conundrum.

The holidays were a couple of weeks away. She was certain they would bring more excitement and anxiety to the classroom. *Yippee.*

The weekend of her next job was quickly descending upon Melanie. Was she having second thoughts? This was an entirely different scenario from the first two. Away from home base. A billionaire entrepreneur. The two of them alone. At dinner. Then his hotel room? Maybe there wouldn't be anyone else. How good was their intel? She knew Patterson wouldn't knowingly put her in serious jeopardy. A little jeopardy, for sure, but serious? Doubtful. She wanted to have another conversation with Gilmour. She sent him a text: **Greek tonight?**

He sent an immediate reply: **Sure. Time? Everything OK?**

She responded: **Great. 6:00. Not sure.**

OK. I'll pick it up.

Melanie was always self-assured, but this job felt different. She couldn't put her finger on it. Maybe Gilmour could diffuse her anxiety.

Like clockwork, Gilmour appeared with two large shopping bags filled with Grecian delights. And a bottle of that special wine Melanie liked.

They unpacked the spread, uncorked the wine, and set the table in relative silence. Gilmour knew Melanie would talk when she was ready.

He poured a glass of wine for both of them, and they sat facing each other at the table. The dogs were comfortable in their beds in front of the fireplace.

Gilmour's curiosity finally prompted him to ask, "What's going on?"

Melanie took a deep breath. "I'm nervous." Gilmour didn't respond. He knew she had more to say. "I'm going to be out of my element. I kinda know New York, but not like I know DC."

"It's not going to be any different. We've got you covered."

Melanie knew Gilmour always had her covered, but this was a whole different ball of wax. "Intellectually, I know that." She was about to say something very foreign to her: "But emotionally, I'm a little scared."

Gilmour wanted to get up and hug her. Instead, he reached out for her hand and looked her straight in the eyes. "I got you. Always know that." He gave her fingers a little squeeze. That's when she knew it was true. Not that she'd ever doubted him, but this was the validation she needed. Or was it something she wanted? Maybe both.

*   *   *

Lynch offered to feed Melanie's dogs while she was out of town. After Lynch had retired, he'd worked for a fellow retired Navy Seal named Terry Magovern. Terry owned and operated a K-9 training center outside of Anacostia. Lynch spent two years learning about animal behavior, with another big dose of human behavior. When Terry had moved the kennels to New Jersey, Lynch went to work as a security guard in the local school district. Now, he was more than happy to spend time with a couple of military vets, canine or otherwise. It was good that Melanie's trip was taking place over the weekend so as not to interrupt their work schedule.

Saturday morning came quickly. Lynch arrived at Melanie's at eight o'clock to go over Cosmo and Kramer's routine. "You are welcome to spend the night if you want. There's a sofa bed in the den upstairs, or you can make yourself comfortable on the couch. Whatever floats your boat. I really appreciate this."

"No problem. My wife is visiting her sister in Atlanta, and the kids are away at college. I just might take you up on the offer, that is if Cosmo and Kramer don't mind." He looked at the dogs, who were looking right back at him.

She gave Lynch a peck on the cheek, and then gave each dog a peck on the head. "You be good for Mr. Lynch, okay?" They both went into a downward dog yoga pose.

Lynch chuckled. "I think we're gonna be fine."

"Thanks again!" Melanie said. She pulled her overnighter behind her and got into the car, driven once again by James. Or was it Charles?

The train pulled into Penn Station right on time. She found her way to the underpass, where her car was supposed to be waiting. It took her a moment to realize her alias would be on the sign in the car window. *Leonora Stavolo*. She gave a wave, and a female driver opened the trunk and got out. "Welcome to New York, Ms. Stavolo. I'm Jennine."

"Thank you. It's been a few years since I've been here."

"It's been a few years since a lot of people have been here." The driver was referring to the extremely slow flow of people returning to the city. "Staying at the Warwick?"

"Um, yes." Melanie, dressed in one of her travel outfits, sported auburn hair, and green contact lenses. She didn't want to seem rude, but she was still a little anxious. New York was a big city, where people could get swallowed up and never be heard from again. But so were Chicago and Detroit. *Can someone say Jimmy Hoffa?* Even though it had happened almost a decade before she was born, the disappearance of the country's biggest union boss was noteworthy. Speculation was rampant, but to this day, no one knows what happened to him after he left that diner outside Detroit in 1975.

The driver looked in the rearview mirror. "Not to worry. We got you." Gilmour's words echoed in Melanie's ears. She relaxed into the seat as Jennine jockeyed her way to 54th between Fifth and Sixth Avenues, just around the corner from the Baccarat. When they arrived, a poshly dressed bellman in a red-velvet uniform greeted them. He took Melanie's luggage and escorted her to the front desk. Jennine called out, "We got you," and waved. Melanie knew that was a message from Gilmour.

Melanie walked to the front desk. "Good afternoon. Checking in. Leonora Stavolo." She presented her fake passport.

"I see you will be with us just one night. We will need a credit card for incidentals." Before Melanie could open her purse, a gentleman approached the counter.

"Please use mine." The nametag said Giorgio Mancini, but the face said Gregory Gilmour. "I'm with Hanover Real Estate. We are taking care of all your needs."

Melanie tried not to laugh at Gilmour's fake mustache. "Thank you, Mr. Mancini. It's totally unnecessary." Melanie played along.

"We insist, and we hope to develop a strong relationship with your firm." He addressed the associate behind the counter. "Please charge everything to my card."

"Of course, Mr. Mancini." The associate typed the instructions into the computer. "Ms. Stavolo, someone will take your bags to your room. Enjoy your stay."

Melanie and Mr. Mancini walked toward the elevator together. "I see we are on the same floor. Splendid," Mancini said with his mustached mouth.

The bellman showed Melanie to her room, and Mancini went in the opposite direction to his. While they were in the elevator, he passed her a note that said, "jewels inside bouquet."

At first, Melanie wasn't sure what it meant, until she saw a beautiful floral arrangement sitting on the small table in front of the window. She tipped the bellman and locked the door behind her. A small pouch containing a pair of gold dangling earrings was stashed among the exotic flowers. She put them on. One side was the microphone, the other was an earpiece. No camera? She fished further and found a gold ring with what appeared to be a very large topaz. She held it up to her eye. She heard a crackling sound, then a voice. "Love the green contacts. They go well with the auburn hair."

"And where will you be during this dinner and soiree?"

"For dinner, I will be in a car outside the restaurant. During the intimate gathering, I will be in the room below with the crew."

"Please don't use the word *intimate*," Melanie requested politely.

Gilmour laughed. "I knew that would get to you."

"You need to get a job at Comedy Central," Melanie barked back.

"Looks like we're all set. See you later."

"I hope so." Melanie smiled into the topaz ring.

She unpacked her clothes, removed the wig, showered,

and began her transformation. Makeup, check. Nails, check. Wig, check. Dress, ooh-la-la. Jewelry, check. Shoes and handbag, check and check. Once again, Melanie looked like a completely different person from the day before. Her phone rang to inform her a car was waiting to take her to the restaurant. And *Sven*.

She wondered if he was in on the scam. Some of these tech guys turned out to be white-collar criminals. Then she chuckled. Most tech guys wear polo shirts or T-shirts. *They're going to have to come up with a new name.*

The driver was Jennine, the same woman who'd fetched her from the train station. She opened the passenger door and handed Melanie a new cashmere wrap. This one was light beige with gold threads running through it. She smiled. *Gilmour.* It was a perfect match for her Dior lamé. The car moved uptown to East 61st and stopped in front of the magnificent beaux-arts townhouse.

The place was stunning. Indirect lighting gave the room a golden glow. She was glad she'd worn the Dior. A finely dressed gentleman greeted her. "Good evening, madame."

"Hello. I am a guest of Mr. Sven Reinhardt."

"Of course. Follow me, please." He escorted her to a table toward the rear of the room. A very tall, very blond man stood and held out his hand.

"Leonora Stavolo. Thank you for joining me tonight." His accent was slight. His diction impeccable. She wondered if he came from money or was a genius who'd made it on his own.

"The pleasure is all mine," Melanie responded, as the maître d' helped with her chair.

Sven Reinhardt had done his homework, learning everything he could find on Leonora Stavolo. "I understand you are in New York to broker a deal on a loft. SoHo?"

"Yes. My clients have very exacting taste. As you know, photos do not tell the entire story, so they asked that I inspect the property in person. With a three-million-dollar budget, I can't blame them." She wanted to get off the subject of Leonora in case she ran out of backstory. "Tell me about yourself. Where did you grow up?"

Sven began at the moment of birth and took Melanie on his life's journey, including many, many details. Too many. *No wonder he doesn't have a girlfriend.* Between breaths, he ordered wine. "I hope you do not mind. I ordered for both of us ahead of time. This way, we can converse without interruption."

"Thank you," Melanie replied. Her thought balloons were saying, *Yep. Control freak.* But he seemed nice enough, though completely self-absorbed. Dinner dragged on for over two hours. Melanie thought how ironic it was that people dream of having dinner in such opulence, and yet she couldn't wait to leave. She had a job to do. She thought dessert would never come. When they finished, he said, "We'll have cognac at my suite." They got up from the table and began to walk out, and Sven bid adieu to the man at the door. Melanie realized Sven hadn't paid the check. *I guess that's how the rich do it.* "*Put it on my tab.*"

A black town car was waiting for them outside the restaurant. It wasn't the same car Melanie had arrived in, but she spotted Jennine in another car a few feet away. As they moved down the street toward the avenue, she noticed Jennine wasn't far behind. *Good to know. Just in case. In case of what? Don't go there.* Her thoughts were spinning.

When they arrived at the Baccarat, two men opened the car doors. "Good evening, Mr. Reinhardt." They spoke one after the other. He smiled.

Melanie followed Sven through the grand salon. It was spectacular. The furnishings were white with wood trim, white area rugs, and crystal everywhere. Crystal chandeliers. Crystal vases. Crystal glasses. Crystal elephants. Melanie was committed to pretending she wasn't impressed and that she was accustomed to being surrounded by beautiful and very expensive things. *Her dogs were beautiful.*

Sven escorted Melanie to the elevator and used his special key card to enable the button for the floor of the largest suite at the hotel. The place smelled rich. She recognized it was a very similar scent to the perfume she was wearing. Of course!

The suite was magnificent. The furnishings were similar to those in the grand salon. White, crystalline, and glamorous. Gilmour was right. It would be easy to get lost. "Please, sit." He swept his arm toward the living room and poured two cognacs into Baccarat crystal tumblers. Within a few minutes, his house phone rang, informing him his guests had arrived. "I am sure you were told several colleagues will be joining us. I want to be sure their wives are comfortable while we discuss business."

Melanie wondered if she was supposed to play hostess. "Of course. Let me know if I can be of any assistance."

"Thank you. If you can make sure their glasses are always filled, I would greatly appreciate it."

So she *was* expected to play hostess. *Okay. Whatever.* She imagined Gilmour and the other agents were listening in, and Gilmour confirmed it. "I'll take a scotch and soda," came quietly through her earpiece earring.

Out of nowhere, Melanie asked Sven, "Did you ever want to strangle someone?"

He looked stunned and appalled. "I beg your pardon?"

"When you're at work. Do people ever get on your nerves?" She knew Gilmour was hearing all of it.

"Constantly. But, no, I never thought of strangling anyone. You Americans handle things quite differently." He smiled.

There were subdued voices in the hallway and then a knock on the door. Sven excused himself to greet his other guests. He made all the necessary introductions. A gentleman named Mr. Chin and his wife Suni; Viktor Reubens and his companion Katarina; Jeffrey Hayward and his girlfriend Bibi; and Isaac Firestone and his wife Carolyn. Melanie waited until everyone was settled and had a drink in hand. "Will you please excuse me?" She had to check out the rest of the enormous suite. Gilmour had shown her a floor plan, but she wanted a three-dimensional view. A hallway led to two enormous bedrooms, each with huge, elaborate bathroom suites. The tubs were also oversized and were positioned against one of the white marble-covered walls. When she returned to the living room, the men were standing together in a huddle. "Ah, Leonora. Would you mind entertaining my guests while we techies have a private conversation?"

"It would be a pleasure." Melanie poured the four other women each a libation of her choice. After a few minutes, she excused herself again. "I am so sorry. I think I left my purse in the loo. Excuse me." She tiptoed toward the room where the men were talking. They were speaking English but with a variety of foreign accents. She heard one of the voices getting louder as he came toward the door. She crammed herself in the adjoining closet that supplied the linens for the two bathrooms and put her ear to the inside wall. Voices were still muffled. An agent spoke into her ear. "We can't hear anything." She looked into the ring, pointed it at the wall, and pressed a finger to her lips. She could make out some of what one of the men was saying. She inched her way from the closet into the bathroom and could see the men through the partially opened door from the bathroom to the master bedroom.

"What I have here is the key to controlling a government. When inserted into the proper module, this small device can jam all security walls protecting the electric grid in North America."

She heard someone ask the same question she had. "What about rolling blackouts?"

"That's the beauty of this. It destroys the path. Wherever there is connectivity, the malware shuts it down."

Another said, "I am not sure I understand. Can you explain, please?"

"We have been working on this for almost twenty years. Do you remember the blackout of 2003? Fifty-five million Americans were without power. Some for up to fourteen days. Since then, utilities have installed failsafe measures, but this little charm can hack right through them. For the right price." It sounded like Viktor's voice, one with an Eastern European accent.

"Which is what?" Mr. Chin asked.

"It's a bargain at five million."

"I am not interested in malware," Sven stated.

"Then why are we here?" Viktor asked.

"I was under the impression you had a new antivirus software that could detect malware threats."

Mr. Chin and Hayward concurred. Perhaps Viktor had overestimated the desire of the wealthy for power.

"Apologies for the confusion," Viktor said in a harsh voice. Melanie heard something click. Metal? He must have put the device in something. He wasn't carrying anything bulky like a briefcase. It had to be on his person. Then she saw him put a silver cigarette case in the inside pocket of his suit jacket.

Melanie saw someone leaving the bedroom. It was Sven. "You can continue your conversation without me." Melanie wouldn't be able to get out of the bathroom right away without being seen by Sven. Her presence would be suspicious. She had to go back into the closet and wait until he was near the living room. She heard him walk past. When she thought he was far enough away, she slowly and quietly opened the door.

Sven turned when he heard footsteps behind him. "I thought I left my handbag in the bathroom," she explained. Sven had an annoyed look on his face. "Is everything alright?" she asked.

"I think we are going to have to conclude our gathering. I feel a migraine coming on."

Melanie had to think fast. One option was to plant a GPS device on Viktor so the agents could track him. With any luck, he wouldn't get out of the hotel with his hideous device. Sven made his apologies, encouraging his guests to stay for as long as they wanted. No one took him up on his offer, and three couples departed. He walked over to Melanie and said goodnight. "It was a pleasure meeting you. I hope we can do this again." He turned to the rest of the group, bade them farewell, and exited in the direction of the master bedroom. Melanie had another idea. As they were walking to the elevator, she touched Katarina's arm. "Do you really need to go? Perhaps a drink in the bar? I was just about to comment on your outfit. Do you have a stylist or are you this fashion savvy?" Melanie was becoming a pro at throwing the bull.

Katarina was flattered. She looked at Viktor, who didn't appear to be very happy. "Why not?" he grumbled. They descended to the lobby, the two women chatting about their latest favorite designers. Viktor stood quietly, his eyes pinched in deep thought. He didn't notice Melanie drop one of the pencil eraser-sized GPS devices in his coat pocket.

The women continued to gab as they walked past the glittering crystal works of art. The walls of the bar were clad in crimson velvet. Leather barstools sat atop a checkered floor, and the wall was lined with dozens upon dozens of crystal goblets, tumblers, flutes, and highball glasses. They each ordered an after-dinner digestif. When the drinks were served, Viktor excused himself. "I am going outside to have a smoke."

Smoking outdoors was tricky in New York. Many establishments had rules about smoking within a certain number of feet of the entrance. He'd figure it out.

Smoking on the sidewalk was the least of Viktor's worries now. His boss had told him on no uncertain terms that he was not to return without a buyer. Viktor's problem was soon solved when two federal agents approached him and summarily took him away in handcuffs.

Melanie heard Gilmour. "All clear. M.A." Which meant she was free to go and mission accomplished. She looked around the bar. "I wonder what's keeping Viktor."

Katarina shrugged. "He is not a nice man. I am glad if he does not return."

"Oh? I thought the two of you were engaged?" Melanie played dumb.

"Him? Never."

They waited for several more minutes. "I really need to get back to my hotel," Melanie said. "Will you be alright here? Alone?"

Katarina looked Melanie in the eye. "I won't be for too long."

Melanie thought she got the gist of what Katarina was saying. If she wasn't leaving with Viktor, she would be leaving with someone else.

Melanie said goodnight and walked through the lobby and out the door. Jennine was waiting for her with a thumbs-up.

Gilmour was in the back seat.

Melanie flung herself onto the soft leather. "Please do not make me do this again."

"Okay. Not this."

Melanie sensed a *but* was about to follow. "What are you not telling me?" She peered into Gilmour's eyes.

"One more. I promise." Gilmour held up his arms in a defensive pose, thinking Melanie was going to beat the tar out of him.

"What is it this time?" She exhaled her words.

"There's chatter about a possible kidnapping."

"Oh, isn't that special." Melanie moaned. "Who, what, where, when, and why?"

"A domestic radical group. A politician's daughter. North

Carolina. Next week on her way home from college. Because they want to show the people that they are being underestimated, disrespected, and are more powerful than we think."

"What's the play?" Melanie asked with very little enthusiasm.

"She's supposed to be going to a holiday party in Miami."

"And?"

"And someone is supposed to abduct her during her travels."

"So why not just keep her from going?"

"Because they'll find something else."

"Then what's the point?"

"If this scheme is foiled, the buddies who are supposed to carry out the plan will no longer be accepted members of the group."

"So they'll find another bunch of crazies to play with."

"I don't think so. If you're called out because you messed up, no one will want to go near you. You're spoiled goods."

"Ah. So we break up these little subversive groups one member at a time?"

"That's part of it. The other part is that we believe these organizations are being funded by foreign money."

"Oh!" Melanie pursed her lips. "If the money people lose confidence in the group, their funds will dry up. Very interesting." Melanie understood the agency's logic. "When is this happening? Soon, I presume."

"Yes. The plan will be launched at a political rally at one of the clubs."

"Please. You're going to make me throw up."

"All you have to do is swap the instructions."

"Swap the what?"

"We know who is supposed to carry out the kidnapping, but we don't know who is handing off the instructions."

"Explain, please."

"A guy named Bennie Wayfair is looking to move up in his band of anarchists. He's been given the task, but he awaits instructions and information. What we could glean from their private server is that someone will hand Bennie a piece of paper at the rally. Your job is to swap that piece of paper with misinformation."

"And that will stop the flood of disinformation."

Gilmour slapped his knee. "You are the brilliant one, aren't you?"

Melanie made a face. "Yeah. Yeah. And when is this little party happening?"

"Next Saturday."

"Oh, geez. Okay, but this is the last one. It's three weeks before Christmas, and I have done absolutely nothing to get ready for the holidays."

"But just think how merry it will be knowing we thwarted these nasty activities."

"What about the daughter? Will she be in any jeopardy?"

"No. Her parents decided to send her to London, where she will be seen on social media."

"And that's when the foreign money will discover their plan went sideways." Melanie finished the concept.

"Yep. You're a genius."

"Well, this genius is going to retire after our next escapade. I can't do both jobs, and I kinda like being a guidance counselor in a small school, in a quaint town, in my cute house with my big dogs."

"I'll let Patterson know. As I said last time, this will surely secure their budget for next year. You will have done your civic duty."

"Again."

Chapter Nineteen

One Last Time

Kids were beginning to get hyped up about the holidays. There was already too much crying, and too many holiday cookies. Audrey explained the routine to Melanie. "You'll probably get at least one crier per day." Melanie shut her eyes, imagining all the tears she'd have to wipe away. Audrey handed her two boxes of tissues. "There are more in the nurse's station."

Melanie rolled her eyes. At least the situations at school weren't treacherous. Just a lot of blubbering.

She spent as much time as she could helping the art teacher decorate the hallways, and all the individual classrooms. It was actually relaxing for Melanie. No sleight of hand required. At least not until Saturday. Thinking about Saturday, she wondered if her Chanel suit would be appropriate? Why not. Just because most of the men in the subversive group looked like they'd crawled out from under a rock didn't mean she had to dress down. And no one would suspect her of being a pickpocket. She thought a moment. *What do you call someone who picks and then plants?*

Gilmour had already briefed her on whom to look for. "He'll be wearing a dark green blazer with a gold crest with I KNOW MY RIGHTS sewn onto the breast pocket. He's in his mid-twenties, shaved head."

"This is a fundraiser?"

"Yes. Ticket price is five hundred dollars to get in the door. There may be some riffraff, but any protest activity will be squelched. This group does not want any negative publicity."

"Wait. This group doesn't want any negative publicity, but they are planning to kidnap someone?"

"That's part of the problem. It's a splinter group trying to gain control, and they are using the kidnapping to draw attention to their cause."

"How many people will be attending this hoop-dee-do?"

"About two hundred."

"You can't be serious."

"He should be relatively easy to spot. You'll just have to keep moving. Plus we'll have several agents there on the lookout. There's a mezzanine where they'll be posted, so they can be on the lookout and guide you."

"Where's my jewelry?" She held out her hand.

When Saturday arrived, she went into disguise mode. This time it was the cream Chanel number, the blond wedge wig, and the violet lenses, and those luscious yellow patent leather pumps. She'd be standing out in the crowd for sure, especially with the additional three inches she'd gain from her shoes.

James picked her up at the designated time and drove her to the venue. It was a large space open to anyone who could afford a ticket. Most of the event was underwritten by big donors.

Melanie handed her ticket to a woman wearing the hall's official jacket and then entered the large ballroom. Two hundred? More like five hundred. She was going to clobber Gilmour. It was a sea of people. She heard a voice in her pearl cluster earrings. "You're in our sights."

She moved through the crowd, pretending she was happy to be there. Then she spotted Shannon. *Not again!* At least she could disappear into the crowd if necessary. As she moved farther into the mélange of people, she also spotted someone else. It was Yassin Cumbe. What was he doing here? It occurred to her he might be the financier of the fringe group.

Now there were two people she had to avoid while trying to find a bald head among many.

Over an hour passed. Her feet were beginning to hurt. She whispered into one of her many strands of pearls. "Anything?"

"Not yet."

Melanie groaned. She needed to sit down, but she knew she couldn't. There were waiters passing small bites and cocktails. There was also a cash bar. Maybe she could lean against it until the bald, green-jacket dude showed up. A "head's up" blew through her ear. "Approaching the bar." At least she didn't have to walk too far. She watched as the young man sidled up to another man. They each ordered a beer and chatted for a minute or two. As the second man was about to leave, he shook green-jacket's hand with a small piece of paper tucked between his thumb and forefinger. Green jacket placed it in his right front pocket and also turned to leave. This was Melanie's opportunity. She squeezed her way through the beer-thirsty crowd and stopped in front of him. "Oh, sorry. I've been waiting forever to get a drink. How did you manage that?" She looked at his beer and gave him a winning smile. "Do you think you could arm wrestle the bartender for me?" She batted her fake eyelashes.

"Er, uh, yeah. Sure." He didn't look like the type who would ever be approached by a stunning woman in need. Any woman, for that matter. "What'll you have?"

"Bourbon. Neat, please." She continued to smile. Green jacket leaned over the bar to get the bartender's attention. Melanie leaned against the bar and brushed up against him. "I really appreciate this." She reached into her purse and pulled out a piece of paper and a twenty-dollar bill.

"It's on me. I don't get to rescue pretty women very often."

"Aren't you sweet?" She placed one hand on his arm and the other in his pocket, swapping the two notes. He handed her the drink. "Thank you." Just as he was about to introduce himself, she said, "Don't go away. I'll be right back." Of course, she wouldn't, but he didn't have to know that just yet. He was basking in the glow of being her hero.

She made her way to the bathroom, but the line was twelve deep. *Why does that always happen?* There was another one on the mezzanine. She took the escalator up to a relatively empty floor. The agents were stationed on the opposite side of the large ballroom. She kept her distance in case anyone was watching. As she went past the janitor's closet, she thought she heard something. It was a muffled voice and kicking sounds. She tried the doorknob. It was locked. She reached under her wig and pulled out a bobby pin.

Uncle Leo, don't fail me now. In an instant, the lock was open. She gasped when she saw Shannon tied to a chair with a gag in her mouth. Even though she couldn't speak, Shannon's eyes screamed her terror. Melanie hoped the agents were still watching, but she couldn't wait for a rescue team. She got within inches of Shannon's face. "It's going to be okay. It's me, Melanie."

Shannon furrowed her brow. Nothing was making any sense.

Melanie untied the handkerchief that covered Shannon's mouth. "Shush." She put a finger over her lips. Melanie looked up and down the long hall. A few people were standing over a hundred feet away, engrossed in conversation. Melanie checked Shannon's restraints. *Shoelaces?* Obviously not premeditated.

Her fake nails were making it difficult to untangle the knots. She stopped for a second to take another look down the hall. No change. After a lot of pulling and squirming, Shannon was able to get one hand out of the makeshift handcuffs. Then the other. Melanie grabbed Shannon's hand. "Come on." She pulled her from the chair. Melanie reckoned Shannon was in a slight state of shock.

They moved quickly without breaking into a run until Melanie heard a voice behind them. "You're not going to get away with this." She looked back. Cumbe, and he was gaining on them. Melanie's high heels were slowing them down. She hated to do it, but she had no choice. It could be life without Louboutin, or Louboutin with no life to wear them. They came to the escalator and bounded down the steps of the moving stairs. There were no other agents in sight, and Alkali was gaining on them. Melanie pulled off the longest strand of pearls. She handed one end to Shannon and told her to squat down on one side of the escalator, while Melanie squatted on the other. "As soon as I say go, pull on it."

Cumbe was almost at the bottom of the escalator when he spotted what they were up to. His ankles caught on the pearls. They broke as he fell forward, smashing his face into the concrete floor. He tried to get up, but he kept slipping on the scattered pearls.

In less than a minute, a dozen police appeared. Two were in riot gear. Melanie flashed her OSI badge. "Take him away, please." They grabbed Cumbe under his arms, zip-tied his hands behind his back, and read him his rights. He was screaming he was a diplomat. "Look! In my pocket!"

One officer patted him down. "Sorry, sir. You've got nothing on you."

Cumbe sputtered and cursed in a foreign language as he was being dragged to a police van.

"Everyone, please stand back." Gilmour had his OSI lanyard on. He squatted down in front of Shannon. "You okay?" She nodded.

"It took you long enough." Melanie pouted.

"And are you okay?" He put both hands on her shoulders.

"Yeah. But no." She looked over at the small koi pond that separated the up and down escalators. Floating in it was her yellow patent leather stiletto. "How sad."

An EMT took Shannon's pulse and gave her a bottle of water. "Do you want to go to the hospital?" he asked.

"Heck, no," Shannon answered. "I want a fabulous dinner and a glass of fine wine."

Melanie turned to Gilmour. "Have you met my sister-in-law, Shannon?"

"I think dinner and wine is on the evening's agenda," Gilmour said. "But first I have a fishing expedition I need to complete." He took off his shoes and socks, rolled up his pants, stepped into the koi pond, and recovered the soggy shoe. He approached Melanie. "You're not going to be able to get into the restaurant without a pair of these." He poured the water out and handed it to her.

"Now you're *my* hero." She borrowed a towel from the EMT and dried the shoe off as best she could. They couldn't stop laughing with every squishy step.

When they were finally settled at the restaurant, Melanie asked how Shannon had got into that situation. "I really don't know. That man accused me of being some kind of spy. He said I hosted an event and something went wrong. Then he saw me here tonight. I really don't understand what he's talking about."

Gilmour and Melanie looked at each other.

"The diamonds," Gilmour said.

"And he's the financier of this gang of hoodlums."

"That about sums it up," Gilmour said.

"Sums what up?" Shannon was still in the dark. "What are you two talking about?"

"We can't tell you," Gilmour replied.

"Highly classified," Melanie added. "Oh, and this thing tonight? It never happened. You went to work. You ran into me. We went to dinner." Melanie was staring at her.

"You're serious, aren't you?" Shannon gave them each a sideways look.

"Yes, Shannon. For real." Melanie placed her hand on top of Shannon's and then smiled. "You gotta admit, that was a pretty good stunt we pulled."

Shannon laughed. "Probably one of the coolest things I've ever done."

"But you can't ever tell anyone." Melanie held up her pinky. "Swear?"

Shannon linked hers around Melanie's. "Swear."

Epilogue

Winding Up and Winding Down

Everyone was in holiday overdrive. The kids were bouncing off the walls. The traffic was crazy. People were everywhere. Chaos abounded.

The school was preparing for its annual holiday play, making a valiant attempt to include every widely known religion in song, dance, and decoration. Melanie promised she would do her card tricks for the holiday play, provided everyone was kind and polite. They had a bake sale, and another food drive in keeping with the tradition of giving.

The activities at school put Melanie in the holiday spirit, and she decided to host a party the week between Christmas and New Year's Eve. Cocktails and appetizers. Shannon took the reins and helped organize the party. She felt it was the least she could do, considering her sister-in-law had probably saved her life.

The guest list consisted of friends from school, family, Patterson and his latest wife, and Gilmour. There would be around thirty people. Shannon ordered a decorated live tree, garland and wreaths, and Christmas vests for Cosmo and Kramer.

The night of the party, the house was shimmering with tea lights and bright shiny things. Giant ornaments hung above the fireplace, and the French doors were adorned with garland wrapped in tiny white lights. It looked like a wonderland while *The Nutcracker Suite* played softly in the background.

Melanie wore her cream Chanel silk suit with the matching bouclé jacket. This time it was her own hair, her own eyes, and her own nails. She looked stunning. Just for a thrill and a bang, she slipped on her yellow patent leather shoes. Every time she and Shannon looked at each other, they laughed.

The party was a huge success, and Shannon and Melanie prepared goodie bags for everyone, each containing cookies, cheese, pizzelle, nuts, and candy.

Gilmour hung around until the last guest departed. "You need anything else?"

Melanie looked around. Everything was tidy and put away. "There is one thing, though."

"Sure. What?"

Melanie pointed up to the ceiling. Mistletoe.

Gilmour pulled her close. "I thought you'd never ask."

The Sisterhood: a group of women from all walks of life bound by friendship and years of adventure. Armed with vast resources, top-notch expertise, and a loyal network of allies around the globe, the Sisterhood will not rest until every wrong is made right.

Payback has its price, and the Sisterhood's last assignment almost landed them in jail. Now the women are fugitives with a bounty on their heads, but they're not planning on hiding out for long—not when good friends need the kind of help only they can give.

Mitch Riley, the ruthless assistant director of the FBI, intends to frame Cornelia "Nellie" Easter, the judge who helped the Sisterhood evade prison, and their lawyer, Lizzie Fox, in order to save his own career. He's created a special task force to hunt the Sisters down. Mitch has the entire FBI behind him, but he's about to discover that he's no match for seven formidable women with an unbreakable bond and a wickedly cunning plan to bring the fight right to his door . . .

SWEET VENGEANCE

A deeply satisfying and uplifting story of one woman's journey from heartbreak to triumph by #1 New York Times bestselling author Fern Michaels.

Tessa Jamison couldn't have imagined anything worse than losing her beloved twin girls and husband—until she was convicted of their murder. For ten years, she has counted off the days in Florida's Correctional Center for Women, fully expecting to die behind bars. Fighting to prove her innocence holds little appeal now that her family's gone. But on one extraordinary day, her lawyers announce that Tessa's conviction has been overturned due to a technicality, and she's released on bail to await a new trial.

Hounded by the press, Tessa retreats to the small tropical island owned by her late husband's pharmaceutical company. There, she begins to gather knowledge about her case. For the first time since her nightmare began, Tessa feels a sense of purpose in working to finally expose the truth and avenge her lost family. One by one, the guilty will be led to justice, and Tessa can gain closure. But will she be able to learn the whole truth at last . . . and reclaim her freedom and her future?